AN UNSETTLING CRIME FOR
SAMUEL CRADDOCK

A SAMUEL CRADDOCK MYSTERY

AN
UNSETTLING
CRIME FOR
SAMUEL
CRADDOCK

TERRY SHAMES

SEVENTH STREET BOOKS®
AN IMPRINT OF PROMETHEUS BOOKS
59 JOHN GLENN DRIVE • AMHERST, NY 14228
www.seventhstreetbooks.com

Published 2017 by Seventh Street Books®, an imprint of Prometheus Books

Cover image © Media Bakery
Cover design by Nicole Sommer-Lecht
Cover design © Prometheus Books

Inquiries should be addressed to
Seventh Street Books
59 John Glenn Drive
Amherst, New York 14228
VOICE: 716–691–0133 • FAX: 716–691–0137
WWW.SEVENTHSTREETBOOKS.COM

21 20 19 18 17 • 5 4 3 2 1

Library of Congress Cataloging-in-Publication Data

Names: Shames, Terry, author.
Title: An unsettling crime for Samuel Craddock : a Samuel Craddock mystery / by
    Terry Shames.
Description: Amherst, NY : Seventh Street Books, an imprint of Prometheus Books,
    [2017]
Identifiers: LCCN 2016032148 (print) | LCCN 2016038748 (ebook) |
    ISBN 9781633882096 (paperback) | ISBN 9781633882102 (ebook)
Subjects: | BISAC: FICTION / Mystery & Detective / General. | FICTION /
    Mystery & Detective / Police Procedural. | GSAFD: Mystery fiction.
Classification: LCC PS3619.H35425 U57 2017 (print) |
    LCC PS3619.H35425 (ebook) | DDC 813/.6—dc23
LC record available at https://lccn.loc.gov/2016032148

Printed in the United States of America

To writers, who light the dark and stormy nights

CHAPTER 1

When I walk into the kitchen Monday morning, Jeanne is standing with her back to me, stirring oatmeal on the stove. She's still in her nightgown, and the outline of her body is visible through the sheer fabric. My breath catches. I walk up behind her, put my arms around her, and nuzzle her neck, where she says it always makes her feel weak. She shivers and nestles back into me. She smells like lemon and soap. I slip my hands up to her breasts, and she whispers, "Samuel, the oatmeal . . ."

I reach over and switch off the burner. She turns around, and her mouth comes up to meet mine. We've been married for six years, and I still can't get enough of her, ever. She steps onto my feet to bring herself up closer to my height, and also because she knows it arouses me. I move my hands over her, and she begins humming that low sound she makes in her throat.

The phone begins to ring, and she stiffens. "Leave it," I say. My voice sounds strange to me, hoarse and urgent.

She clamps her arms around my neck, and I pick her up so she can wrap her legs around my waist. I carry her to the bedroom like that and slam the door to muffle the sound of the telephone. I hear the sound of the volunteer fire department whistle starting up. Thank goodness that's not for me.

When we get back to the oatmeal, she says, "You're just wound up because the cattle are coming today."

"If owning cattle gets me that wound up, I'm going to buy more," I say.

She's right. I'm happy. Ever since we moved back to Jarrett Creek, I've been planning to buy twenty head of cattle for the pasture behind the house. It's why we settled on this house to begin with. We weren't in a hurry, thinking we'd start a family first, and then add the cows after we knew what we were up against with raising a child. But no children have come along yet, so we decided a few months ago to start shopping for cattle.

The phone starts up again. "You better get it," she says. "The people bringing the cows may be lost."

She knows that's not true. It'll be work. Something's happened, and I'll have to go in. Earlier this year I was appointed chief of police here in Jarrett Creek, the youngest chief they've ever had. When Hazel Baker, the city administrator, called me into her office and suggested it, I laughed.

"Why me? I don't know anything being a police officer, much less chief."

She didn't laugh with me. "Don't play dumb with me, Samuel. I've known you since you were a little kid, and you're too smart not to know we've got a drug problem here." She was right, I did know. If I hadn't been so unprepared for her suggestion that I take over as chief, I would have asked her why she thought I was the one to solve the problem. Maybe I was too flattered to think carefully about the city council's reasons for choosing me.

The whole country went through a big upheaval after President Kennedy was shot and the Vietnam War heated up. That was almost twenty years ago. It's like a whole generation ran off the rails and straight into drugs. You wouldn't think a small town like ours would attract drug dealers, but it was looking like we weren't immune.

"Jack Knight is too old to get a handle on what's going on with all the young people," Hazel said. "You're young and smart and from around here, so you know everybody. And I can guarantee you that Jack is going to be glad to get out from under the job."

"Can't one of the deputies take over?"

She snorted. "Eldridge is older than Jack, Doug Tilley is moving to Waco, and the less said about Johnny Pat Hruska, the better." Johnny Pat was legendary for taking six years to complete high school. A sweet man, but not the brightest candle on the birthday cake.

"How does this work? You hand me a badge and tell me I'm the police chief?"

"It's not quite that easy, but almost. Roland Newberry is the Bobtail County sheriff, and he'll have to okay it, but I don't expect he'll put up a fuss."

Seeing that I hadn't exactly figured out what I was going to do now that I was back in my hometown, I consented. Only after I said yes, without consulting Jeanne, did I find out she was opposed to it. She made her peace with it, but she's short on enthusiasm.

After I agreed to take the job, there was still the matter of me having no training, so the county paid for me to take a three-month program in Austin. Jeanne stayed in Austin with me and often drove up to see her mother in Fort Worth.

Hazel was right. Jack Knight didn't let the door hit him on the way out of office. It turned out that Tilley decided not to move to Waco after all, but he seems fine with remaining a deputy, as do the other two. I worried that the three deputies might be surly about having a chief as young as me and without a shred of experience, but if they are unhappy, they keep it to themselves.

It's Tilley on the phone. In addition to being deputy, he's also a member of the volunteer fire department. "Where the hell have you been?"

I'm startled. Tilley is a deacon in the Baptist church, and he rarely curses. "I was outside. What's the problem?"

He breathes hard for a couple of seconds before he speaks. Outside,

I hear sirens in the distance, which means they've called the Bobtail Fire Department for help. Must be big. "We've got us a situation. It's bad."

He's so agitated that his explanation is garbled, but when he says *bodies*, I interrupt. "Where are you?"

"Out in the woods in Darktown, across the tracks and south. Past the old Mitchell place."

CHAPTER 2

All the black people in town live across the tracks in a place that's been called "Darktown" since before I can remember. After I cross the tracks, I turn south and speed along the gravel-and-dirt road that borders the railroad tracks. Ahead of me, a plume of smoke rises through the trees. To my right, the fenced-in property is strewn with equipment and leavings from the abandoned railroad-tie plant that kept this town thriving when the railroads were big. Ties dark with creosote preservative lie scattered among knee-deep weeds. A few old railroad cars lie rusting alongside the fence.

On the other side, shacks are lined up close to one another. Most people who live here can't afford paint, so the houses are whitewashed and weathered. They're small but mostly kept up, although a few lean as if they are tired from the effort to stay upright. Many have late-season flowers blooming in the yards—zinnias and climbing roses. Several people are standing out on their porches, eyes trained in the direction of the woods, toward the smoke. I pass the Bennett house, where Truly Bennett lives with his daddy and sister. His mother died last year— one of the kindest ladies you'd ever meet. I'll be seeing Truly later. He's coming to help me get the cows settled. I don't think he's twenty, and he already has a reputation as somebody who knows his cattle. His daddy is standing on the porch, and I wave to him. He half lifts his hand, but he's focused on what's happening in the woods.

I'm driving pretty fast, but a highway patrol car overtakes me, siren blaring, and speeds on by, leaving me in a cloud of dust. I get a glimpse of two officers, but I don't recognize either of them. I follow the patrol car as it turns down a dirt road that's rutted and barely passable. Scrub brush scrapes the patrol car and my pickup. We pull into a clearing at the side of the road where a path leads off through the woods.

There are already two fire trucks here. In addition to our yellow Jarrett Creek truck, there's a red one from Bobtail. The Bobtail fire chief's pickup is here, too.

I park next to the highway patrol car and lean over to grab my badge out of the glove box and pin it to my shirt pocket. Tilley's call sounded so urgent that I didn't stop to put on a uniform. I leave my pistol there. I expect there's enough firepower here already.

As soon as I open the door, the smell hits me. The smell of burning creosote is strongest, but there's another smell underneath that turns my stomach: burned flesh. Somebody didn't make it out alive.

The highway patrolmen are out of their car before me and don't pause long enough for me to catch up. I follow them along the path through the woods until we reach the scene of the fire.

The fire crew got here in time to save part of the house, but a good portion of it is a charred mess. From the stink of creosote in the air, I figure the reason it didn't burn to the ground is that it was built with stolen treated railroad ties. A lot of the illegal residences around here are built with lumber filched from the stack of railroad ties left behind when the plant shut down.

Tilley spots me and comes over right away. His face is an unhealthy color of gray/green. He's a hefty man, under six feet but with a lot of extra pounds on him, and a couple of extra chins. He once told me his favorite food was pancakes, and it's pretty clear he has eaten more than his share.

"What happened?" I ask.

He groans. "It's awful. At least four bodies."

"Four!" I'm staggered. How did a fire happen so fast that four people got trapped?

"Tilley," somebody calls, "We need you over here." A firefighter wearing a Bobtail Fire Department baseball cap beckons to him.

I hear another car out on the road, and in a few seconds a lanky, energetic woman in her forties hurries into view with a notebook and pen in her hand, and a camera slung around her neck. We don't have much of a newspaper in town, the *Jarrett Creek Tribune*, but Bonnie Bedichek struts around as if she's the editor and chief reporter of the *Dallas Morning News*.

"What have we got here?" She strides toward the two highway patrolmen, ignoring me. She has never made any secret of the fact that she has no respect for me as a lawman, because of my age and inexperience.

"Hey, little lady, back it up." One of the highway patrolmen puts up both hands to stop her. He's at least three inches shorter than she is, stocky and red-faced. His gray hair is cut military-style. His eyes are what they call gunfighter blue—cold and unrelenting.

I flinch, knowing how "little lady" is going to go over with her.

"I'm not your 'little lady,'" she says. "I'm a reporter for the *Jarrett Creek Tribune*, and I have every right to be here."

He raises his eyebrows. "You have a right to be where I say you can be. I determine whether it's safe for you, and I'm telling you it's unsafe. Now back away, get in your car, and clear on out."

"I'll do no such thing."

Before this can get into a pissing contest, I step up. "Bonnie, how about if you stand back here with me? We'll find out what's going on together."

"Who the hell are you?" the patrolman asks.

I thumb my badge. "Samuel Craddock, chief of police here in Jarrett Creek." As if he couldn't tell from seeing the badge.

"Looks like they robbed the cradle when they found a chief," he says. "It's nice for you to take the trouble to come out, but we've got this under control. This is going to be a state matter, and we're going to cordon off the area. So you can run along."

I bristle at his tone and his words. "This fire happened in the city limits and is part of my jurisdiction."

He puts his hands on his hips and moves a step closer. "Your jurisdiction be damned. As you may or may not know, in the state of Texas, the highway patrol investigates suspicious deaths in small towns. And if this little bump in the road isn't a small town, I don't know what is. Which means you have no standing."

His partner, a man of about sixty, has stayed in the background, as if he's used to his partner's ways and isn't of a mind to interfere. I noticed that his eyes follow everything, though, and I expect he doesn't miss a thing.

The patrolman is stretching his facts. The highway patrol is usually the first to be notified of major crimes, but the Texas Rangers generally take over when an investigation is warranted. On paper, the highway patrol has the authority; but the Rangers have superior resources.

"I didn't get your name," I say.

"Sutherland. Now I'll thank you to step aside." He glances over at Bonnie, who is writing furiously in her notebook. "And take that . . . lady with you."

Just as I'm ready to incite a turf war over my right to be here, Tilley comes back, shaking his head. "Craddock, this is a bad business."

"You say there are four bodies?" I ask, ignoring Sutherland.

"They just found a fifth one out behind the house."

I shudder, thinking of someone on fire fleeing a house, and then Tilley says, "But this girl wasn't burned. She was shot."

"Goddammit, I told you to stay out of this," Sutherland says to me.

He's got more authority and experience than I do, but his attitude aggravates me. "I understand you're in charge, but I'm the chief here, and I want to be kept informed of what you find out."

"What the hell do you care about a bunch of niggers killing each other, anyway? Probably all drinking and got into a fight over some whore."

I've heard that kind of language my whole life, but it never sits well, and it sounds especially hateful coming out of a lawman's mouth.

"I don't think that's likely," Tilley says, shooting Sutherland a hard look. "They're all youngsters."

CHAPTER 3

Right then, two Texas Rangers arrive on the scene, and the dynamic changes considerably. They hold themselves with the air of men sure of their status and used to commanding respect. There's a reason for that. By reputation, the Rangers trump all other lawmen in the state of Texas.

Unlike Sutherland, the older Ranger introduces himself immediately. "I'm Curren Wills, and this is my partner, Luke Schoppe. We were in the vicinity and heard what was happening and thought you might be able to use a hand."

The Rangers' handshakes are firm, and they both look me in the eye. Schoppe is about my age and gives me a complicit smile. We're the low men on this totem pole, although he has a lot more training than I have, which makes me the lowest of the low.

"John Sutherland." The patrolman not only doesn't tell the Rangers to shove off but also seems to have lost his swagger.

Wills sniffs the air, his nose wrinkled. "From the smell of things and the way you fellas look, I expect things are looking bad. Somebody want to fill me in?"

Sutherland doesn't jump in, so Tilley says, "I guess that's up to me." He explains that he's a police deputy and in the volunteer fire department. "Somebody passing by on the highway early this morning saw smoke. He stopped at Town Café, and they called me and we got out our volunteers. We saw right away it was more than we could handle, so somebody went back to town to call the Bobtail Fire Department and the Texas Highway Patrol. We got it under control an hour ago. That's when we spotted the bodies inside the front room."

"How many bodies are we talking about?" Wills asks.

"Five so far," Tilley swallows. "Looks like kids."

"Damn." Wills takes his Ranger hat off and scratches the back of his neck.

"And at least one of them was shot."

"The hell you say! Let's get on back there and take a look. Mind all of you not to tramp around too much, although between the fire and the firefighters moving around, I expect there's not much left of the crime scene."

We move through the trees. I admit my heart is pounding pretty hard. In the months I've been chief, the only bodies I've seen are a glimpse of someone laid out at the side of the road after an automobile crash, and a couple of old people who died of natural causes. In a town of three thousand people, you don't get much in the way of murder—or at least I haven't had the misfortune to see it.

It's full daylight now, but the sun hasn't hit the house, surrounded as it is by tall post oak trees. Although the house stands in a cleared area, some of the trees close by are blackened from the fire. Several firemen are standing in a huddle, looking shocked and grimy. Some are smoking cigarettes, most likely to rid themselves of the awful smell of creosote and burned flesh. The smell has a bad effect on the oatmeal I ate earlier, making it tumble around like a live snake in my stomach. I grit my teeth, determined not to disgrace myself by losing my breakfast in front of these men.

The house is a single story cobbled together and sprawled out probably without much regard to building codes. But it looks more substantial than some of the houses built in this area. There was a wide porch, and the beams holding up the roof over it are still standing, although it looks like a good push could knock them down. The house is big enough to have two or three bedrooms in addition to a kitchen and a living room.

Schoppe falls into step beside me, behind the others. "Man, this is a tough one." He coughs and spits to one side.

A man in a Bobtail Fire Department jacket peels away from the huddle of men and walks over to us. "I'm Bob Koontz, fire chief over in Bobtail."

"Have you called the ambulance?" Wills asks.

"Didn't see any sense in it. It's too hot for them to get in there yet. You all stay back. That porch looks like it might collapse, and if it does, embers could get scattered."

"Would you mind taking us as close as you consider a safe distance?"

I like Wills. Reputation has it that Rangers are arrogant and pushy, but I see none of that in him. I read somewhere that they are trying to clean up their image after a handful of shameful scandals. Maybe this is part of that effort, or maybe it's just Wills's usual way.

As we move closer, Koontz coughs deep in his lungs. "Right inside the door there, you see what looks like three bodies, and then around back there's another one near the kitchen door."

The door is hanging partly open. "It looks to me like they were trying to escape the fire. Is that your assessment?" Wills's voice is steady, although I don't know how he stays calm. What happened here makes me tremble with anger.

"We're not sure. The body in the yard puts a different light on it. The girl was shot."

We file by the precarious porch. The door has been torn off its hinges and bears evidence of being chopped at by an ax. The doorway and walls inside the entry are charred. Each man in turn peers into the house where a slant of light illuminates three shapes tangled together in a sprawl by the front door. Whoever set the fire didn't bother to pretend it was a natural disaster. Three gas cans lie on the ground near the front door. Wills points at them. "We're going to need those taken in for prints."

"We'll take care of that," Sutherland says.

Wills hooks his thumbs in his belt and gives Sutherland a speculative look. If I had to interpret his expression, I'd say he knows Sutherland and doesn't like him.

I hear a squeak of distress. Bonnie Bedichek has crept along behind us, and despite the horror of what she's seeing, she's scribbling madly in her notebook. Then she hoists the camera that's slung around her neck and begins taking snapshots.

"Ma'am, I'm going to have to ask you to desist from taking photos. We'll let the press in as soon as we've had time to process the scene." Wills is quiet, but somehow he projects authority. I can learn something from this man.

Maybe because he addressed her with respect, or maybe because the scene is more than she can take in, Bonnie lowers the camera.

We proceed around back, and when I see the form laid out in the weeds, I hear a roaring in my ears. Schoppe is beside me again. "How long have you been chief?" he asks.

If he hadn't asked me a question to take my mind away from the body, I might have fainted flat out, but I feel an urgent need to answer the question. "A little over six months. How long have you been a Ranger?"

"Two years, but the first one was all training. Never seen anything like this. Never wanted to."

I put in my time in the US Air Force and then went to Texas A&M for four years, so I'm not a kid, but all that experience seems to drop away at the moment. I feel like Schoppe and I are two high school boys tagging along behind the grown-ups.

The body in the yard is a girl with mahogany-colored skin, a teenager by the looks of her thin, gangly legs and skinny little body. She's clad in short shorts and a brightly colored, striped top. Her hair is fluffed out from her head like an electric shock went through her. I've seen that style on TV. It looks like she was fleeing from burning clothing—the worst thing you can do. But, looking closer, I see that the clothing is charred and not burned off her body. She was rolling around, trying to smother the flames, and somebody shot her just off the center of her forehead.

"Close range," Schoppe says in a whisper. "See the powder burns?" I nod, grateful that he pointed it out.

Everybody is whispering. I suddenly realize that Sutherland is not with us. I see him off in the trees, bent over. I look back to see his partner gazing at me coolly. "He has a sixteen-year-old daughter," he says.

CHAPTER 4

I've never been a big drinker, as my daddy drank himself to death and my brother is well on his way to doing the same. I enjoy a beer in hot weather, and maybe a shot of bourbon to be sociable, but that's about it. After what I've seen this morning, though, I understand why somebody would get drunk enough to numb his senses. I'd like nothing better than to go to the Ten Spot on the outskirts of town and spend the rest of the day hoisting one beer after another.

Of course I'm not going to do that. Something tells me that while my conscious mind would be tamped down, I'd still be left with images seared on my retinas. Not only that, but I'd be playing right into Jeanne's misgivings about me being a lawman.

After I leave the crime scene, I go back to what we call headquarters, a ramshackle building that used to be a hardware store right next to the Texaco station. The city council is always planning to build a new police station, but then something comes up that's more important. The recent project that has me steamed is the building of a museum right in the center of town. True, the Santa Fe Railway paid for most of it, since it mostly consists of memorabilia from when the railroad was the heart and soul of central Texas. But the rest of the money came from Biddy White, whose husband was the foreman of the tie plant and a big cheese in the town at one time. Somebody could have persuaded her to pay for a decent police station.

Tilley drives in right behind me, and we walk up to the door together not saying a word. I tear a note off the front door that says Susie Lassiter's dog has gone missing again. Yesterday I would have called her straight off and offered my help, but this morning's events have put the missing dog in perspective.

Tilley and I slump into our chairs like we're old men. He lights up a cigarette, and for once I don't mind. It's a clean smell by comparison. He sighs. "I need a shower."

"I know what you mean."

"What are you going to do?" he asks. I notice he doesn't say *we*. "You going to leave it to the state?"

I'm not sure what to reply. I suppose that's the easiest way. Despite my annoyance at the highway patrolman, he's right; I don't have jurisdiction. But I feel like it's a cop-out to simply walk away and hand off the investigation to people who don't live around here. Not that I have the resources or the experience to investigate myself, but at least I ought to know what they find out. Wills said he'd keep me in the loop, but if Sutherland has anything to say about it, I imagine I won't be included. I just can't quite decide if I want to push it.

The phone rings. It's Jeanne, and her voice is cheerful and excited. It's like hearing someone from another time and place. "Where have you been? I've been calling you. If you don't get on over here, you're going to miss the unloading." I notice the light blinking on the answering machine.

"Is Truly there?"

"He just drove up."

"I'll be there in a minute."

It's probably wrong to assume that because Truly Bennett is black, he knows all the other black people in town, but I can't help dreading telling him about the scene out at the burned house. Of course, he might already know. His daddy was still standing on the porch when I drove back by, keeping vigil. This time there was a young girl with him. I assume that was Truly's sister.

Leaving his earlier question unanswered, I tell Tilley what's going on at my house. He forces a smile. "So you're going to be a cattle rancher."

"I wouldn't go that far. I just want to keep a few cows."

Tilley sniffs his armpit. "I think I'll duck on home and get a shower and then come back, if it's all the same to you."

It still gives me a funny feeling for a man ten years older and more experienced than me asking my permission to leave work.

I listen to the phone messages. Two are from Jeanne, sounding impatient the second time. The other one is a panicked voice asking if I know what the sirens are for. It's Verna Price. She calls every time the volunteer fire siren goes off. She's stuck in the fifties, when everyone was afraid Russia was going to bomb the United States. Why she thinks anybody would target a small town an hour and a half's drive from the nearest city, which is San Antonio, is anybody's guess. Reasoning with her never gets me anywhere. But her panic is real, so I call her back and tell her it was only a fire.

I live five minutes from the station. When I drive up, Jeanne is standing next to a big truck that has brought the cows. She runs to my pickup and looks as excited as a child. "We got some good-looking heifers. I was afraid you wouldn't get here to see them unloaded."

I look inside the cattle truck and see there are a good dozen still unloaded. Truly's truck is parked next to the cattle truck, but I don't see him. I assume he and the truck driver are getting a batch of cows herded into the pasture.

I kiss Jeanne and try to bring my attention back to the excitement of the moment.

"Phew, you smell awful," she says.

"It was a bad fire," I say. "I'm going back to the pasture to see if they need any help."

At that moment, though, the two men come around the side of the house and head toward me. Truly is quiet, as always, and I can't read his face.

"How can I help?" I ask.

"This boy has been helping me," the driver says. "We're taking them down a couple at a time. He seems to know what he's doing." The driver looks around the same age as Truly, early twenties, and him calling Truly a "boy" irritates me. Maybe it's just my mood.

"Truly helped me pick out this bunch," I say. "He's a good man with cattle."

Neither the driver nor Truly seems to notice my correction, but Jeanne gives a little snort of amusement.

I love the look of a Hereford cow—its snowy white face surrounded by red. As a breed they look solid, and they have fewer health problems than some other breeds. They take the heat well and fatten up readily. It takes only a half hour for us to finish up getting them down into the pasture. By then I'm feeling less agitated.

After the driver leaves, Jeanne says she's going in to make some lunch. Although I know she won't approve, I ask Truly if he'll join us. It's a token request. I know he won't stay. It wouldn't make him any more comfortable than it would Jeanne. Sure enough, he says he's got to be somewhere, and Jeanne goes into the house.

"Truly, I need to talk to you."

"Yes, sir?"

"You know there was a fire out in the woods beyond your place this morning?"

He nods and looks down at the ground.

"Would you happen to know who lives out there?"

"Not right off," he says. His voice is so quiet, I barely hear him. He lifts his head and looks off into the distance. "I heard talk, though."

"What kind of talk?"

He shakes his head and doesn't look at me. "I'd rather not say. It's better you leave it."

"What do you mean 'leave it'?"

He shakes his head again. "It's rumors. I'd best be getting on now."

To my surprise, he walks swiftly away, toward his truck.

"Truly, I owe you money."

"I'll get it later," he calls over his shoulder.

I watch him drive away and wonder what's gotten into him. He has never been much for chatter, but he is always polite and respectful—almost deferential.

I walk on back to the pasture. To the north I see that the sky has darkened. We're going to get our first norther of the season. The cows will like that. They're probably hot after being cooped up in that truck for the last few of hours.

"Your mother called this morning."

Jeanne and I are sitting at the little table she set up on the porch so we can have occasional meals here when the weather permits.

She insisted that I take a shower and change clothes before eating lunch. I didn't think I could eat after what I've been exposed to this morning, but I find I'm starving. She's heated up roast beef from last night. She's a good cook. Nothing fancy, and that's fine with me. When we visit her family in Fort Worth, they always take us to some fancy restaurant. Jeanne loves it, but I'm more of a meat-and-potatoes man.

"What did she want?"

"She wants you to come by. She said she has something to tell you."

I grunt in reply. She always has something to tell me. Always a complaint against me; my brother, Horace; or our dead daddy.

"Don't be that way. She's old. She just wants attention."

I don't know why, but Jeanne has taken it on herself to be friendly to my mamma. I've told her how mean Mamma was when I was growing up. She nagged and belittled my daddy and brother pretty much nonstop. Neither of them ever did a thing that pleased her. Maybe because I was younger than Horace, I escaped the worst of it, although it seemed like plenty. But it was almost worse, having to witness what she did to the two of them. I always felt guilty being spared. As nice as

Jeanne is to her, you'd think that Mamma would be kind back, but she barely gives Jeanne the time of day and is downright cruel about the fact that we haven't produced any children. I can't see why Jeanne acts like everything is fine.

"I'll go see her," I say.

"Today?"

"I don't know. Now let me alone."

I know better than to snap at my wife like that, and she usually pops right back, but now she's quiet and I can feel her eyes on me as I shovel my food in.

"What happened this morning?" she asks. "You've been jumpy as a cat ever since you got back."

I lay my fork down. The image of those bodies heaped in the front doorway overtakes me and I run my hands over my face. "I'll give you the easy version. There was a fire and we found bodies."

She gasps. "Oh, Samuel. Where was the fire? Who was killed?"

I need to choose my words carefully. I don't want to start a fight. "It was a black family over in Darktown. The dead appear to be young."

"How young? You know how they are." For some reason, Jeanne has taken up her father's line that black people neglect their children. I don't know where it comes from. I told her I never saw anything like that around here, but she said that was because I didn't pay enough attention. My feeling is that I'd rather have been neglected by my folks than subjected to Mamma's unrelenting criticism and Daddy's drunken rambles.

"We'll have to wait for the autopsy to find that out."

"I mean little kids?"

"No, I don't think so."

"What do you mean you don't think so? The bodies would be little. If it's teenagers, you'd wonder why they didn't have sense enough to get out of the house."

I know she doesn't mean it that way, but she sounds hard-hearted, as if she's not talking about real people. But maybe I'm too raw at the moment and her words hit me wrong. I don't want to describe the heap of bodies and tell her that there was no way to see how big they were because they were a burned mass, fused together in a doorway. Maybe later I'll be able to tell her that I hope to God they were shot like the girl outside was before the fire got to them. But I can't talk about it now. I push my plate away and get up. "I have to get back," I say.

I don't know if we've actually had a fight, but it feels that way when I drive away. Maybe to appease her I'll stop by and visit my mother later. But there's a lot to take care of between now and then. I realize that I didn't go back and take another look at the cows before I left. I'm sure they'll be fine. But my lapse tells me what kind of mood I'm in.

CHAPTER 5

Tilley is back at headquarters after his shower. Normally, as head of the volunteer fire department, Tilley would have stayed at the site of the fire, but with bodies involved, the Bobtail fire chief is in charge. It is his responsibility to get state forensic fire examiners out here, though who knows how long it will take?

Tilley says he had lunch at Town Café and the whole place is buzzing about the fire, wondering exactly what happened. He's leaning back in his chair, his hands crossed over his bulging belly.

"You didn't tell them the girl was shot, did you?" I ask.

He gets a peeved look on his face, and his chins wobble as he replies. "I believe I did mention it. I didn't see any reason to keep it a secret."

"I'm sure you're right." For some reason, I want to protect everybody from knowing that something so terrible happened.

He tilts forward in his chair. "Craddock, there's no way to keep something like that quiet. People are going to find out."

"But there's no need for a cop to be passing out the information before we've had a chance to digest it ourselves."

Tilley shrugs like it's no big deal, but his eyes are narrowed.

"I'm going back out there to take another look," I say.

"Be my guest."

When I step outside the station, I find that the temperature has dropped about thirty degrees. That's what happens when a norther comes in. It's like a wall of cold air. It may only last a day or two, since it isn't fall yet, but for now it feels downright wintry.

I rummage around behind the seat of the pickup and pull out a jacket that hasn't seen action since March. I shake it out and put it on.

Even if it looks and smells like something a bum would wear, I'm glad I have it.

Darktown has an air of desertion. I expected to see people outside, standing in clusters, talking to one another about what happened, but I don't see a soul. It gives me an uneasy feeling. When I get close to the scene of the fire, I find out where everybody is. There must be thirty, forty people, mostly black, gathered on the side of the road near the path through the woods that leads to the burned-out house. I recognize a few of them, but most are strangers. I don't know what has drawn them here. In the past few years, there have been TV images of black protests in cities, so I'm used to the idea of protest. But I don't know why these people would be protesting. It isn't as if white citizens are to blame here—or, if they are, at least it's too early to tell.

I park next to a highway patrol car that is probably Sutherland's. There are several other cars parked haphazardly along the road as if people rushed up to the scene, slowed their cars to a stop, and jumped out in a hurry.

I climb out of my pickup, nodding to the Pearl brothers, who are standing at the edge of the crowd. They put up the fence for my pasture last month. Frank looks down at the ground, and his younger brother, Erland, gives me a stone-cold stare. I consider asking them what's going on, but there'll be time for that when I've had a look around.

When I arrive at the burned-out house, Sutherland and his partner are standing with Bobtail Fire Chief Koontz. Not only that, but a pack of reporters and photographers are spread out, taking pictures from every possible angle. I'm sorry they're here. If I had thought about it, I should have known they would be, but this is my first experience of such a big crime. Reporters and highway patrolmen don't show up when somebody is arrested for being drunk and disorderly.

"Anything new?" I ask.

"Looks like you got what you wanted," Sutherland says with a smirk.

"And what would that be?"

"All your fine, upstanding citizens gathered around near the road back there could use a little policing."

"Have they done something wrong?" I ask.

"I don't know. Does this hick town have a law that they have to have a permit to assemble?"

It's pretty clear Sutherland is making fun of me. I'm trying to keep my cool, but I have an edge to my voice when I say, "Isn't there some way to keep these news hounds from trampling the crime scene?"

"They aren't going to do any more damage than has already been done by the firemen," Koontz says. He's looking off into the distance, trying to ignore our exchange.

Suddenly the newsmen all surge in our direction. Sutherland and Koontz look at something over my shoulder, and I turn to see a stocky man with a bristly mustache and hair that looks like porcupine quills charging up to us. It's Roland Newberry, who has been the county sheriff for a long time. He's wearing his uniform and badge, which is unusual. He's usually dressed in civilian clothes. I'm glad to see him. Newberry has been cordial to me since I became chief, and early on he offered to help without being condescending to me.

As county sheriff, he is in a tricky position. He doesn't have any authority to investigate, but he needs to make sure the investigators can do their jobs. He is a liaison between police chiefs of small towns and the THP and the Texas Rangers, and he provides whatever logistical support he can to the investigators.

"Hey, are you the county sheriff?" One of the newspeople hollers.

Newberry strides toward them. "I'm not wearing this uniform and badge to play-act," he says. "I'm the sheriff and I'll thank you all to move back away from the building. This is an active crime scene."

"Nobody said we couldn't take a closer look," says a skinny guy wearing a hat that makes him look like a reporter out of a 1940s movie.

"Can't you read? That yellow tape says 'Crime Scene' all over it."

The reporters pepper him with questions. "Who first spotted the fire? This land is part of Cato Woods, isn't it? Who owns the house? Did they know somebody was living out here? Was this part of a drug deal? Who's investigating? Will that be the Texas Rangers?"

Newberry waves his hands in the air. "All right, goddammit, settle down. You're like a pack of hyenas."

"What can you tell us?" one of them shouts.

"Not a damn thing. As you can plainly see, I just got here."

"What are you going to do with that mob out there on the road?"

"Nothing, as long as they stay orderly. They're not hurting anybody as far as I can see."

"Yeah, but you get your niggers all riled up, and next thing you know they're going to be burning people's houses down."

"What's your name and where are you from?" Newberry barks the question.

"Pete Wallace out of Houston. I'm from the *Chronicle*."

"Well Pete, just because you all can't keep things under control in Houston doesn't mean we can't keep everything in order here. Now, if you'll give me a while to get caught up, I'll have a statement for you. I'll be holding a press conference at the courthouse in Bobtail."

There are a few groans.

"I'm sorry if that doesn't suit you, but I'm the boss here and I get to make the rules. Matter of fact, that may give you an indication of how I plan to keep order. Now I suggest you get in your cars and head back to Bobtail and wait for me. I'm done talking to you."

He turns his back on them. "Hi, fellas. Chief Craddock." He nods all around. "If you all ignore them, they'll lose interest and get on out of here." He offers his ham hock of a hand to Sutherland, "I don't believe we're acquainted. I'm Roland Newberry, County Sheriff."

Everybody introduces themselves.

"Koontz, have you been able to do any preliminary investigation on this fire?" Newberry asks.

"It's still too hot, though this norther is going to cool it off fast. But I can tell you right now the fire was set to cover the murders of the kids in this house."

"Was it all kids that was killed?"

Koontz winces. "Hard to tell. One of 'em was big enough to be a grownup, but you know how that goes."

"Some of these black kids can be as big as me by the time they're twelve," Sutherland offers.

"How do you know it was set?" Newberry asks.

"Whoever did it didn't try to cover it up," Koontz says. "There were gas cans all over, and you can smell the gas strong back there."

"Hmph. Somebody sending a message of some kind, if we can manage to decipher it."

"You leave that to me," Sutherland says.

"You mean the highway patrol is going to be in charge?" Newberry sounds startled. "You aren't calling on the Rangers to investigate?"

"That's right," Sutherland says, resting his hand on his gun. "I don't think it's necessary to get Rangers involved. The THP ought to be able to clear this up."

"Well, that's between you and Wills." Newberry's expression is unreadable, but his response lacked enthusiasm, and I can't help thinking he doesn't much like Sutherland. "Anybody talked to those people milling around on the road to find out what they're up to?"

It strikes me that I can extricate myself from Sutherland's presence and at the same time put myself in charge of something. "I'm going out there right now to have a talk with them," I say.

Newberry nods. "Let us know if you need any help."

Sutherland snorts. "Good luck with that. Those people will close up ranks. You'll be lucky to get the time of day."

"I'll be fine," I say, addressing Newberry, but the truth is I have no idea what I'm going to do. I just know I have to put my stamp on this somehow.

The trick is to find somebody in the crowd who knows me. When I approach, everyone is facing the same direction, toward where somebody is speaking in a voice loud enough that it could be coming from a megaphone. I scan the crowd for Truly Bennett. I know him better than any other black man in town. But I don't see him. I do see his daddy, though, a big man who hunches over as if he's got back trouble, even though he can't be more than midforties. Some of the people have come out without coats, which means they got here before the norther blew in. Must be something important that keeps those people here huddled against the cold.

Skirting the group, I walk toward the commanding voice, surprised to see a few white faces. As I get close, I hear what the speaker is saying. "They're not going to do a thing to catch whoever did this. We're going to have to protest and stay after them to see to it that justice is done."

The crowd murmurs, and I get an uneasy feeling. I see situations like this on TV news, where people get riled up and nothing good comes of it. But if you told me it could happen here, I wouldn't have believed it. And then I remember Truly Bennett's cold shoulder this morning.

Until now, I thought I had everything buttoned down with regard to law enforcement. Since I took the job, I've had to arrest only a couple of dozen people for one thing or another—most of which involved a night in jail. I had to haul a couple of men up to Bobtail for serious charges when I found out they were selling lots they didn't own. But mostly it's been men drinking too much and getting rowdy. Even the drug problem seems to have settled down, or at least no one has complained.

Confronted with what might turn into a mob, I stay quiet and listen, wondering if I ought to get Sheriff Newberry to come over and say a few words. But I've lived here all my life. If I don't have the guts to confront this situation, I should turn in my badge.

I listen a few more minutes, edging closer to the speaker. I realize

I've seen him somewhere before, most likely on TV. I wonder where he's from and what brought him here so fast. He's whip thin and as tall as me, about six feet, and he's so black his skin is almost purple. His eyes are fiery, and even though I don't like what he saying, I feel the power of his personality.

It's now or never. I step up closer and then into the space that has cleared around him. "Excuse me, if I could interrupt for a minute."

The look he sends my way is calculating. I don't want to give him the chance to use me, so before he speaks I say, "I'm Samuel Craddock, chief of police here in Jarrett Creek."

He looks me up and down, and again I am aware of my youth. He's no older than me, but he exudes self-confidence. "Are you asking us to disperse?" he asks, challenging.

"Doesn't look to me like that's necessary," I say. "I didn't catch your name."

A couple of young men in the crowd snicker, which leads me to believe that the man is well-known among them. "I'm Albert Lamond."

"From Houston," I say, recognizing the man that the *Chronicle* calls "abrasive and obnoxious."

He nods.

"Mr. Lamond, I'd like to say a couple of words to these folks, if you don't mind."

Of course he minds. I've seen him on TV strutting and preening for the cameras. "You have every right to interrupt me, if you think anybody will listen." A tic at his mouth signals that he's annoyed, but he opens one arm wide to invite me to stand next to him. "The police chief wants to talk to you folks," he says loudly. His voice couldn't be more condescending. I'm glad it's chilly because it keeps my cheeks from turning red. I'm not good at handling being mocked.

"I don't know a lot of y'all," I say. "All I want to say is that I intend to do everything I can to make sure the authorities find out who did this horrible crime. That's my pledge."

"That ain't sayin' much," somebody mutters loud enough for me to hear.

I swallow. "I can't do it alone," I say. "I need anybody who knows anything about this to talk to me. Call me, come by headquarters, or . . ." I hesitate, thinking of how Jeanne will react. "Come by my house. Everybody knows where I live. The Texas Highway Patrol will be in charge of the investigation, but I'll see to it that they get any information that might help." I step back a couple of feet and say, "Thank you," to Lamond.

And that's when I see a man with a camera taking one photo after another, and a man standing next to him taking notes. I take my eyes off them when Lamond comes up close and says, "Talk is cheap. I'm going to keep an eye on this town."

I suddenly think that Lamond might be useful to me in a pinch. "How can I get in touch with you?"

"My man Juno will give you a phone number." He beckons to one of his black-suited aides, who hurries over. "Juno, give this lawman a card."

Juno makes a big show of pulling a silver card case out of his pocket and handing me a card like it's pure gold. "You can reach me with this, and I'll pass a message along to Mr. Lamond."

I tuck the card in my shirt pocket and walk away, skirting the crowd. When I arrive at my truck, I notice that a few people are walking back toward the road.

The two reporters who were taking snapshots hustle over to me. "You know who that was?" the man taking notes asks.

"You a reporter?" I ask.

"Niles Morgenstern, *Dallas Morning News*. You know who that was?"

Despite the cool, I break out in a sweat. In the police training I had, they told us always to be wary of reporters, that they could make you look like a fool. I laughed at the idea, thinking I'd never be in a position to worry about that kind of thing.

"I do know. Now if you'll excuse me."

"You know he can fire up people and make life hell for you."

"I'll have to take care of that if it happens," I say. "Now if you want to know anything more, Sheriff Newberry will be giving a press conference at the courthouse later today. You'd be better off talking to him."

Morgenstern smiles. He's got kind eyes. "Newberry isn't the one who just confronted Albert Lamond. I'd like to interview you."

I shake my head. "I don't have any more to say. My encounter with Mr. Lamond was not a confrontation. I just wanted to say a few words. I'm sure you're aware I don't have any authority over how this investigation goes, so I'd best keep my two cents' worth out of it."

Morgenstern laughs. "Okay, we'll leave you alone for now. But a word to the wise. You've put yourself in it, whether you like it or not." He flips me his card, motions to the photographer, and they leave.

CHAPTER 6

After the episode with Lamond, I'm so rattled that I figure I might as well face my mamma and get all the unpleasantness over in one day. I pull up to her apartment and sit for a few minutes, trying to decide whether to go in. I'd rather face that crowd again than face my mamma, but Jeanne will keep after me until I make good on my promise to go see her. Besides, I'm already here.

The apartment building is only a few years old, but the construction is so shoddy that it's already falling apart. I've tried every way to get Mamma to move to a better place nearer the middle of town so she won't have so much trouble getting groceries, but she stays here because my brother, Horace, has one of the other apartments. It's a step up from the trailer they used to live in when they were first married. I don't know why it matters to her to be close to Horace. They don't get along, and she treats Horace's wife, Donna, two degrees worse than she treats everybody else. As far as I know, Jeanne is the only person who gets along with her. Jeanne brings her groceries once a week and makes sure she has everything she needs.

The reason Horace lives here is it's close to the liquor store.

I sigh and get out of the truck. Horace's beaten-up old Ford Falcon is not out front. Maybe Mamma has gone somewhere with him. I can always hope. Then, if she complains that I didn't come to see her, I can tell her I did but that she was not home. That's not likely. She hardly ever leaves her apartment.

When I knock on the pressed-board door, she calls out, "Hold your horses!" I hear her shuffling toward the door and I steel myself.

"Look what the cat dragged in," she says. She's wearing a gray-and-yellow striped housedress that hangs on her, and a frayed pink sweater. "Coming by to see if I'm dead yet?"

The mere act of opening the door has let out a pent-up cloud of cigarette smoke. She has been a chain smoker my whole life. I don't know which is worse, the liquor that eventually killed my daddy or her cigarettes.

"Jeanne said you called, and I thought I'd stop by."

"You might as well come on in." She turns her back on me and shuffles into the living room. She has the heater on and it's at least eighty degrees in here. She's always been thin, but now her arms and legs are like sticks. She looks twenty years older than she is. I wonder if a nasty attitude ages a person. She eases herself into her rickety rocking chair that has a quilted seat cushion and back. It's positioned to watch the black-and-white console TV that Daddy bought right before he got sick. I don't know where he got the money for it. Some things you don't ask.

"You want me to make some coffee?" I ask.

"Go ahead. Make yourself right at home in my house."

If I hadn't asked, she would have complained that I never did a thing for her. She's the original "damned if you do, damned if you don't." I've learned not to bite back, but it exhausts me to resist.

The kitchen is small but adequate. I'll say this for her: she has always kept a clean house. I smile at the school picture of my nephew, Tom, that she has taped to the refrigerator. It's from a year ago, when he was in the second grade, and in the last year he has sprouted considerably. He's grinning a mile wide. I don't know how Horace and Donna managed to produce such a smart, friendly kid. I put the coffee on to perc and sit down, choosing a leatherette side chair rather than the saggy sofa with the nubby weave.

"It's cold outside," I say.

"Humph. You got nothing to talk about but the weather?"

My conversation choices are limited by what I can stand to hear her go on about. If I tell her that my cows arrived today, she'll declare that they're a waste of time and money. When I first told her I was going to buy some cattle, she said, "That's nice. You're going to be a gentleman farmer." What she meant was that I was a phony, trying to look like a cattle rancher when I'm nothing but a boy who grew up poor and married a rich wife.

If I tell her about the fire, she'll blame the victims, and when she finds out they were black, she'll rant that "coloreds" have it better than her and don't know how to take care of their goods. "Well, it is cold," I say. "Norther came in and the temperature dropped thirty degrees."

"I heard all that racket out there this morning with the fire trucks. What happened?"

I don't have the heart for this. "It was a fire, but it's out now." Before she has a chance to pump me, I say, "Jeanne said you had something you wanted to talk to me about."

"I doubt it would be of interest to you."

"It might. Why don't you try me?"

"You going to let that coffee sit in there percolating until it's scorched?"

I go into the kitchen and pour us each a cup. "Cream and sugar?"

"Not too much cream," she says.

When I hand it to her, she eyes it with suspicion.

I sit back down. "Go on, tell me what it was you wanted to talk about."

"I guess you didn't hear that Donna got beat up over the weekend."

"No, I hadn't heard it." This is news. Donna isn't one to take anything off anybody, and I'm surprised somebody got the better of her.

"Of course not. You're just the chief of police. Why would you know when somebody's going around attacking women?"

"Somebody attacked her? Did she say who did it?"

"I know what you're thinking, but it wasn't Horace that beat her up."

"That wasn't in my mind. Did she go to the hospital?" I don't know exactly what "beaten up" means. It could mean anything from somebody slapping her to having bones broken.

"I told her she looked so bad that she ought to, but she said she was all right."

"I'll stop by and see if she wants to file a complaint," I say.

"La-di-dah, ain't we official. I don't expect she'll appreciate you sticking your nose in."

She's probably right. Donna and I have an adversarial relationship due to some history that I prefer not to dwell on. But regardless of what Mamma thinks, I am the chief of police, and I can't have people getting beaten up and not reporting it. "Have you seen Tom?"

"He don't ever come by here to see me. Lives right downstairs, and I hear him run out hollering with his friends, but he doesn't have the time of day for his old granny, even though he's the apple of my eye."

He could come by every day, and she'd say the same thing. All I know is when I was that age I stayed out as much as I could to escape her tongue.

I get up and tell her I need to go. "Thank you for telling me what happened to Donna. I'll talk to her or Horace to make sure she's all right."

I'm surprised when the sharp retort I expect doesn't come. Instead, she nods and looks off toward the front door with her head cocked. "You watch. There's more to that story than she's telling."

After I perform all the little rituals of leave-taking I head downstairs to the apartment where Horace, Donna, and Tom live. I knock on the door and hear footsteps. Donna opens the door, and I can't help letting out an exclamation of surprise. Someone has made a mess of her face. Her left eye is black and swollen almost shut, and she has bruises all over, including around her neck. It looks like somebody tried to strangle her.

She shrinks back when she sees me. "I didn't expect to see you here," she says, sweeping her long mane of hair back over her shoulder. Her hair is naturally brown, but a year ago she went blond. She's short and stacked, with a tiny waist and curved bottom. She's not exactly pretty, but she has a way of pouting her lips and lowering her head to look up at you that gives you ideas.

"What in the world happened to you?" I ask.

"I guess *she* told you."

"Mamma was worried about you."

"Don't give me that BS. She just wants to gossip." She steps back. "It's cold! Now that you've seen me, you might as well come on in." No wonder she's cold. She's wearing tight pants and a short-sleeved shirt with a plunging neckline that exposes a lot of skin. She puts me on guard.

I close the door behind me. "Who did this to you?"

She gives her usual roguish smile. But the effect is grotesque, given the state of her face. "You gonna go beat him up for me?"

"Donna, just tell me what happened."

"I hitched a ride from the wrong person."

"Why were you hitchhiking?"

She licks her lips. "I went out to get some milk for Tom. Horace had the car, so I figured it wouldn't hurt to thumb a ride. It's only a mile down the road to the grocery store."

Something sounds fishy, but I don't want to directly accuse Horace of hitting her. To tell the truth, Horace may be shiftless and he drinks too much, but I've never known him to be violent.

"Did you know the guy who picked you up?"

She touches the skin above her eye. "Never laid eyes on him."

"What kind of car was he driving?"

She shrugs. "I don't know. A Ford, I think. A lot newer than ours. It was dark-colored."

"What time was this?"

"Late. About ten o'clock at night. That's what time I realized we didn't have any milk for Tom's breakfast." Her eyes cut to the side, which makes me suspicious. Shifty eyes. Could mean she's nervous because I'm asking all these questions. But could also be that she's lying. But why? It's not as if it matters what she was doing out. But then an uncomfortable thought strikes me.

"Where was Horace?"

"He was over in Bobtail, having a beer with some guys."

Horace isn't a particularly friendly guy, and I wonder who he could have been out drinking beer with. I have a feeling that Donna is lying, but I'm not sure what about exactly.

Could she be cheating on Horace? If he found out, it's possible that he's the one who hit her. And I know from firsthand experience that she cozies up to other men. Right after she and Horace were married and I was in college, I came home for a visit and she cornered me in the house when everybody was out. If she'd been married to anybody but my brother, I might have been tempted, but that was one step too far. We've had an uneasy relationship ever since, and she's downright cold to Jeanne, although I don't think that bothers Jeanne one bit.

"I'm sorry that happened to you, but you shouldn't be hitchhiking late at night," I say.

"How else am I going to get to the store if Horace is gone?"

I know what she wants me to say, but I'm not going to offer to come take her to the store late at night. "Don't run out of milk," I say.

She laughs. It's a throaty sound. She knows how to be sexy, even with a torn-up face.

"If you see the guy who did this again, call me."

CHAPTER 7

It's almost five o'clock, so it's likely I missed Newberry's press conference. Not that he had much to tell the press, but it might have been interesting to see how these things are done. I wonder if that reporter from the *Dallas Morning News* went. It's a four-hour drive from Dallas to Jarrett Creek. I guess they monitor reports that come in to the highway patrol and the Rangers, and a bulletin about five dead bodies is worth traveling down here to check out.

I can't get the crime scene out of my mind. Even if it isn't my place to investigate, I want to go back there and took a look at it. I'm afraid Albert Lamond is right. From the way Sutherland talked, since the victims are black, I'm pretty sure he isn't going to put a lot of effort into the case. It has been a while since I left there, and maybe everyone has cleared out until the fire cools down enough to go inside. I'd like a chance to look over the site without others milling around.

First I stop by headquarters. No one is there, but Tilley has left me a note saying he's gone off to help his wife get their cat out of a tree. There are three messages on the answering machine, all asking about this morning's fire. One of them is Bonnie Bedichek, wanting an update for the newspaper. None of them needs to be answered at the moment.

The fire chief's truck is still parked on the road near the path that leads to the house. He and another man are sitting in the truck, eating hamburgers. They greet me with a gloomy air.

"Still too hot to get close?" I ask.

"Nothing we can do anyway. That's up to the fire forensics team from Austin. They'll be here first thing tomorrow. We're waiting for

THP to send somebody out to keep an eye on the place overnight. You get looters and curiosity-seekers at something like this. That structure is not safe and somebody could get hurt."

"I'm going over there to take another look around," I say.

"Let me get you a hard hat," Koontz says. He climbs out of the truck and sizes me up. "You okay staying here until the THP man arrives? I'd like to get on back."

I tell him I'll stay. He doesn't have to hear it twice. As he's climbing back into his truck, I ask him what to do with the hard hat when I'm done.

"I'll get it from you next time I see you. No doubt we'll run into each other again."

I don't know what I'm looking for. Maybe I'm overstepping myself and ought to leave this to the experts, but at the very least I want to get a good look at the scene. I want to know how they lived and what was going on inside when the murders occurred. Did they know the person who killed them? Did they have a meal together? Or were they rousted out of bed? The stench is still hanging in the air from the fire and the bodies, but it has come down a notch in the chill air. The scene has a feel of doom, trees at the perimeter of the clearing drooping from the heat and the smoke of the fire. I have to remind myself not to get caught up in the desolation of the scene. That's what they told us in the scant training I received—that your investigating is best done with a neutral attitude. Still, it's hard not to react when children are involved.

Wisps of smoke still rise here and there from the embers. There's a big area of bare ground surrounding the house. Nobody bothered with a garden here. Why would anybody go to the trouble to clear such a big area and leave it bare? It makes the house look stark, standing in the middle of the clearing. It looks suspiciously like whoever lived here wanted to be sure they didn't get snuck up on.

I first walk the perimeter of the clearing, keeping my eye on the ground to see if anything is out of place. A lot of the area is trampled with the footprints of the men who responded to the fire. There's a variety of discarded items—a lone sock, half buried in the dirt; a paper cup; several feet of frayed rope; a bangle bracelet; and a comb with half its teeth missing. All of this has obviously been here for a while.

More interesting is a pile of beer bottles and cigarette butts, newer, next to what looks like a campfire. It's possible that a bit of drinking turned into an argument and an argument into gunplay. I crouch down and hold my hand near the ashes. The remnants of wood are cold. I use a stick to sift through the ashes of the fire and find a marshmallow, charred on one side, uncooked on the other. I peer off through the trees, picturing the scene. A kid cooking marshmallows and this one slipping off the stick. Adults standing around, drinking beer, watching the kids cook over the fire. There might have been hot dogs, too. Animals would have eaten any remains of that, but no self-respecting animal would touch a marshmallow.

Footprints around the fire indicate that there were women here as well as men. There's a track of a high-heeled shoe very clearly marked. But I don't have a way of making this mean anything.

I rise, dusting my hands on my pants, and continue my walk around the clearing, getting closer to the house. There are more cigarette butts and a few more pieces of detritus, but nothing that strikes me as of great interest.

The back of the house is the most intact, and I wonder why. From the way the house is damaged, it looks like whoever lit the fire came up to the front door and started it. So why were the bodies at the front of the house? I get a sick feeling at what occurs to me as the most likely scenario. Someone at the back of the house was stationed to keep them from escaping out the back, so they ran to the front. There they either ran into the fire or were mowed down by gunfire. One body was found inside the back door. When that person was killed, the others must have fled toward the front.

There's a concrete slab for a porch at the back door, scuffed and with dried dirt on one edge where someone scraped their shoes. The door is closed, but it opens readily and I step into the kitchen. It's chaotic, as if someone had served a meal and hadn't gotten around to doing the dishes. Everything is covered with soot, so it's hard to tell if these are dishes accumulated from several days or if it's a recent meal. I stand still, getting a sense of the scene. There's an area on the floor in front of me that has less soot on it, and a messy area of overlapping footprints where the body must have been retrieved. I wonder if anybody noted any footprints present before the ambulance crew arrived. No way of knowing.

I step around where the body was found, and I walk over to the kitchen counter. There are beans in the bottom of a large pot, and a couple of pieces of cornbread in a metal pan. Another pot is empty, but there's a green leaf sticking to the side—collards, most likely.

The dishes are mismatched, mostly melamine, but with a couple of chipped china dishes. They are spread haphazardly across the counter with remnants of the meal. One person scraped their plate clean, and one hardly ate anything. Most didn't leave much. The glasses are jelly jars. Two of them have traces of milk in the bottom—or at least I take it to be milk. It's cloudy with ash. Children. I wonder if there was an adult here to cook this meal.

And then it strikes me: The fire happened this morning. What kept them from doing the dishes last night? It's possible that they left the dishes every night and washed them the next morning. I know some people do that. But the rest of the kitchen is relatively tidy. I don't get the sense that this is a household that would have left the dishes like this. So what happened?

I step into a hallway. The air stings my nose, and the smell is nauseating. It's dark in the hallway, but every surface is covered with soot. I look up at the ceiling. The soot is darkest there.

There are three doors off the hallway, all closed, and an open entry into the living room, which took the brunt of the fire. I open the closest door and peer in. It's a girl's bedroom with two twin beds without headboards, made up with sheets and no bedspread. On one of the beds there's a stuffed animal that has seen better days. Hard to tell what kind of animal it was originally. Between the two beds there's a wooden crate for a bedside table. It has a lamp on it with no shade, just a bare bulb. Clothes are strewn across one of the beds, and there are tattered magazines on the floor, as if the girls had looked at them again and again. There's a plain mirror propped up on a wooden chest of drawers, and various bits of paraphernalia are scattered in front of the mirror. Makeup and nail polish, and cologne. So not really young children anyway. I don't know why, but that makes me feel a little better.

The next room is a small laundry room that smells of cat. I haven't seen signs of a cat. Probably ran off into the woods when the fire started. There's a scrub tub and an old wringer washer that looks like it hasn't been used in a long time. A piece of twine is tacked up across the room. It's hung with a few underclothes.

The third room is completely different. It is tricked out like someone's idea of a New Orleans bordello. The room is papered in red-flocked wallpaper, and the double bed is covered with a red-and-gold spread and decorated with gold and black satin pillows. There's a fancy, old-fashioned chest of drawers with carved handles and legs, and a mirror across the top. I use my handkerchief to open the top drawer. It's warped and hard to open. It contains women's undergarments. The other drawers are a jumbled mess of blouses and slacks that don't look like they belong to children. A straight-backed chair in one corner has a worn, red velvet seat cover. Next to the bed is a carved round table with an ornate glass lamp with a red-fringed lampshade.

This room puts the residents in a different light. Why were there children living here in what looks like a bordello? Another thought makes my skin crawl. Were the children here for sex? I wonder what Sutherland or the Rangers will make of that. I remember what Albert Lamond ranted, that no one would bother to investigate. Will Sutherland shrug off the whole episode as beneath his interest? I remember him off in the woods, retching. He may have had a personal reaction, but my gut tells me that doesn't mean he'll take the deaths here seriously.

Much of the living room is charred, and the rest is sooty and singed. I suspect the sofa and chairs were saggy and worn before they were damaged. The big console TV is old. It's set in a corner with all the seating facing it. There's a big hole in a burnt-out front window. I walk over gingerly, avoiding charred places in the floor that might give way, and look out to see a window air-conditioner that has fallen to the ground. I don't know how I missed seeing that outside.

Some photos taped to one wall escaped the fire. Some are school pictures of young girls and one of a boy. There are also group photos, but taken from such a distance that it's hard to see any faces. They are all black people. In one, everyone is dressed up like it's a wedding or a Sunday church meeting. If it's a funeral, everybody was glad the person died, because they're all looking cheerful.

One picture was taken out front of this house with two youngsters standing in front of it, grinning. The house looked brand-new. How is it that it was built and I knew nothing of it? I think I know what goes on in town, but obviously I don't know as much as I thought I did. I have a sudden desire to leave. I feel a little ashamed that these people came here under what was supposed to be my watch, and not only did I fail to protect them, I didn't even know they existed.

Before I leave, I suck up my courage and peer into the front hallway. It's a burnt-out shell. The bodies are gone, so there's nothing to see, but that doesn't keep my mind from manufacturing images of bodies heaped up near the door.

I hear voices outside and go back out the back door to find two young highway patrolmen I don't recognize smoking cigarettes and drinking beer.

"Whoa!" one of them says. "I didn't know anybody was inside. What's it look like in there?"

I ignore the question since I get the feeling he's looking for a thrill rather than for information. Instead, I introduce myself.

"I heard you were a kid," the older of the two says. He's tall and blond, with a blond mustache and ice-blue eyes. He can't be more than a few years older than me.

"Must have been Sutherland told you that," I say.

Both men laugh. "Yep. He's an ass," the other one says. He's got red hair and freckles. "Don't let him get to you. Everybody knows he likes to ride greenhorns."

"You fellas spending the night?"

"Unfortunately."

"You need anything?"

They tell me they don't, that they'll take turns napping in the car, and go for supplies as need be. They've clearly scouted out the liquor store.

CHAPTER 8

On my way home, I stop at Truly Bennett's house, hoping to have a chat with him to find out what inspired his cold shoulder toward me, but no one answers the door. In fact, the whole neighborhood seems quiet after today's excitement. I'll come back and talk to him tomorrow.

As soon as I step into my house, I feel a chill that matches the weather. I call out, as always. Jeanne's reply has frost around the edges.

I follow the sound of her voice to the spare room, where she has a sewing machine set up. I have no idea why she insists on sewing. She seems to hate it, and the only thing I've ever seen come of it are the kitchen curtains, and they hang crooked. Not that I've mentioned it. She's bent over some unfortunate piece of cloth and doesn't look up. I go over and slip my arm around her shoulders and bend over to kiss her, but she shakes me off. "Can't you see I'm busy?"

"Sorry, I didn't mean to interrupt." I don't hear that tone often. The question is, do I acknowledge it and ask what's wrong, or do I pretend I didn't notice and hope it goes away? I'd prefer to do the latter, but I suspect it will prolong the situation.

The silence persists, so I take a sideways approach. "What are you working on?"

She sighs and lets it fall to her lap. When she looks up, I see that her eyes are red-rimmed, which punches me in the gut. "What difference does it make? It's going to turn out awful."

"No, it won't. But why don't you put it down and come on in the living room? We can have something to drink." I take the pitiful rag out of her hand and pull her up. Something has brought on this mood, and I think I know what it is.

"I'm going to build a fire in the fireplace and then have a beer. What can I get you?"

She waves her hand. "I don't care. A beer, I guess."

She hates beer. I don't know why this mood comes as a surprise to me every month, but it does. For two years now we've been hoping to get pregnant, and naturally she's more attuned to the failures than I am.

It isn't really cold enough for a fire, but it will feel cozy, so I wad up some newspapers and tuck them under the log set up left from last winter. I set a match to it, and it whooshes to life. I sneak a look at Jeanne, who has come into the room and is gazing morosely into the fire. The burning newspaper reminds me of today's fire. I get up and back away. In the kitchen I make her a gin and tonic, and pour myself a couple of fingers of bourbon. Being reminded of the fire, I need something stronger than beer.

When I bring in our drinks, she is sitting on the sofa in front of the fire and greets me with a determined smile. That's the way she is. She may have disappointments, but she's not one for wallowing. One of the first things that attracted me to her was her good cheer.

I hand the drink to Jeanne and sit down next to her, kiss her gently, and brush the hair back from her face. I feel her shrink away, but I know it's not me she's upset about. She feels like a failure in the one thing she wants so badly. She has big brown eyes, and I can hardly stand it when they are sad. She isn't beautiful by magazine standards. Her face is round and her hair is a plain color of brown. But I love her impish smile and the way her eyes crinkle up at the corners when she laughs. I normally do what I can to make that happen. But now it's best if I just sit with her.

I slump against the back of the sofa and can't help letting out a weary sigh.

"Oh, I'm so selfish," she says. "Here I am pouting and you've had a hard day."

"All that falls away when I'm here with you. You know that."

It was the wrong thing to say. Her eyes tear up.

"I should go down and take a look at my new toys before it gets too dark," I say. "Why don't you come with me?" I get up and reach my hand out to her.

"I went down there earlier. They were pining away for you," she says, and smiles.

The phone rings. I groan.

"Don't answer it," she says.

"Got to," I say. I get up and go into the hall to answer it.

It's my brother, Horace. "I'm wondering if me and Donna can bring Tom by to stay with you for a while. Me and her have somebody we need to see in Bobtail."

"Tonight? Why don't you have him pack a bag and stay overnight."

"That sounds like a good idea. I'll see if he wants to."

With everything on my mind this afternoon, I had forgotten Donna's beating. She's vain about her looks, and it surprises me that she's going out of the house with her eye swollen shut and bruises on her face. But I'm glad they're going. We love it when Tom comes over. He's a bright little kid who deserves better than what my brother and his wife do for him—which seems to be the minimum. But they do love him, and that counts for a lot.

I go back into the living room. "Guess what? That was Horace. Tom's coming to spend the night."

"Really? I'd better get some supper on." Jeanne jumps up with new light in her eyes.

I follow her into the kitchen. She opens the refrigerator and starts getting food out. "You think he'd rather have fried chicken or chicken-fried steak?" Her face is pink with happiness.

I know which one I'd rather have. "What do you think?"

"I know you'd rather have the steak," she says. "But he loves fried chicken."

"Then make that. I like it, too, especially the way you make it."

"And some mashed potatoes and gravy and peas," she says. She's on high speed now.

"Something I need to tell you," I say. "I saw Mamma today."

She pauses and cocks her head. "Good for you."

I tell her about Donna's injuries.

"Oh, my goodness. Poor Tom." She turns to face me, leaning back against the counter. "I bet he's worried about his mamma. Did she say . . ." She hesitates. "Never mind."

She turns back to the counter and spends a few minutes hacking the chicken into pieces. When she starts dredging them in the flour-and-egg mixture and has the oil heating up, she says, "You don't suppose Horace did it, do you?"

"I've never known him to be violent toward a woman. I expect it was somebody passing through. She said she was hitchhiking and didn't recognize the guy."

She looks toward me and lifts an eyebrow but keeps whatever she's thinking to herself. She doesn't have much use for Horace. She thinks he's lazy and uses any excuse to make people feel sorry for him. "Donna said she was hitchhiking? That doesn't make sense. Why didn't she call us if she needed a ride?"

I shrug. "What can I do to help you?"

She turns around and gives me a stink-eye. "Stay out of my way, that's what."

I tell her I'm going to go pay my new cows a visit. "Send Tom down when he gets here."

I can't help getting a silly grin on my face when I get to the pasture. The cows are huddled together, and they give me a suspicious look when I get to the fence. "I'm not going to hurt you," I say. "You'll get used to me pretty fast."

I remember the snide comment Mamma made about me wanting to be a gentleman farmer. Suppose I do? Why is that so bad?

Before I can start brooding about it, I hear Tom hollering, "Uncle

Samuel!" I turn to see him sprinting toward me. I run to greet him and grab him up and twirl him around. He's breathless when I set him down, and he reels around like he's dizzy for a minute. Then he charges over to the fence, grinning a mile wide at the new arrivals. "Them are some good-looking cows," he says, confident in his opinion. "What kind are they? Are they boys or girls?"

"These are Herefords. White-faced. And these are all females. I'll be having a bull delivered before long. He's the male."

"Can I watch them have sex?"

I bust out laughing. "What do you know about that?"

"I saw Cootic Barton's dogs having sex. His mamma told us what they were doing. So can I?"

"We'll see when the time comes. Is your daddy up at the house?"

"No, he let me off and went on. He said to tell you hi. Did you know Aunt Jeanne is making fried chicken? I *love* fried chicken." He clutches his chest, squeezes his eyes shut, and wiggles.

"Let's get on back to the house, then. If we're not there when supper's ready, she'll throw it out."

His eyes pop open. "She wouldn't do that."

"I don't want to test her and find out. Come on, I'll race you."

CHAPTER 9

I'm up early the next morning, my first day as a gentleman farmer. Mamma meant the phrase as a jibe, but the idea is beginning to grow on me. As perky as Tom usually is, he isn't a morning child, and I leave him to Jeanne to try to coax some breakfast into him while I go down to the pasture.

Truly Bennett told me to give the cows half feed this morning, since they'll still be unsettled from their move. The cows all keep an eye on me, as if they're not quite ready to trust me. Most of them crowd up to the feed station, but a couple of them hang back. I need to keep an eye on them to make sure they aren't ailing. I thought I'd have trouble telling them apart, but already I see differences, everything from markings to the distribution of their weight to the way they look at me. And of course they aren't all the same age. There are several settled breeders and a few yearlings and some calves.

The next order of business will be to get a bull, but Truly said the best thing to do is get the cows comfortable and then hire a bull after the first season. He knows a couple of ranchers who could use the breeding money and who have good breeders. He says not to rush it.

As soon as I drop Tom off at school, I head into work early. As tired as I was after the grim day yesterday, I still tossed and turned all night, chasing the images of those bodies and the stink of the fire from my senses. This morning Jeanne said if I kept that up, I was going to be banished to the sofa.

The cool spell is short-lived, as they tend to be this early in September, and by eight a.m., it's already warm. By afternoon it'll be back up in the eighties.

I'm glad no one else is in the office yet. I need to figure out a few things. I may not have much experience, and I may not have any standing in the investigation, but I don't like being pushed aside in my own town. It's up to someone else to investigate who did it, but I want to know who was living out there and why they were murdered.

It's likely that if the THP is going to hold onto the case, Sutherland will be the lead investigator, and he made it clear that he's not volunteering information. I could ask Curren Wills, but I'm leery of looking like a hanger-on, somebody who doesn't have the guts to confront Sutherland. I could also call the county morgue in Bobtail and ask for the autopsy results.

The phone rings. It's Mickey Wells, a chronic complainer, who wants to know why the town hasn't cleared up the smoke from yesterday's fire. I don't know what he has in mind. Maybe setting up a big fan on one end of town and blowing it out the other end. I tell him I'll take it up with the fire department.

I've barely hung up when Bonnie Bedichek calls. "Anything new?"

"Not anything concrete, but even if I did know something, I couldn't tell you. You have to get official information through the THP."

"You're kidding, right?"

"No, I can't be blabbing to the press."

"It could be a two-way street."

"What do you mean?"

"I mean I could give you information in return."

"Bonnie, all due respect, I don't think I can use your information since I'm not officially part of the investigation. You better save up anything you hear to feed to John Sutherland."

She chuckles. "I've got nothing to say to that man. 'Little lady,' he calls me."

I tell her I have work to do and I wish her well with her reporting and hang up with her still protesting.

The next call surprises me. It's John Sutherland. "If you're so all-fired anxious to be involved in the investigation of the murder in your territory, I have a lot going on and I may turn a little something over to you."

I don't give a damn if he's up to something; all I care about is getting to be involved in the case. "What might that be?"

"I'm thinking you might want to be in on a couple of the autopsies. They're doing some of them today, and the others tomorrow. It's too late for you to get in on them today, but it occurred to me you could get up to Austin for the ones they're doing tomorrow." There's a hint of a smirk in his voice. Finding out what I'm made of. The idea of viewing those burned and twisted bodies gives me a knot in my belly. But I have to prove to myself and to him that I can face whatever is necessary to get the job done.

"When and where?" I ask.

"That would be in Austin first thing tomorrow."

"You have a phone contact?"

He gives me the name of Clinton Haywood, an assistant to the medical examiner.

"I'll be there." If I'm going to be there first thing in the morning, I either have to leave at five a.m. or go up to Austin tonight. Maybe Jeanne would like to go to Austin for the day. But then I stop short. I've got a new responsibility: the cows. Although Jeanne reminded me that having cattle would tie us down, I didn't take it seriously. Even if Jeanne stays home, I can't very well ask her to feed the cattle. This is my responsibility.

But I have an even-greater responsibility as chief of police. Then it strikes me that I can kill not two but three birds with one stone. I'll ask Truly Bennett if he'll take care of the cows, which gives me an excuse to go by and see him. When he knows why I'm going to Austin, he'll let his people know that I'm making good on my vow to take the murders seriously.

I jump in the car and head for Truly's place. It's a modest house, probably no more than four or five rooms, though I'm guessing. I've never been inside. The only times I've been here is when I needed his help. He doesn't have a phone, so I have to drive over here to hire him. He not only works with livestock but also does some repair work, and people say he's good at painting.

I get out of the car feeling uneasy, remembering how curt Truly was yesterday. He has always been mild-mannered and easy-going, no kind of rabble-rouser, and I wonder what's eating at him. I don't think I said or did anything to offend him, but I'll get a chance to find out.

His daddy, Ezekiel, answers the door. An older version of Truly, he's wearing overhauls over a worn blue work shirt. He greets me gravely, looking me straight in the eye. No challenge there, but he appears to be watchful and maybe wary. "Mr. Craddock, everything okay with them cows?"

"Yes, but I need some help from Truly. Is he here?"

He screws up his face and looks past me, reaching up to scratch the side of his neck. "He's gone out for a while."

"You know when he might be back? I need to ask him to take care of my cattle tomorrow morning."

He clears his throat. "When he gets back, I'll ask him to come over to your place and talk to you."

His eyes have a pleading look to them, and then I realize: He doesn't want me hanging around on his front porch where the neighbors can see me talking to him. I realize that if he won't talk to me, then no one will, and I don't have much of a chance of finding out what was going on out in the woods. "Mr. Bennett, I don't want to impose on you, but can I ask you a question?"

His wariness increases. "What about?"

"I think you know. I've got to have some help, or there's no way I'll find out what happened to those young people who died."

He looks me up and down, and it's almost like I'm looking in a mirror, seeing what he sees: a tall, lanky white boy who could as easily be working on a farm somewhere. The only difference is I've got a badge and not a bit of experience. "I don't know a thing about those people back there," he says. His voice is so soft I can barely catch the words.

"Tell me who might." I can't help the pleading sound in my voice. "You have a young daughter, don't you? Maybe she knows something."

"Best leave Alva out of it," he says. "She working over in Bobtail at the Motel 6. She not hanging out with no lowlife. Sorry I can't help you. I got things to do. Now you go on."

He steps back into the house.

"You'll tell Truly I came by?" But the door is closed gently, but firmly, in my face.

I stand on the porch for a minute, bamboozled. It never occurred to me that people would turn their backs on me. "You're a fool," I mutter to myself. Back in the pickup, I ponder my next move. I could go door to door asking questions, but something tells me I wouldn't get anywhere.

CHAPTER 10

Since I'm out near Cato Woods anyway, I'm drawn back to the crime scene. A black Cadillac Eldorado is parked off the road near the house. You don't see cars that fancy around here.

When I arrive at the house, I find two men standing with their arms crossed, gazing at the damaged structure. One is a white man dressed in a western-style black business suit with wide lapels and flared-bottom pants, a ruffled white shirt, and bolo tie. The other man is black with a tight, curly Afro and a goatee. His clothes grab my attention. The soft, pleated pants and black silk T-shirt are expensive. Like some rock stars I see on TV, he's wearing a clutch of gold chains around his neck and one gold earring. What kind of work must he do to be able to afford those clothes? What are these two dandies doing here?

"What can I do you for, Sheriff?" the white man asks. He's trying to be cute.

He's got my title wrong, but at least since I wore my uniform today he knows I'm a lawman. I introduce myself and tell him I'm the police chief. "Thought maybe the forensics people would be here by now. Since this was arson, they'll be sending out a team from Austin."

"We haven't seen them." Up close, the white guy has a seedy look to him, his eyes with pouches under them and broken veins around his nose. The signs of a hard drinker. "Barton Dudley," he says, sticking out his hand for me to shake. "They call me 'Blue.' I'm the insurance man for this property, and this is Freddie Carmichael. He owns this house."

I try not to show that the information startles me. I assumed the people who lived there owned it or rented it from the Cato family.

"Shame what happened here. A tragedy. But I'm glad you're here. Can you tell me the names of the people who were living here?"

The two men exchange glances. Carmichael's lips lift in a sneer. "Until this fire, I wasn't aware that anyone was living in the house. It appears that they were squatters. Of course I'm sorry for what happened, but they had no business being here."

His voice startles me. I haven't run into a black man with his smooth way of talking. "You sound like you're not from around here," I say.

"I live in Houston, but I'm originally from Chicago."

"How long have you owned this property?" I ask.

"Is that an official question? Should I have my lawyer here?"

The question throws me off. What would somebody like Curren Wills, the Texas Ranger, say? John Sutherland would probably have him in cuffs by now for having an insolent attitude. "I don't know why that would be necessary," I say. And then I add, "Do you?"

"No, but it has been my experience in Texas that the law doesn't always work the same for white men and black men."

"That's not the case in Chicago?"

"There are some differences," he says. "But as for your question, I bought this house about a year ago."

"Who did you buy it from?" I'm genuinely curious. It's like a whole different world out here in this part of town, people owning and selling property I didn't know existed.

"I didn't deal with him personally, so his name slips my mind, but I can find out for you if it's important."

"Did you go through a realtor here in town?"

He strokes the side of his cheek as if making sure that his goatee has been properly groomed. "You know, I wish I could be of more help, but that has slipped my mind as well."

I could list the names of all the realtors in town and jog his memory, but it would be futile. I don't know exactly why he's lying, but he is. Did someone else actually sell the house to him, or did he have it built? Were squatters living here, or did he know who they were? Maybe he doesn't even own the house and both of them are lying.

I'm going to have to get to the truth from someone else. But I learned in college that acting like a rube can sometimes work to my advantage. I may run into them later and it would be best if they think I haven't got much of a brain. "Never mind," I say. "Your friend Blue here can tell you that in small towns we're always nosy. Anything you tell me wouldn't be of use to me anyway. The highway patrol will be investigating this, and I sure don't want to step on their toes. They know I'm wet behind the ears."

Blue laughs and claps me on the side of my arm. "You stick to catching teenagers pulling down the goalposts after a football game."

"I think that's about my size," I say, with a big grin. "If you'll excuse me, I'm going to leave you to it. Nice meeting you, Mr. Dudley, Mr. Carmichael." I turn like I'm going to walk away and then turn back. "Blue, would you happen to have a card on you? I know somebody who might give you a good price on clearing out this damage and fixing it up."

Blue Dudley hands me a card, which I stick in my shirt pocket. I nod to both of them. Neither of them gives me a particularly friendly look in return for the small-town-hick smile I bestow on them.

I'm walking back toward my truck when two men pull up in a panel truck.

One of them, a grizzled, red-faced man with white hair in a military-style buzz cut walks over to me.

"I'm Kelly Place," he says. "I'm the regional fire inspector with the state. This is my partner, Johnny Carson." He waves his hands. "I know, I know, not that Johnny Carson." His partner grins and ducks his head. He probably gets tired of that old joke from his boss.

"I assume we're in the right location."

"You are." I introduce myself and he seems satisfied. It's a relief to run into the occasional person who doesn't seem bothered by my youth.

"You been inside the crime scene?" he asks.

I tell him I have. "I didn't get much out of it, though. I'd like to shadow you, if you don't mind. I've got a lot to learn."

"That's a breath of fresh air. Most people turn tail and leave it to us. Ours is not the exciting part of the job."

"There's one thing I want to mention," I say. I tell him about Dudley and Carmichael. "I don't have any reason to be suspicious of them, but I've never heard of them around here."

"Let me take care of it. You'd be surprised how often you get real-estate people trying to make a quick buck off a tragedy."

He directs his assistant to bring some equipment and then follows me toward the house. Halfway there, we meet Dudley and Carmichael.

"Mr. Carmichael is the owner of the house," I say.

"Not exactly the owner," Dudley says. "Mr. Carmichael is the owner's representative."

"What does that mean, exactly?" Place smiles, but that doesn't quite smooth away the steel in his question.

"The owner is not from around here," Carmichael says. "He has a lot of interests, and I take care of the details for him."

"Mr. Carmichael," Place says, "I don't know who your employer says he is, but I looked up all the relevant information on this property, and it's part of a large tract of land called Cato Woods. If the man you're working for isn't named Cato, he's putting one over on you."

"Sorry for the confusion," Blue Dudley says, "It's all on the up and up. The Cato family leased the property out."

"If you say so. But I want to be sure who I'm dealing with here. Somebody has to be responsible for the property if it's declared unsafe. Plus, the highway patrol is in charge of this investigation, and they'll need to get in touch. I'd like to see some identification and get your contact information."

Carmichael leaves the matter to Dudley. I can tell that Place is not totally satisfied with the exchange, but like me he can't think of any reason to bear down.

After Dudley and Carmichael leave, we head on over to the house.

Place stands for a couple of minutes with his hands on his hips, surveying the damage. "It's not as bad as I expected."

We go in through the back door and I see he's making the same kind of assessment I did. "Beans and greens and cornbread," he says. His voice is so matter-of-fact that I don't have a clue what he's thinking. Poor folks' meal? Same kind of food he likes to eat? Food he hates? Hard to tell.

We start to walk away, but then he stops. "There were five bodies found and I count seven plates. Who else ate here?" He looks at me. I'm stunned because I didn't notice that the first time I came through.

"Good question," I say.

"Lord have mercy," he says. "Could the killers have got up from sharing a meal with them and then shot them? If not, why weren't they killed along with the other five? Or maybe the killers took them out of here and we'll find more bodies somewhere else on the property." He's talking low in a monologue, thinking out loud. I'm soaking it in, mad that I didn't see all that myself when I went through yesterday. I can learn, though. A mistake like that won't happen again.

"There'll be fingerprints on the plates. I'll get them bagged up and send them off for printing, although I doubt anything will come of it."

"Why is that?"

"This is likely to be a local dispute, not done by somebody with a criminal record."

I shrug because I don't know how to judge it.

"Let's see how far we can get into the fire area."

It takes the rest of the afternoon for the fire inspectors to do their work. They are thorough and careful, and he's right, it's not the most exciting thing I've ever seen. Even though he quickly agrees that the gasoline cans tossed out front were the cause of the fire, he still does all kinds of measurements and assessments of exactly what the sequence of events must have been. A lot of it seems to consist of standing and staring at charred areas. What I learn from the experience is that in the future, I'll leave fire evidence to the experts.

I head back to town to do some research. At city hall I find no record of any such place having building permits out in Cato Woods, which means it was an illegal dwelling. As to whether Freddie Carmichael or his "employer" actually owns it, since the place doesn't actually exist on paper, there's no evidence of who owns it.

Cato Woods is a huge tract of land, and it could contain many of these types of dwellings without anybody being the wiser. The Cato family lives in Dallas. I don't know that I've ever set eyes on any of them. There is a farmstead on the Cato land directly south of Cotton Hill. It's worth a drive out there to find out what the farmers might know, if anything, about the house.

Back at the station, as I'm walking out the door, Truly Bennett drives up in his old pickup. I wait for him to come to me. "Let's go inside where it's a little cooler," I say. He looks at the door as if he really doesn't want to come inside. I ignore his reluctance and hold the door for him so he can't very well refuse.

Inside, I offer him a seat, but he's says he'll stand. He wears a straw hat and he takes it off and clutches it in his hands. "Daddy said you wanted to talk to me?"

"I'd like to hire you to do something for me. I've got to go to Austin tonight. I'm going to observe the autopsies of those young people killed in the fire. Can you feed my cows for me?"

He nods. "I'll see to it," he says. "Is there anything else?"

I let a little sigh out. "Truly, I've always thought we got along okay, but recently I've had a feeling you've got a problem with me. Have I said something to offend you?"

He looks at me for the first time today, startled. "Oh, no, sir. I've got some things on my mind, that's all. I'm sorry. I didn't mean to . . ."

"No need to apologize. I just don't want there to be bad feeling between us."

"No, sir." He's back to staring at his feet.

"Did your daddy tell you I was asking about the people who lived out there in the woods?"

"He told me that."

"Do you know any of their names? If I'm going to attend their autopsies, I ought to at least know who they are."

I can tell he's thinking over his answer, so I stay quiet. Finally he says, "Folks don't want anybody talking."

"They don't want the people who did this horrible thing arrested? Did you know that one of the victims was a young girl who was shot while she was trying to put out the fire on her clothes? Do you know that somebody trapped them in the front hall so they would burn to death? And nobody wants whoever did that to be punished?" I don't mean to be yelling, but my frustration has taken over.

At my words, his chest starts heaving. "It's not that," he says.

"Then what is it? Why won't anybody talk to me? I promised I'd track down who did it, but if everybody clams up, how am I supposed to investigate anything?"

"You best leave it alone," he says. He claps his hat on his head and starts for the door. When his hand is on the knob, his head drops. I think he's about to say more, but he apparently thinks better of it.

I say thank you, but I'm speaking to the door. I hear his truck start up and he drives away so fast, he spews gravel.

CHAPTER 11

The Cato farm is up on a hill. The lawn in front of it is lush and green even after the heat of summer, making it look like a model place. They must have sprinklers going for hours every day. The land below the lawn and house is farmed with cotton almost ready to pick.

It's a long drive up the hill. What kind of people live in a place that looks like a magazine idea of a farm? Whoever it is, I doubt they have the slightest idea that a bootleg house exists on the opposite end of their thousand-acre plot.

As I drive up to the front porch, a rowdy black-and-white farm dog comes racing around the side of the house, barking like he means business. But his tail is whipping from side to side, as frenzied as he is. I get out of the car and tell him to calm down, which he does. The screen door opens and a tall, bony woman wearing khaki work pants, a long-tailed man's shirt, and work boots walks out. "Scout, hush!" She's a little late. The dog is frisking around me like we're old friends.

"Can I help you?" Her expression is stony. "If the dog bothers you, I'll put it away."

"I don't mind dogs," I say. I advance to the bottom step of the porch. "I'm Samuel Craddock, police chief over in Jarrett Creek. I wonder if I might have a word with you?"

"About what? We're a busy farm."

"I didn't get your name."

"Judy Montclair." She gives up the name like she's handing out gold.

"I'm investigating an incident that happened yesterday on the Cato farm property. I need some information."

"I don't know what I can tell you. We don't own the farm. We've got a lease on it."

I lean forward. "Do you know how I can get in touch with the owner?"

"I don't see why you can't get it from the county records."

A tall man wearing blue jeans and a well-worn, faded shirt walks from around back. He glares up at the woman, but she answers the hard look with one of her own. He turns the glare to me. "What is it you want?"

"Owen, this is Mr. Craddock. He's chief of police in Jarrett Creek."

He nods, but his expression tells me he doesn't care who I am, I'm in the way.

"I was telling Mrs. Montclair I'm hoping to get some information. There was a fire yesterday at a house on the edge of the Cato property over in Jarrett Creek."

"We don't get much gossip out here. We work a long day."

I begin to understand that their grim behavior toward me isn't personal. They're half dead from hard work, trying to keep up this farm. I wonder why they don't let some of the cosmetic work go.

"I understand," I say. "I wanted to know if you were aware of the house and if you know who has been living there."

The man gives a snort. "Way you're describing it, it must be Darktown. That's the only part of the property that's in Jarrett Creek. I don't know who you think you're talking to, but I wouldn't have anything to do with that type of person."

"Do you know how I can get in touch with the owner?"

"Judy, will you go in the house and get this man what he wants so I don't have to track my muddy boots inside?"

She gives him a hateful look, then turns without a word and heads into the house.

Trying to think of something friendly to say, I remark, "You sure keep the place up nice. How often do you see the owner?"

A bitter twist contorts the man's mouth. "Once a month, when he comes to collect the lease money."

That startles me. "He drives here once a month? Seems kind of unnecessary when you could just send it in."

The man walks a few steps toward me. His eyebrows bristle and his eyes are fierce. "The son of a bitch wants the property back. Thinks he can get more money from the government letting it lie fallow. It's in the lease that if we don't keep it up, he can cancel the contract."

"You have any children?"

"Boy and a girl. In school over in Bobtail." A spark of pride flares in his eyes and then dies.

His wife comes back out and hands me a piece of paper. It occurs to me that she's angry with him because he refuses to back down and abandon the place. They are wearing themselves out on this farm.

"I'll let you get back to it," I say. "Sorry to have bothered you."

The dog trots to my car with me. I lean over and give it a friendly pat. He might not get too many of those.

Back in the office, I put in a call to the Bobtail sheriff's office. Roland Newberry is out, but the officer manning the front desk seems willing to help.

"I'd like to check up on a couple of men."

"What do you mean check up on them?"

"I mean, do they have a criminal record or been in any trouble."

"Where are they from?"

"Houston. One of them is named Barton Dudley." I read his business address off the card he gave me. "The other one is a black man. Freddie Carmichael."

"That his real name, or is it Frederick?"

"I don't know. He said he was from Chicago but lives in Houston now."

"I'll run it through the criminal records in the state public safety archives and see if I can get you anything."

I hang up as Bonnie Bedichek whirls in and plants herself in front of my desk. "It's time for you and me to have a talk," she says.

"I thought we already did," I say. "Why don't you sit down?"

She sits, but I have the impression that she could bounce off the chair any minute. She's a bundle of energy, even though she's got to be at least forty. "I want to know everything you know about that fire," she says.

"Whoa," I say. "I may not have a lot of experience dealing with homicide, but I don't think it works that way between the law and the press."

She cocks her head to one side. "How do you think it works?"

"For one thing, you and the law are after two different things. We want to catch who killed those children and you want to tell people about it."

"I don't see that as being all that different."

"Let me ask you this. Suppose I knew an important clue to solving a case and I let that information slip to you. Are you telling me that you'd keep quiet?"

She opens her mouth like she's going to say something and then shuts it again and narrows her eyes at me. "A free press is important."

"So is getting criminals off the street. You didn't answer my question."

"Are you telling me that you have a suspect?"

"No, hell no. If you print something like that, you'll make a fool out of both of us. Like I told you, I'm not even part of the investigation."

"You really think that highway patrolman gives a damn who killed those people? As far as Sutherland is concerned, this is a little bump in the road and whatever happens here is of no consequence. It will be forgotten in a few days."

"I'll keep after them," I say.

"You think that's going to matter to him?"

"Why does it matter to you? You don't even know if those people are from around here. Someone said they were squatters."

"Who said that?"

I feel my face getting hot. I don't know how to handle a woman like her. She doesn't back down an inch. "Just somebody," I say.

She narrows her eyes. "Whoever it was, it happened in your town and you're never going to be much of a lawman if you don't take what happens here seriously."

Now I've had it. "I don't need you telling me how to do my job." I get up. "Now I've got work to do."

She stays seated and grins up at me. "You do have a little fire in you. I'm glad to see it." She jumps up. "I want an exclusive when you figure out what happened out there."

I can't help laughing. She sounds like somebody on TV. "I don't even know what that means. You're the only newspaper in town. Who else would I tell?"

"You're kidding, right? Yesterday that Albert Lamond was here. Before long, all the big newspapers are going to be nosing around."

"Reporters from the *Houston Chronicle* and the *Dallas Morning News* were already out at the crime scene."

"Goddammit," she says. "That's the problem with being the one and only reporter. I had to interview the football coach yesterday afternoon. If this town didn't get their football news, I'd be run out of town."

"I don't think they got much out of their visit," I say. "Nobody knows anything yet."

CHAPTER 12

In the few months' training I had, it was mandatory to view an autopsy. I got through it, but I can't say it was an experience I want to repeat. I have an uneasy feeling that viewing an autopsy on burn victims is going to be a whole different thing.

Although I slept all right in my motel room in Austin, I'm up at six a.m. and wish I had something to do to calm my nerves. The desk clerk tells me there's a good walking trail down by the lake. I spend an hour with the walkers, runners, bicyclists, and dogs. I'm usually a good breakfast eater, but I keep it light this morning, eating some toast and bacon in the gloomy motel café. Something tells me I better not push my luck with food.

I asked Jeanne to come with me, but she said it was a good chance to go and visit her mother in Fort Worth, so we have gone our separate ways. I would have been poor company last night anyway.

The medical examiner's office is in Breckinridge Hospital. Clinton Heywood told me to find him and he'd take me to the autopsy room. His office is on the third floor.

Heywood looks like he escaped from the cadaver room himself, a hunched, bony man of about fifty with a prominent jaw and brow and oversized hands. He shakes my hand and offers me a seat and a cup of coffee. The coffee I drank this morning is sitting sour in my gut, so I decline. He peers at me from under shaggy eyebrows. "You ever see an autopsy on a burn victim?"

"No, sir, I haven't."

He sighs. "I can tell you right now it isn't going to be a pleasant experience. You sure you want to go through with it?"

My heart is belting out a good rhythm, but I'm determined to see this through, otherwise I'll never be able to look Sutherland in the eye. "I'm ready."

"Let me just say this: If you think you're going to lose your breakfast, try to make it outside the autopsy room. And don't be embarrassed."

I'm not a timid man. With a set of folks like mine, I learned to roll with all kinds of mayhem, from shouting matches to cleaning up after my daddy's binges. I remind myself of this as I head down to the basement with Heywood.

We go through a metal door into an entirely different setting. The smell hits me as soon as Heywood opens the door. It's a combination of strong lemon scent, mold, and something darker, more primitive, that the disinfectant can't overpower.

"We only have one autopsy room," Heywood says, "and it's crowded down here."

We pause at another metal door, and Heywood glances back at me. I must look like I'm reasonably in charge of myself, because he nods and opens the door. We enter a small room furnished with a rolling chair, a couple of small sinks, and a lot of cabinets with the contents identified with labels. I take note of gowns, gloves, caps, and then all manner of equipment from saws to scalpels.

Heywood jerks open the gown drawer, takes out two stiff green gowns, and hands them to me. "An extra one just in case," he says.

I don't even want to consider what "just in case" means. He starts putting on his gear, and I copy what he does, shaking out the gown, pulling it on with the opening in the back, and tying it at the waist and neck. He directs me to wash my hands, and then we finish up with a cap, a mask, and rubber gloves.

Once we're suited up, he pushes open the swinging doors, introducing us to even stronger smells and to chilling cold. At this point I have two choices: either be overcome by the drama, or get a grip on my emotions and be cool while I observe the proceedings.

My eyes are first drawn to the metal table in the center of the room and the unnaturally lumpy mound covered with a sheet. A fully-gowned man is already waiting at the autopsy table. A black man. When he introduces himself, his voice matches the chill of the air. "I'm Dr. Allingham, one of the medical examiners employed by the state of Texas. May I remind you that the bodies are to be treated with respect. I realize that you may feel uncomfortable at some points in the procedure, but I do not tolerate disrespect in any form, including crude humor. If you are unable to continue observation, please leave the room and do not attempt to return." With that, he pulls his mask up high on his face and nods to Heywood, who reaches over and pulls back the sheet. Then Heywood steps to a side table and picks up a chart and pen, poised to take notes.

I am thankful that someone has already performed the awful chore of pulling apart the twisted mangle of bodies that I glimpsed in the hallway of the burned house. I can tell that this victim is a young female, and that the reason she loomed so large under the sheet is that the arms and legs are charred into place. From my limited knowledge of what happens to bodies after death, rigor should have relaxed by now and the bodies should be limp. I assume that the fire welded the bones into this grotesque position.

Even worse is the blackened, charred flesh. It's impossible to tell how much of it is the natural color of the girl's skin and how much is due to the fire. I try to imagine that I'm reading Allingham's descriptions, not observing them. In language I can barely comprehend, the examiner confirms my understanding that the fire is responsible for the rigid limbs. He then proceeds to manually force the limbs flat with Heywood's help, a process that makes a horrible sound like the crack of tree limbs. The only indication that either man is aware of the sound is beads of sweat that pop out on Heywood's temples above his mask. I can't help an involuntary shudder, but it's as much from the cold as from what I'm witnessing.

After that, I watch the rest of the procedure with such detachment that I'm barely aware of time passing as Allingham's voice drones on, describing his findings. A tape-recorder hums quietly on the counter nearby. I note that the girl's approximate age is seventeen and that she was sexually active. Allingham also says that the state of the organs makes it impossible to determine the health of the girl prior to her death. He discovers a bullet hole in the left chest and comments that the bullet probably killed the victim before the fire got to her. I think of it as a small mercy.

When he completes the autopsy, I'm surprised to see that three hours have passed. My body is rigid with tension. Both Heywood and Allingham step back, and they're in a similar state. "Let's take a lunch break," Allingham says, nodding to me and then moving to a trash can where he strips off his gloves. "We'll resume at twelve thirty. We'll be running late today because I want to finish up." He strides out of the room.

Heywood pulls the sheet back over the girl, and I have to fight off an impulse to tear up. To steady myself I concentrate on Heywood's movements as he walks over to the counter and pushes a button. In the distance I hear a bell ringing. Within moments, a shaggy-looking man comes into the room. He and Heywood move the shell of the body onto a gurney and push it into another room. As the door opens, I see a bank of square drawers that must be where bodies are kept before and after autopsy.

Desperate for fresh air, I don't wait for Heywood but push open the swinging doors, yank off my gown and lay it on the counter, and head for the front of the building. I glance at my watch, determined not to keep anyone waiting. At a coffee shop a couple of blocks away, I force myself to eat a plain chicken sandwich and to down a good strong cup of black coffee.

The break is over too soon, but when I return, I find that the next autopsy doesn't give me as much trouble. I hate to think that I'm already

74

hardened to the fact that a young girl has been murdered, but I'm grateful for whatever steadies me. This autopsy doesn't take as long, as if now Allingham is in the groove. He finds that this young girl, a chubby child, approximate age sixteen, was also shot, and that she was sexually active. We take another break mid-afternoon, and then another doctor, Dr. Ferris, shows up to take over for the third autopsy. My feet ache from standing on the concrete floor, and my eyes are watering from the intense fumes of the formaldehyde used to preserve the bodies.

This body is that of a boy about eleven. While Dr. Ferris continues his precise business, I consider why a young boy would have been in the household of young women who may have been prostitutes. The possible explanation makes me sick until Ferris comments that there is no evidence of sexual abuse on the boy's body. Another feature: his body isn't as badly burned as the others, as if one of the victims threw herself across him to protect him.

When the ordeal is over, Heywood follows me out and shakes my hand. "This was a long day. You handled it well. I can guarantee you're rarely going to have to witness an autopsy this hard to take."

I thank him for his help and he says, "I don't know if I ought to tell you this. I know the highway patrol has decided to take on this investigation, but . . ." He pauses and runs a hand through his hair. "Sometimes they get busy and things fall by the wayside." I realize he's trying to tell me that Sutherland isn't going to put much manpower into investigating this. Why it matters to Heywood isn't clear.

"I understand." I wait, sure he'll go on.

"During yesterday's prep of the bodies, we found a name and phone number in one of the girl's pockets."

"Where is it now?"

"All the effects were given to the highway patrol."

"You remember which victim it was?"

"The one that wasn't burned so badly. Another teenaged girl."

"Who was the other victim autopsied yesterday?"

"A woman a little older than the others, early thirties. Allingham said she had borne a child when she was young. We speculated she might be the mother of the boy we worked on today."

After parting ways with Haywood, I waste no time getting to my motel room, where I immediately strip down and shower. After I'm in clean clothes, I consider trashing the clothes I was wearing during the autopsies, but I put them in the laundry bag provided in the room and take the bag outside and throw it into the bed of my pickup.

Surprisingly, I'm famished and eat a rack of barbecued baby back ribs with potato salad. Later, back in the motel room, I can't sleep. I go outdoors and walk around until a lot later than I usually stay up, then come back and fall asleep in front of the TV. But my sleep is restless and punctuated with murky dreams. I'm up at five and on the road headed for home by seven.

CHAPTER 13

When I pull into my driveway mid-morning, I'm surprised to see my brother's car in front. He's sitting on the porch. My first thought is that whatever problem he has, I don't need it. But I instantly feel bad for the thought. He is my brother, and his life has been harder than mine in every respect. Our mother was harder on him than she was on me, and he has taken after our daddy in easing his unhappiness with alcohol.

I hope it's nothing to do with his wife showing up with bruises. When he's drunk, Horace is maudlin and self-pitying, but I've never known him to become belligerent or violent when he's drinking. Still, there's a first time for everything.

"Hey, I didn't expect you. What's up?"

"Where have you been? I was here last night and again this morning, and the place was locked up tight. That boy you have working around here told me he didn't know when you were coming back. I figured I'd better wait it out." As always, his tone is aggrieved, as if I should be here at his beck and call.

"I had to run up to Austin. I'm here now. Come on inside and I'll make some coffee."

Horace follows me inside, but as usual he seems uneasy in my house. I live very differently from my brother. I married a woman whose family is wealthy, and they shower us with gifts. I had a hard time with it at first, feeling it's up to me to provide for my family. But Jeanne is frugal in most ways, not showy at all. She isn't interested in wearing expensive jewelry or having a grand house. The only thing she spends money on is art.

In fact, that may be what makes Horace uneasy. Our furnishings are plain, and the house is nothing more than a spacious farmhouse, but our walls are hung with modern and abstract paintings that make no sense. They are expensive, and I know some of them are by well-known contemporary artists. The paintings are full of shapes, and some of them have nice colors, but they aren't pictures of anything recognizable. Although Jeanne has tried to tell me why some people appreciate them, I don't get the meaning of them, and I pretty much ignore them. But sometimes people who visit us are startled.

I make the coffee and scare up some cookies, and we take them out onto the front porch. Horace visibly relaxes and settles into a chair.

"What did you want to see me about?" I ask.

Horace is a few years older than me, but he looks a lot older. His hair is lank, his face deeply lined, and his body hunched as if he's in pain. But the real difference is in his haunted eyes. He looks like a man who has lost hope. Except that I don't remember him ever having any. "I wonder if we can leave Tom with you for a few days."

"Of course you can. You know we love to have him."

"Maybe even a week."

"You going on a trip?"

I don't mean anything by the question, but it brings a suspicious look to his eyes. He sets his cup down hard. "If I had knowed you would give me the third degree, I would have asked somebody else."

I hold up my hand. "I didn't mean to pry. It was an idle question, nothing more. Just being sociable."

He rolls his shoulders and sits back. I know why he is so defensive. Our mamma questioned his every intention, needled him, and never let him have a thought she didn't shoot down. She seemed to have softened by the time I came along. At least it didn't eat at me the way it has him. Maybe he defended me when I was young enough not to know I needed defending, or maybe it's our different natures.

I clear my throat and try to think of a way to ask a question without giving more offense. "When is this going to happen?"

"You don't have to do it at all, if you don't want to. I know it's a burden."

"It's not a burden. We love Tom. You know Jeanne dotes on him. We both do."

He pulls a pack of Lucky Strikes out of his shirt pocket and lights one. "Me and Donna were thinking maybe this weekend we could ask you to keep him." He takes a long drag and blows the smoke out away from me. He avoids looking at me, and I wonder what he's up to.

"That's fine," I say.

"You said you was in Austin last night?" he asks. "Doing what?"

I could point out to him that his questions are nosier than mine were, but I tell him I had to attend some autopsies.

"Jesus H. Christ. You couldn't pay me enough to do something like that."

I want to ask him something, and I know I'm only going to get one chance at it. "You hear anything about those people that got killed? I'm trying to put a name to them."

"Who, me?" He grinds the cigarette butt out on the bottom of his boot and flicks it out into the yard. "Why would I know anything about people like that?" He stands up. "I got to go. I'll bring Tom by on Saturday."

I stand up. "Good. We'll try to keep him entertained."

"He's spoilt enough as it is. You don't need to do nothing special."

I watch him tromp down the steps, climb into his old beat-up Ford, and speed away. I know Horace pretty well. He answered my question with another question. That usually means he's lying, either by omission or commission. What has he got to lie about?

Horace's visit kept me from what I had planned to do as soon as I walked in the door, which was change clothes and go spend some time with my cows. I take off my uniform, pull on some short-sleeved coveralls, and go down to the pasture. It gives me a good feeling to see that the cows have scattered out. The first couple of days, they huddled together, but now they look more relaxed.

I go into the barn and get a bag of grain and walk out among them. I take a little grain in my hand, and sure enough the youngsters come pushing up to me the way Truly said they would. I like the feel of their noses nuzzling for the bits of grain. Pretty soon a couple of the bolder cows saunter up to get in on the action. The little ones buck and jump around like they're jealous when one of the larger cows muscles in.

I could spend the rest of the day this way, but I get back into my uniform and head down to the station to find out what's going on. I don't wear my uniform often, since it isn't a requirement, but I didn't like getting caught in civilian clothes when I encountered John Sutherland for the first time. For now, I'll dress the part of chief.

Johnny Pat Hruska is on duty. He tells me there have been a couple of phone calls for me. One is from Alvin Beck, the officer in Bobtail whom I asked to research the realtor, Blue Dudley, and his client, Freddie Carmichael. The other is from the high school secretary asking if she can arrange a meeting between me and the principal. I've been expecting this call for weeks, but it comes at a bad time. Is there ever a good time to discuss drug problems at the school?

Beck comes right to the point. "Dudley has a list of complaints against him for shady dealings, but no record."

"And Carmichael?"

He chuckles. "That's where things get a little strange. There's no such person, in Houston or in Chicago."

"He's using a false name."

"Sounds like it. Question is, what do you want with him? Is it important enough to dig deeper?"

"I'm not sure. I think so, but give me time to decide." I thank him and hang up. I'd like him to keep digging, but I'm afraid it'll get back to Sutherland that I'm interfering with his investigation. If I'm going to nose around Carmichael, I need to be discreet.

I return the school secretary's call, and she asks if I can squeeze in a meeting this afternoon. I tell her I'll be there at two o'clock.

I'm hungry, but before I can escape, Bonnie Bedichek flings open the door. "Were you going to call me and tell me how the autopsies went?"

"Bonnie, I just walked in the door. As hard as it may be for you to accept, you aren't the first person I think of morning, noon, and night."

She grins. "One of these days, I'll get you trained. So what did you find out?"

I can't imagine that it will hurt for me to tell her. "Let's go over to the café and I'll tell you."

"You buying?"

"Seems to me you ought to be the one buying, but I won't hold you to it."

Before we can sit down at Town Café, we have to greet people and field questions about the fire and the people killed. I'm impressed by Bonnie's ability to deflect questions and become the questioner. Eventually we sit down at one of the scarred wooden tables.

The café won't ever win any decoration awards. It consists of four walls painted white, wood tables and chairs, and pictures of football teams hung all over. The place has changed hands half a dozen times since I was old enough to notice. I don't think any owner has ever bothered to change the menu. They serve fried chicken and fish, hamburgers, a couple of different kinds of sandwiches, chicken fried steak and smothered steak, plus a standard selection of Mexican food. Although I've never noticed any difference in the food from one owner to the next, it's always pretty good.

Over enchiladas, I give Bonnie general information about the autopsies, figuring she doesn't want to know the gory details any more than I want to describe them. "The victims were three teenage girls, a woman in her thirties, and a boy around eleven years old."

Bonnie has a habit of running a thumb under her bottom lip when she's thinking. "Strange mix. What do you suppose their relationship was?"

"Without knowing any of their names, I don't know how anybody's going to find that out," I say.

"You think Sutherland is going to care enough to do a proper investigation?"

"How should I know? All I know is that it isn't my business."

I fork in a last bite of enchilada and look up to see her eyes blazing at me, and her nostrils flared. "So if the highway patrol doesn't see fit to make it their business, and you're too timid to step in, I guess whoever killed those people will get off scot-free."

"Hold on a minute. There's no need to insult me. I'm not timid, I just don't know how this fits with my jurisdiction."

She settles back and folds her arms across her chest. She hasn't got a lot of meat on her bones, but her chest makes up for it. "So that's the kind of lawman you intend to be? Don't step on any toes, keep your head down, and do the least you can to justify your salary?"

"I don't know the first thing about how to investigate something this big. How am I supposed to find the names of those poor people who got killed? I've asked around and I got nowhere. Nobody's talking, and let's face it, the resources of the Jarrett Creek PD are a little limited."

Bonnie holds up a finger. "Fingerprints. You have every right to send off fingerprints for identification." She flips up the second finger. "Public records. You can find out how to contact the Cato family and ask them if they knew who was living there." Third finger. "Reward. Not publicly, but privately let it be known that there's a reward for information about the victims." Fourth finger. "Contact that Ranger who was here. Wills? Tell him you are concerned that the THP is lacking fire in the belly. He had some history with Sutherland and he wasn't all that impressed." On five she spreads her fingers wide. "Number five, use the press!"

She's right and I feel embarrassed. "If you're so all-fired smart, why aren't you the chief of police?"

"Because no way in hell are they going to hire a woman for the job. But there's an even bigger reason."

"What's that?"

She leans in close across the table and says in a fierce voice, "Because I'm a journalist."

My dignity and pride are wounded. I throw a twenty on the table and get to my feet. "I have to go," I say.

She looks me up and down and grins. "I'm going to whip you into shape yet."

I stalk out, hoping nobody notices that my cheeks are flaming and I'm mad as hell.

CHAPTER 14

The school principal, John Gilpin, was principal when I went to Jarrett Creek High School a dozen plus years ago. At that time he was a big, fat man who wore his pants up high on his massive belly, which made him look like Diego Rivera. The only difference now is that he's even fatter and his hair is liberally peppered with gray. He shakes hands and motions for me to take a seat in one of the severe-looking wooden chairs facing him across his desk. He has to wedge himself into his wide-seated rolling chair. He doesn't seem to notice the grunt he lets out as he hoists one cheek and then another into position.

"Samuel, you've done all right for yourself. I wouldn't have given a plug nickel for your chances of making it through college when you were at school here."

He never was one to waste encouraging words. "Yeah, it took some doing." It wasn't the college part that gave me trouble, but the paying for it. That's why I went into the US Air Force first.

"You went to Texas A&M, right? Remind me what you majored in."

I sigh. Although I ended up liking the classes, it was a choice initially dictated by the necessity to find a scholarship I had a chance of getting. It made paying for my classes doable. "Geology," I say.

"That's right. I remember it was some foolish degree. What in the world did you ever think you were going to do with a degree like that? To do anything in science, you need a master's or even a PhD."

I can't help snapping back. "I assume you didn't ask me in here to discuss my education. Your secretary said you wanted to see me. Let's get to the problem."

He narrows his eyes and I can tell he doesn't like me taking that tone. He folds his hands across his massive belly and tips his head back to peer down his nose at me. "I have to say I'm disappointed in you."

"Oh?"

"When you were hired, I expected you to tackle some of the drug problems we're having at the school, and I have yet to hear a word from you on that matter."

This is the second time this afternoon that someone has scolded me for not doing my job properly. The fact is, I was waiting to be asked rather than jumping in. It was probably the wrong way to approach it, but it's too late to worry about that now. "I apologize. It has taken me some time to settle in and get acquainted with the job."

"You thought it was going to be easy?"

I remember him raking a teacher over the coals once, and he reminded me of my mother. I'm not willing to let that be our relationship. Even if he is a lot older than me, I have some small bit of authority, which I dredge up from somewhere. "Why don't you tell me what has been happening, and we can get down to business taking care of it."

Another long-nosed look, but he seems unable to find fault with what I said. "Somebody is selling drugs to these kids, and I want it stopped."

"How do you know the kids are buying drugs?" I ask.

"What do you mean, how do I know?"

"Are they showing up stoned in class? Skipping class? Cutting up in class? Stealing?"

"All of the above," he says.

"Who's giving you the most trouble? Seniors? Juniors?"

He blinks a few times. "I have to look into that. Off the top of my head, I'd say it's juniors. I expect by the time they're seniors, they've learned to hide their habits."

"Habits? You mean you think some of these kids are habitual users?"

"I don't mean habits per se," he says. He struggles to sit forward and plunks his meaty hands onto his desk. "I mean they don't show it so much."

"Or maybe they try it out when they're juniors and by the time they're seniors they lose interest."

"Dream on," he says.

"Have any of them been caught with drugs in their possession?"

"Once or twice. It's sometimes prescription bottles from their folks' medicine cabinets."

"What did you do with the kids? Did you notify us down at the police department? Because if you did, I didn't get the message."

"No, I called them into my office and gave them a good talking-to. I told them that the next time I'd be calling their parents and suspending them from school."

"But you didn't talk to the parents?"

"I confiscated the pills, and I thought a warning would work."

I reach in my shirt pocket and pull out a little notebook I carry. "I need the names of the kids."

"Whoa. That isn't going to happen. I told them it would be confidential."

Suddenly I'm feeling more in charge of myself. "It can't be that way," I say. "They're breaking the law."

"They're minors," he says.

"Any of them eighteen?"

He hesitates. I see by his eyes that he's calculating his answer, as if he doesn't want to give away too much of his control over the situation.

"One of them," he says.

"Then I have to have the name. This is nonnegotiable unless you want me to subpoena your records."

His eyes bug out and his mouth falls open. "Who do you think you are?"

"I'm the chief of police," I say with steel in my voice. "You asked me to help you with the drug problem, and this is what it's going to take." And I think, *Did you imagine the problem was going to be solved by magic? That I wouldn't arrest anyone using drugs? That you wouldn't have to be involved?*

What I'm thinking must be on my face, because he looks embarrassed all of a sudden, grabs a pad of paper, writes a name down, and shoves it over to me. Now I understand his desire to keep the name to himself. Ben Morgan. The Lutheran preacher's son. "He's a senior. I can get him out of class."

Ben Morgan is a shambling hulk of a kid with shaggy hair that flops over his forehead, and a face like an angel. He has perfected the art of looking innocent. He offers his hand for a handshake. "Howya doing?" His tone makes it sound like we're old friends.

"Doing okay." I match his folksy tone. "I have a few matters I want to chat with you about."

"Oh yeah?" Innocent smile in place, but his eyes slide sideways to take in Principal Gilpin, and back to me.

"Sit down." I gesture to the other straight-backed wooden chair. He perches on the edge. "What are your plans for after you graduate?" I'm settled back, with my leg crossed at the knee. Casual.

He looks startled. His senior year just began and he sees it stretching in front of him endlessly, no thought as to what lies at the other end.

"College, I guess."

"You make good grades?"

He shrugs. "Pretty good."

"Better keep them up. Competition is fierce out there." I sit forward. "And if you have a drug arrest on your record, it's going to be hard for a college to get excited about you."

He shifts in his chair but keeps his angel face in place. "I expect so."

"I've been hearing rumors this summer that kids are experimenting with drugs. You know anything about that?"

His eyes flick to the principal. Gilpin says, "You might as well tell him."

"You said you wouldn't take it to the law."

"I said as long as it was one incident. But what I hear is that nothing has changed."

"I don't know what you mean. It was only that one time. We were trying it out, that's all."

"Marijuana?" I ask.

"Just one joint, that's all."

"Anything stronger?"

"Hell, I mean heck no."

I hope he's telling the truth. "Where'd you get it?"

"Umm, one of the other kids had it."

"You hiding behind somebody else?"

My first score. The kid's neck gets red. "I don't know who it belonged to, all right?" A bit of grievance in his voice.

"What did your folks say when they heard?"

Again the eyes dart toward Gilpin. "They were okay. I mean they didn't like it, but I promised I wouldn't do it anymore."

Now I know he's lying. His daddy, Reverend Oliver Morgan, is even more straitlaced than the Baptist preacher, and that's saying a lot. No way would he be "okay" with his son taking even a drag off a marijuana cigarette.

I get up from my seat. "All right, you can go. You know where I am. If you think of anything you want to tell me, give me a call."

He springs out of his chair, looking like he could shout, "Hallelujah!" and shoots out of the room. I turn on Gilpin. "You didn't tell his folks? Did you notify any of the parents?"

"I thought we ought to handle it internally."

"And how well did that work out for you?" I remember now why nobody ever had any respect for Gilpin. He let kids get away with anything.

"That's why I've called you in." His face is beet red. As fat as he is, I worry that he's going to have a stroke.

"If I don't get a little more cooperation from you, the problem is gonna get worse."

"What do you want me to do?"

"Call in the parents of any kid that gets caught and tell them to contact me. I've got to find out who's selling the drugs."

Gilpin is the picture of unhappiness, but he nods.

"Let me know when you've had the meeting." I start to walk out, but I come back to his desk. "One last question. Where have the kids been doing this? On school property?"

"Out back of the gym."

"So right out in the open?" I can't believe it. The gym is on the street.

"Kids these days have no respect."

If they get away with everything short of murder, it's no wonder they don't.

CHAPTER 15

I don't feel like talking to anybody at the moment. I need to think some things over. Usually when I want to be alone, I head up to Lakeside Park and stare at the water, but this time I go home and check up on my cows.

I stand at the fence, and a few of the cows amble over to see what I'm up to. One stands in the middle of the pasture, bellowing. I hope there's nothing wrong with her. She looks fine, just seems to be letting off steam. Kind of what I'd like to be doing.

Between Bonnie Bedichek and Gilpin, I'm feeling raw. This is the first time I've been pushed to tackle a real crime. I've hauled in a few drunks and kept them in jail overnight. There've been some minor thefts and a couple of cases of vandalism. But how much trouble can a town of three thousand people get into? That's what I told Jeanne when she protested my taking on the job.

Now with Gilpin pushing for me to investigate, and Bonnie demanding that I act like a real chief of police, I wonder if I've got the gumption to stand up to Jeanne and let her know I'm fully committed to being chief. When I married her, her daddy gave me a stern lecture, admonishing me not to let my pride get in the way of accepting money so Jeanne could live the way she was used to under her folks' roof. He said, "I've spoiled her, and it's not her fault if she wants the finer things."

In our four years in the US Air Force, I was happy to find that Jeanne didn't seem to mind living in shabby housing on the base. She swore she was happy with me, and I was sure as hell happy with her. It took some time for me to realize that the way she was spoiled was subtle: She's used to getting her way.

I'm not sure why she didn't want me to be chief of police. She isn't a snob, but I wonder if she thought the job was beneath a man she married. As I stand looking at the cows, I admit to myself that I've let her become the boss. Being brought up with a mother like mine, I prefer not to make a fuss.

I took on the job to make a statement that I am a man and I can make my own way, and I haven't lived up to that ideal. I have ignored the drug problem because I felt guilty taking on a job Jeanne didn't want me to do. I've embarrassed myself, and it's time to remedy that.

Bonnie had some good suggestions this afternoon, and first thing tomorrow morning, I'm going to implement them. It's only four thirty, and there's one thing I can do tonight.

In the house I find the note I got from the Montclairs farming the Cato land. I dial the number and get an answering machine. "You have reached the offices of Ronald Cato. Please leave a message and Mr. Cato will return your call at his earliest convenience."

"This is Samuel Craddock. I'm chief of police in Jarrett Creek. I'm sure Mr. Cato is aware there was a criminal act on his property a couple of days ago. I'd like him to call me back on that matter, if he doesn't mind. I have a couple of questions to ask him."

As soon as I hang up, I'm annoyed with myself. Asking him to call "if he doesn't mind" sounds like a wimp.

I stare at the phone wondering if it's a good time to call Jeanne, when the phone rings.

"This is Ronald Cato. I'm calling for Chief Craddock." He sounds like an old man. The property out there has been called Cato Woods for as long as I've been alive. I wonder if he's the original owner.

"This is Craddock. Thank you for returning my call. You heard about that bad business out on your acreage?"

"Damn squatters. Not that I wanted anything like that to happen, mind you, but they shouldn't have been there."

"So you didn't know they were there?"

A long pause. "How old are you? You sound mighty young to be holding down the job of police chief."

"I'm old enough." I've had it with that line of inquiry. "Let me repeat the question: Did you know there was somebody living there?"

"Well. You're a feisty one. I have to admit, I did know there was somebody squatting out there."

"Do you have a name?"

"I sure don't. I wish I could help you, but I turned a blind eye to the squatters, thinking they weren't going to cause me any trouble. Now look what I've got to put up with."

"When are you going to be in town next? I understand you come down once a month."

"Who, me?" His laugh is harsh. "I'm in a wheelchair. I'm not the one who comes. That would be my son, George. Named after my daddy. He takes care of most of the business these days."

"I understand he's trying to get the tenants on the farm to leave."

This time his voice has a steel edge. "Like I said, my son is handling the business. He's got a good business sense, so if he wants them to clear out, he must have good reasons."

"You happen to know when he'll be here next?"

"I'm afraid I don't."

I wonder, is there a problem between him and his son, or is he protective of George? "You have a number where I can reach him?"

He's quiet for a moment. "I'll tell you what. How about if I have him call you? This number okay?"

I give him the number at headquarters in addition to my home number. He hangs up before I can ask when I might expect a call.

I get a beer out of the refrigerator and check to make sure there is a frozen beef pot pie in the freezer for later. Jeanne can't stand them, so the only time I get to eat one is if Jeanne is out playing bridge or at a church meeting.

I'm of two minds about spending an evening without Jeanne. I miss her, but there's a certain freedom to it. I can leave manners out of the equation and put my bare feet up on the coffee table if I want to, and I might even have a second beer.

Beer in hand, I stroll onto the front porch and sit down to mull over how to implement Bonnie Bedichek's idea of a reward for information about the fire.

CHAPTER 16

I wake up feeling uneasy, as if I've had a bad night's sleep. I remember waking in the night and thinking I heard a fire siren, but it was far away, and since no one called me, I must have been dreaming. But when I step outside to go down to the pasture, I smell a hint of smoke in the air. It could be from the Cato Woods fire, but I haven't noticed it before. While I'm feeding the cows, I think about Tom coming this weekend. I haven't told Jeanne. She's going to be happy.

I don't expect George Cato to call me back, so if I'm going to talk to him, I have to catch him. When I get to headquarters, I call Judy and Owen Montclair to ask when they expect him to show up for the rent money. There's no answer. I'll have to call this evening. I doubt I'll get much out of George Cato anyway, and that discourages me. There's a good reason the highway patrol and the Texas Rangers investigate crimes. They have the manpower, the training, and the experience.

Still, I could put together a flyer advertising the reward. Is five hundred dollars enough? That's all the money I'm going to get from the state, and the town coffers are always on the brink of empty. I could toss in some money, but I'm not part of some private law-enforcement agency. I'm still mulling it over when I hear the crunch of gravel outside and the sounds of an engine. It's Truly Bennett's old pickup parking. One of the men I wanted to see today.

But when the door opens, it's Truly's daddy, Ezekiel, looming in the doorway. His hat is in his hand and his eyes are wide open and wild-looking. "Mr. Craddock, you've got to help Truly."

"Come on in here."

He shuffles in, looking lost and bewildered.

"Let me get you a cup of coffee."

"No, sir, that's okay. There's no time for that. They have my boy and I don't know what they're going to do with him."

"Who has him?"

He blinks. "You don't know?"

"Know what?"

"They arrested him early this morning. The highway patrol sent four men out to the house."

"Arrested him for what?"

"They say he's the one that killed those people out there. He wouldn't do that. He's not like that. He didn't know those people, and he had no reason to kill them."

My heart thumps so hard I could pass out. What the hell does Sutherland think he's doing? "There's got to be some misunderstanding. I'll make a call. Did they say where they were taking him?"

"No, sir. They wouldn't tell me nothing."

"Did you get their names?"

"No, sir." His breath is coming hard. He has good reason to be terrified. Young black men don't fare well in custody, especially if they are suspected of a capital crime.

"Calm down. It won't do Truly any good if you have a heart attack." My heart is pounding, too. It's not like Truly Bennett and I are friends, but I've known him my whole life. Everybody knows him, and everyone knows he wouldn't hurt anybody, let alone kill them. "I want you to sit down." I point at the straight-backed, metal chair next to my desk. He shakes his head and stands there, miserable, terrified for his son.

The first person I call is John Sutherland. I'm told he's out of the office.

"I need to reach him right away. Can you patch me through to his patrol-car radio?"

"Hold on a minute."

It's longer than a minute, but it gives me a chance to consider my approach to Sutherland. I want to do the best I can for Truly. Eventually a woman comes on and says she's the dispatcher and she can patch me through to him.

"Sutherland? This is Samuel Craddock over in Jarrett Creek."

The line is crackling. "What do you want?"

"There's seems to be a misunderstanding. Somebody who said they were Texas Highway Patrol came out and arrested one of our residents. I figured that can't be, because protocol says I should be notified if one of our residents is picked up."

"That's a damn shame," Sutherland says. "I guess somebody forgot to call you. Anyway, it's all taken care of."

"What's taken care of? Where is he?"

But the line is dead. Fury rises up in me. I dial the number again. My inclination is to spit fire at the man who answers, but I figure I'll get farther if I keep my temper. "I was talking to John Sutherland and we had a bad line. He was going to tell me where he was taking a man he arrested. Wonder if you can help me out with that."

"What's the prisoner's name?"

"Truly Bennett."

"Just a minute." He doesn't put me on hold, and I hear him ask somebody for a list. A minute later he says, "I don't have anybody by that name. He must not have been processed yet."

"Where do they usually take prisoners?"

"Pretty much always to the closest county jail, and then, depending on the crime, they may be taken to a more secure facility."

I thank him for his information and hang up. My ears are ringing. I've known of cases where black men were taken away and never seen again. In my mind's eye I can imagine Truly in the back of a squad car, taken out to a wood somewhere and beaten. Even killed.

Ezekiel Bennett stands over my desk. I hope he doesn't see my hands shaking. "Did you locate him? Can we get to him?"

"Hold on. I'm not sure. I have to think for a minute." I get up and pour two cups of coffee and bring Bennett one. My mind is working furiously. I need to get this right. It occurs to me that the former chief could tell me what is likely happening. And then something else occurs to me. It wouldn't hurt to have Bonnie Bedichek on my side. I phone her and it's obvious I've woken her up.

"I only got to bed at four," she grumbles.

"I'm sorry, but I need you here."

"What for?"

"I don't have time to tell you, but I've got the makings of a hell of a story. Don't stop for coffee. I've got a pot made."

She coughs. "Is it really urgent? Never mind, I'll be there in fifteen minutes."

"Make it ten."

I call former chief Eldridge. He listens to what I have to say. "I don't know what you're so fired up about," he says. "If they arrested somebody, they must have a pretty good reason." He talks so slow that in my current state of agitation, I want to tell him to hurry it up.

"Eldridge, I know Truly Bennett, and I don't believe he would do something like this."

He chuckles long and low. "You think you know him, but you can't really know what a colored boy is thinking. I understand there was some young girls out there. He probably got a notion to bed one of them and she wouldn't have anything to do with him, and the rest followed."

He isn't saying anything that half the people in town aren't thinking, so there's no use arguing with him. "Do you know where they're likely to take him?"

"Over to Bobtail, or maybe San Antonio. But I'd try Bobtail first."

Sheriff Newberry is a good man, but normally the whereabouts of a man arrested by the highway patrol would not be of much interest to him. However, this is a high-profile case. I don't know whether he'll take me seriously when I tell him they've arrested the wrong man.

"What can I do for you?" Newberry sounds distracted, which isn't good.

I tell him that the THP arrested someone without notifying me and that I don't buy the claim that Bennett is guilty.

He doesn't say anything for a minute. "I know you're worried there will be a repeat of what happened up in Georgetown a couple of months ago, but I run a better jail than that. I hate to say it, but I didn't have much regard for Sutherland when we met the other day. Still, it's his call. All I can do right now is make sure your man is treated fairly when he's here."

"I trust you. I'm worried that they'll take him somewhere else."

"Let me call and find out if they're bringing him here. I'll get right back to you."

"I don't want you to think I'm horning in on your territory, but I'd like to come over and talk to Truly if they bring him there."

"That may take some doing. It's Sutherland's call. But I tell you what. Come on over here and we'll see what we can do."

When I hang up, I tell Ezekiel what's going on. "It's the best I can hope for. Newberry is a fair man, and I'll get as close to Truly as I can."

The door bangs open and Bonnie charges in.

"Don't you ever just walk into a room?" I ask.

"Not when I've been told my presence is needed urgently," she says. Her eyes are puffy and her hair could have used another lick with the comb.

"Now you're here, let's get going. I'll explain on my way."

"Wait a minute. You promised me a cup of coffee."

I pour the last of the coffee into a cup and hand it to her. "Drink it on the way," I say.

I introduce her to Ezekiel Bennett. "Mr. Bennett, I think maybe it's best if you don't come with us."

"I understand. But I'm going to follow you over to the jail. I'll feel better if I'm near my boy."

CHAPTER 17

In the car I tell Bonnie what I know so far. "Oh, my Lord. I wonder what they have on him?"

I've been wondering the same thing. There hasn't been enough time for an in-depth investigation, so Sutherland must have some strong evidence to stick his neck out far enough to arrest Truly.

I glance off to the east and notice a haze on the horizon. "Looks like there was a fire somewhere," I say. "I smelled it in the air this morning."

"That's where I was until early this morning," Bonnie says. "The Bobtail Fire Department handled it. I guess they didn't see any need to call Jarrett Creek volunteers."

"Where was it?"

"Cato Farm. Up on the hill."

"What? You mean the place the Montclairs are farming?"

"You know them?"

"I just met them. Was anybody hurt?"

"No, they lost part of their cotton crop. They were pretty shook up. It's a financial blow."

I'm reminded that George Cato is trying to run them off the farm. Suddenly my desire to meet him ramps up a notch. "Any idea how it started?"

"Not that I heard. Why?"

"No reason. Seems strange, two fires on the Cato property within a few days."

"Hmm. Now that you mention it, it is strange. I guess I wasn't thinking about the fact that that's all part of the same property." She's got her journalist look on her face. Her eyes are sharp and she seems more awake than she was five minutes ago. "Do you think there's a connection?"

"I don't know. I'm just wondering; that's all. Right now my mind is on what we can do for Truly."

By the time we've driven the fifteen miles to the courthouse, I'm no better off than I was before we left headquarters. This is new territory for me and I don't have any idea what to expect when we arrive. "Have you ever covered a murder arrest?" I ask.

"I was here a couple of years ago when they brought in that guy from up in East Texas who was hiding out here. You may not remember it. He killed a couple of hitchhikers up around Nacogdoches."

I shake my head. "I don't remember hearing about it."

"Oh, wait a minute. It was four years ago. You weren't back here then."

I drive slowly past the front of the courthouse. Somehow I had it in my head that there would be crowds gathered, patrol cars and TV vans parked all over the place, reporters at the ready. As far as I can see, there's nothing going on. My heart sinks. Maybe they've taken Truly somewhere else. I glance back and see Ezekiel's old truck behind me, and I wonder what he's thinking.

"Let's park around back," Bonnie says. I turn the corner, and sure enough there are three highway patrol cars parked up next to the back door. "Bingo," she says. She's halfway out of the car before I even have the motor turned off.

My heart is pounding as we approach the back door. I don't want to have a run-in with Sutherland, but I have to be prepared.

We go up to the back door, Bonnie striding in front of me like she's queen of the world. She reaches for the doorknob, and the door opens, almost throwing her backward. I grab her arm to steady her.

A highway patrolman I don't recognize comes out and makes to close the door. Bonnie lunges for the knob. "You can't go in there," he says.

"The hell I can't," she says and scoots through before he can stop her.

"Hey, now," he says to me. "You've got to get her out of there. What do you think you're doing here anyway?"

She sticks her head back out. "You coming?" she asks me.

I don't need a second invitation. Her boldness is contagious. I march right in with the patrolman behind me. He grabs my arm and I whirl on him. "I'm chief of police of Jarrett Creek," I say. "Now take your hand off me."

He glances at my badge. "You're fine, but the lady has to leave."

Except Bonnie is nowhere to be seen. "If you can catch her, you can throw her out," I say.

"Goddammit," he mutters. "Let Sutherland sort her out." He heads back out the door and I'm left to figure out where Bonnie has gone.

Three doors branch off the short hallway, none of them marked. I open the first one. It's a cleaning closet. The second one leads to a larger hallway, this one swarming with patrol officers. Bonnie is in the thick of them, hands on her hips, and practically nose to nose with Sutherland. "Here he is," she says when she spots me.

"Good," Sutherland says. "Now I can throw both of you out at the same time."

I head straight for them. I have no intention of leaving. "Where is Truly Bennett?" I ask.

"He's locked up," Sutherland says. "We've got him dead to rights. You're wasting your time here. You and your newspaper-lady buddy can beat it out of here."

"I'm not going anywhere," Bonnie says loudly. "Not until I get an interview."

Roland Newberry breaks away from a nest of officers and comes over. "Miz Bedichek, you know you can't stay here. Let me escort you outside." He takes her elbow in a courtly gesture. "And, Sutherland, you know damn good and well that Craddock can see the prisoner. He may look like a kid, but he is lawful chief of police."

He turns to me and points to a doorway. "Craddock, go on in there and tell the guy behind the desk that you want to see the prisoner."

As he escorts Bonnie away, she gives me a furtive wink, and I realize that some of her bluff was for my benefit. I owe her, whether I like it or not.

In the room Newberry pointed me to, an older officer in a Bobtail PD uniform sits behind a metal desk. His look of disinterest doesn't change when I tell him I'm here to see Truly Bennett. He hoists himself up from behind the desk as if his joints are creaky, and shuffles around in front of me to a metal door, which he opens with a key. He leads me over to one of the five cells.

"You can't go in the cell because he's considered dangerous. You have to talk to him from outside. There's a chair you can bring over here if you want to." He points to a rickety-looking chair at the end of the row of cells. "Bang on the door when you're ready to come out."

Two cells down from Truly, a big, angry-looking white man with arms like tree trunks slams the bars of his cell. "You can't leave me in here with that nigger. A white man ought to have a separate area."

"Shut up, Carl," the jailer yells and goes out.

He slams the door behind him, and I walk over to the cell where Truly is sitting, hunched over. "Truly," I say quietly. "Come over here and talk to me."

He shakes his head, not looking up.

"I need you to talk to me."

He looks up, and I've never seen a more defeated look on anyone's face. "What good is it going to do to talk to you? They've got their minds made up."

"I don't."

He sighs and eases himself off the bed. He walks over to me like he's a hundred years old. "You might as well save your time. It's not going to do any good."

I wish he was wrong, but I'm pretty sure he's right. What have I got to offer? What he needs is a good lawyer. At least I can help with that. He grasps the bars, and I say, "Listen, I'm going to find out who really did this."

"Mr. Craddock, I do appreciate your interest. But I have to ask, why would you bother with me when it's likely to cause you nothing but trouble? Folks aren't going to like you putting yourself out for somebody like me."

"I've got my reasons."

He looks me straight in the eye for the first time, and he must see that I mean it, because he nods. My reasons are not for anybody but me to know, but it's the only chance I may ever have to pay a debt I owe.

"At the very least, I'll see to it that you get a good lawyer."

His smile is tired. "I'll be dead by then. Did you see that man over in the next cell? He told me if he gets a chance he'll rip my head right off. You know if he kills me nobody will do a thing to him."

"Sheriff Newberry runs a tight operation here. Try to keep calm. Now let me ask you, Sutherland said he had good evidence to charge you. Do you know what his evidence is?"

He shakes his head.

"What did he say when he came to your house?"

Holding onto the bars with both hands, he leans forward with his head hanging. "It made no sense. He asked me if my sister was a prostitute."

"Your sister. How old is she?"

"Sixteen."

"She's in school?"

He looks up. "No, sir. She thought high school was a waste of time. Daddy was awfully mad at her for up and quitting."

"I don't know any other way to ask this, so I'll ask straight out. Is there any chance that she's . . ." I shrug. "You know."

"No way. She's a church-going girl. Baptist. Same as my daddy and me. She's trying to save money to go to beauty school, you know, to do hair. She doesn't even have a boyfriend."

"Did Sutherland say anything else when he was arresting you?"

"He asked if I knew any of those people that died. I didn't. Then he asked me if my sister knew any of them. I told him I didn't have any idea if she did."

"What's the name of the motel where she works?"

"It's the Motel 6 out on the other side of Bobtail. But I wish you wouldn't go over there. The lady she works for won't like her being called on by the law."

"Listen, I'm going to get to the bottom of this. And I'll tell Sheriff Newberry what that guy said." I nod toward the man the jailer called Carl. "I want you to keep your spirits up."

"Yes, sir, thank you for coming." I don't think he believes for one minute that things are going to go his way.

I bang on the door and go back to where I last saw Newberry. Everyone is gone, including Sutherland. I go back outside and find Bonnie waiting. I tell her that I saw Truly, but I don't tell her what he said about his sister. That's something I need to dig into on my own. "Now I need to go find Newberry."

"Me, too," she says.

"Listen, I appreciate what you did this morning, but Newberry didn't look like he's going to give up much to you."

She gives a cackle. "You think I'm not used to that? My job is a matter of push, push, push. If I don't push, I get nowhere. If I do, I still may get nowhere, but at least I know I did everything I could." She cocks an eyebrow at me, and I know she's laying some philosophy on me that she thinks I need to take on.

We head around to the front of the station, and inside I tell the duty officer that I need to talk to Newberry.

"He's in a meeting."

"I'll wait."

He makes a call and says, "Go on back. He'll see you. Not you," he says to Bonnie.

"I'll go out and keep Ezekiel company," she says.

As I approach his office, Newberry steps out into the hallway and closes his door behind him. "Make it quick," he says.

I tell him about the threat to Truly. "You have to understand, I know Truly. I don't believe he could murder somebody, especially not the way those people were killed."

"Maybe not," Newberry says, "But the highway patrol does have some evidence."

"What?"

He looks off, his hands hitched in his belt. "I can't tell you right this minute." He nods to his closed door. Sutherland must be in there and there's a lot going on.

"I'm going to find out what really happened," I say. "And I won't let them railroad Truly."

He looks surprised. "You do what you can, and I'll see to it that he's kept alive."

I'm still worried. On the way out, I stop at the front desk.

"The man in the cell close to Truly Bennett's. What's he in for?"

The duty officer laughs. "Rooney? He got drunk and stole a county earth-moving machine off a road crew in the middle of the night. Not the first time he's done that, but this time his wife said he could rot in jail, that she wasn't going to pay his bail."

"How much is it?"

"Five hundred."

"Is he a flight risk?"

"If he left, he'd have to hitchhike because his car was repossessed, and besides, his wife would hunt him down and haul his ass back here."

I go out the front and walk over to city hall to bail out Carl Rooney. If they won't let me bail out Truly, at least I can get Rooney away from him.

The pinch-mouthed woman behind the desk says, "I'm sorry, Eleanor went home sick, so we can't process any bails."

"This is an emergency."

She smacks her lips as if she has eaten something tasty. "I don't know what to tell you. Judge Orlander is off fishing this weekend, so he can't order it. Not that he would anyway."

CHAPTER 18

When I walk back to the police station, Bonnie and Ezekiel are standing in the back parking lot, Bonnie smoking a cigarette.

"Did you see my boy?" Ezekiel asks.

I tell him what went on and that Sheriff Newberry assured me he would keep an eye on Truly's safety. He doesn't look particularly comforted by that, but it's all I have to offer. Bonnie is itching to hear more, but I hold back the information that Sutherland asked Truly about his sister. I may tell her eventually, but I don't need to be too quick to hand out information.

I think about asking Ezekiel to give Bonnie a ride back to Jarrett Creek, but before I have a chance, he says he's going to stay in Bobtail for a while. "I feel better staying close to my boy for now."

It's afternoon when we get back to the Jarrett Creek station. To my relief, Bonnie jumps out of my car, saying she has to get home to write up what she knows. I go inside and find Tilley eating tacos at his desk and reading the *Houston Chronicle*. "I have an article here about the fire," he says.

"How did you get a hold of it?"

"My wife was visiting with her sister in Sugarland. She saw the article and brought the paper back with her this morning."

"Anything in it we didn't already know?"

"I guess I didn't know Jarrett Creek was such a hick town. That's the way they make it sound, anyway." He tosses the newspaper onto my desk.

"There's more news on that front," I say, and then tell him that Sutherland arrested Truly.

He sits bolt upright. "Truly Bennett? What have they got on him?"

"I don't know, but I'm worried about him. Newberry said he'd make sure Truly is safe, but I don't know how far that goes."

He shrugs. "Newberry's a good man, but . . ."

"You know anything about a fire last night out at the farm on the hill above Cato Woods?"

He's still frowning about Truly, and now his mouth drops open. "No. I didn't hear anything. Why didn't anybody call me?"

"Bobtail Fire Department was called out to deal with it. I'm going up there to talk to the people who farm the place. What are you up to?"

"You want me to go along?" His eyes have a pleading look that isn't like him.

"I don't think it's necessary. Why?"

He grins. "I was hoping to get out of going over to Sledge's. He had another break-in last night."

I laugh. "Too bad. I'm afraid you're up, though." Donnie Sledge owns a convenience store out at the lake, and every few weeks he calls to say that someone has broken into the store and stolen a few six packs of beer. The problem is, it's bogus. Sledge gets drunk and invites his friends to raid the beer refrigerator and then forgets he did it. But if one of us doesn't go out there and act like we're taking it seriously, he comes into the office here and raises hell. It's easier to go out to his store and get it over with.

I pick up the newspaper to read the article.

Five Found Slain After Jarrett Creek Fire

The sleepy central Texas town of Jarrett Creek got a rude awakening Monday morning when someone called in an early-morning fire. Volunteer firefighters discovered the bodies of one adult, three teenagers, and a young boy. State Highway Patrol, Texas Rangers, and county law-enforcement officials were called in to the town of 3,000 people.

Officials confirmed that all the victims had been shot. It was speculated that the fire was set to cover up the murders.

As of Wednesday, the bodies were unidentified. It appeared that they were residing in an illegal dwelling. The owner of the property, George Cato, could not be reached for comment.

The article identified the names of the county law-enforcement officers but made no mention of the town police. Not that I have any interest in seeing my name in print, but I don't like the implication that we have no police presence. There's also no mention of the gathering of black residents and the presence of Albert Lamond.

There are quotes from Sheriff Newberry's press conference, but much longer quotes from John Sutherland. "This is a terrible crime, and we're going to make an arrest right away. People can't feel safe in their homes with a cold-blooded killer on the loose." And more words to that effect.

This is Wednesday's newspaper. I wish I had the ones from yesterday and today. I wonder if Bonnie has seen them.

The tacos Tilley was eating made me hungry, and I grab a quick bowl of chili at the café before heading up to the Cato farm. On the way, I realize that I'm not likely to find anyone available there to talk to before dusk, so I head to Bobtail and the Motel 6.

The motel is a small, two-story L-shaped building on the outskirts of town, the kind of place people turn to if they're traveling and run out of time and energy. There are only a dozen rooms, but the place is kept up, painted olive green with white trim.

A cart is parked outside one of the rooms upstairs, and I wonder if the maid cleaning the room is Truly's sister.

A large, cheerful woman with a big dimple in her chin greets me behind the desk. "You need a room?"

I tell her who I am. "I need to talk to one of your employees."

"Which one. We only have two."

"Alva Bennett."

Her good cheer is swallowed up with a dark look. "Is she in some kind of trouble?"

"Not at all. I don't know if you heard about the fire we had over in Jarrett Creek?"

"Where all those people were murdered?" The woman grabs her throat like she thinks I might jump across the counter and strangle her.

"That's right."

"What does Alva have to do with that?"

"Nothing personally. We're trying to identify the victims and not having much luck. Alva lives not far away, and I thought maybe she might be able to give me a name." I make it as vague as possible. I hate to have the girl lose her job simply because I'm here to question her. There's a good chance that news will get back of Truly's arrest. She won't stand a chance of keeping her job after that, but I'll try not to make things worse.

"I'll tell her she better cooperate. I won't have any troublemakers here."

"As I understand it, she's a good, church-going girl. I don't think I'll have any trouble from her."

"She's cleaning a room. I'll call her down." She lumbers around the desk and goes out into the parking lot and hollers up for Alva to come down.

In a minute, the woman starts talking, I presume to Alva. I hear the haranguing tone of her voice, but not her words. When the two come in, it's obvious that whatever the woman said, Alva is terrified. She's a skinny girl the same age as the girls who were killed. Her eyes are so wide open that the whites are showing and she's wringing her hands.

"Alva, do you mind if we step outside so I can ask you a few questions?" I speak gently. She won't be any use to me if she's paralyzed with fear.

"What do you want with me?" she asks, darting a glance at her employer. "I didn't do nothing."

"I told you not to give this man any sass." The woman's voice is stern.

"It's fine," I say hastily. "Of course she wants to know what I'm here for. Alva, I'm investigating that fire that happened in Cato Woods, and I'm talking to everybody who lives close by. I need to ask you a couple of questions."

"I don't know nothing," she says, barely above a whisper.

"Alva!"

"Let's go outside. I'll only take a few minutes of your time and let you get back to work."

She lets me prod her outside. I beckon to her to come farther away from the door, out of earshot of her employer. "I have something important to tell you," I say quietly. "I didn't want to tell you inside."

"What do you want to tell me?" She's trembling. Happily, a car wheels into the parking lot and a man gets out and goes inside. I hope he wants a room and that the transaction takes a few minutes.

"Alva, you need to be strong. Your brother has been arrested."

She squeaks in fear. "For what?"

"They think he had something to do with the people who were killed."

"No! No! He didn't do that. He couldn't . . ."

"Hush now. I know he didn't do it. I'm working to figure out who did. But for now, you need to be strong for him and for your daddy."

"And my daddy? Did they arrest him, too?"

"No, but he's upset about Truly, and you need to help him stay calm."

"Calm! You crazy! How can we be calm? You know how they do us. They just want to arrest somebody, and the best somebody they can come up with is a nigger. They don't care who really did it."

"I do."

"Who are you? What do you have to do with anything?"

"I'm chief of police, and I know Truly. I don't want to see him falsely accused. I know this is a bad situation, and the more you can help me, the better chance I have of getting your brother released."

"I told you I don't know nothing."

The man comes out of the office and gives us a curious look. He gets in his car and moves it a few spaces away.

I lower my voice. "Listen to me. The Texas Highway Patrol officer who arrested Truly questioned him about you. How would he know that Truly had a sister?"

She stares at me. "How do I know? I don't know any highway patrolman." She begins to weep, her chest heaving and tears running down her cheeks. "They're going to beat him like that black man they killed in Georgetown. He's going to die. I know he will."

"No. The sheriff here is a good man. He doesn't want anything like that to happen. But the faster I can help get Truly out, the better. I need help from anybody who can tell me something about those people."

"Oh . . ." she squeals. "I swear I don't know them." She chews on her fist and then brings her chin up in defiance. "Why do you care what happens to Truly?"

That's the question a lot of people are going to ask. "I just do, that's all." At first it was personal, but now something is stirred up in me and I need to know what really happened out there. "Are you going to help me or not?"

The motel owner takes that unfortunate moment to stick her head out the door and send a fierce look in our direction.

"I've got to get back to work," Alva says, avoiding my eyes. She starts backing away.

"Wait." I open my wallet, fish one of my cards out, and hand it to her. "A name. That's all I need." Then louder I say, "Thank you very much for your help. I'll let you get back to work."

Back at the motel office, I stick my head inside. The woman is standing there absolutely still. "Thank you. Sorry I disturbed your girl. Everything's fine. I won't need to come out here again."

"I guess that's all right then."

CHAPTER 19

Before I leave Bobtail, I stop at a phone booth and call home. I don't expect Jeanne until this evening, but if she has come back early, I want her to know where I am. The phone rings and rings, and I'm oddly relieved that I don't have to explain to her why I'm stopping off to see the Montclairs.

It's not hard to see where the fire was. A whole section of crop is charred, and you can still see wisps of smoke here and there from some of the remaining seared plants. I spy Owen Montclair out on the edge of the field with a hoe. Is he going to turn the soil under by hand? It's a wrenching thought. A tractor could do the work in no time.

He raises his head and watches me as I drive up the long, rutted road, but he doesn't acknowledge me and quickly returns to his work.

At the house, I walk up onto the porch and rap on the door. There's movement inside and the door opens to a boy Tom's age. He's nothing like Tom, though. Despite my brother's unhappiness, Tom has an irrepressible good nature. The Montclair family's struggle to make ends meet is reflected in the disappointment on this boy's face.

The boy stares at me silently. I ask if his mamma is in.

"She's out back seeing to the chickens," he says.

"Would you tell her Mr. Craddock is here and that I'd like to talk to her when she has a minute?" Before the boy can close the door, a young girl a couple of years older than him hurries into the front room, wiping her hands on an apron that's too big for her. "Who is it, Cal? Oh, can I help you?"

I repeat my request.

"You can come inside if you want," she says.

"That's all right, I'll stay out here."

The girl glances past me and freezes. I look behind me to see Montclair striding toward the porch. "Get on into the kitchen, Cal," she says in a tense voice.

I go down the steps to meet Montclair. "Sorry to bother you," I say.

"What is it you want?"

There's no need to ease into the subject of why I'm here. I have no doubt it would aggravate the man further. "I heard you had a fire, and I couldn't help thinking it was something of a coincidence to have two fires on the Cato property in one week. I wondered if you know how it started."

The anger in his eyes lowers a notch. "Fire chief seemed to think it was carelessness."

I look past him toward the scorched land, and then meet his eyes. "I only met you once, but from what I saw, it seems unlikely you'd be careless. How do you think it happened?"

"I think somebody set it."

"How? Gas? Kindling of some kind?"

He swallows and his expression sags with naked defeat. "If you're interested, come with me."

I follow him down to the field where he was hoeing. He crouches down next to one of the plants. "It's close to harvest, so the plants are dry. All it takes is for a few of them to be kindled." He pulls one of the ravaged plants from the ground, sniffs it, and hands it over. "Gasoline."

"Did you show this to the fire chief?"

"I only just now found it. I knew there had to be a starter somewhere, so I began clearing around the perimeter to see if I could find something." He stands up and wipes his hands on his pants. "Not that it matters." He says it so low, he could be talking to himself.

I don't need to ask what he means. He was counting on every one of these cotton plants to give him the slim margin he needed to keep going. The loss of even one field tips him off the edge. It might be for the best. His stubbornness has not done his family any good. I don't know what drives a man to dig in his heels the way he has, and I don't see how I can make it my business. But one part of it is my business. Somebody set this fire. You can't go around torching someone's livelihood just because you have other plans.

"When is George Cato set to come out here?" I ask.

He blinks at me. "George? He comes the first of every month, so it'll be another couple of weeks. You're not thinking he's responsible for this, are you?"

"It occurred to me, since you said he wanted you off the property."

His mouth turns down in a sneer. "This isn't Cato's work."

"Why do you say that?"

He takes a while to answer. "It was like the two of us were in a standoff. He didn't believe I could make a go of this farm, and I was determined to show him I could. I think he was too anxious to prove me wrong to do anything underhanded. He wanted to make me understand fair and square that I was a fool."

"Sounds personal," I say.

"Oh, yes, it's personal all right. Him and me are half brothers. We have the same mamma but different daddies. He always thought he was the smart one."

He seems convinced that George Cato didn't have a hand in the fire, but I'm not. I remember the implied smirk in the voice of George Cato's father. "George's daddy had money and yours didn't."

"My daddy was a high school teacher, and George's daddy is a real-estate tycoon in Dallas. Which one do you think is rich?"

"You said your daddy 'was.' Is he deceased?"

"Long time ago. I was a young boy. My mamma went to work as Ronald Cato's secretary, and he married her."

"You've got a different name. He didn't adopt you?"

"No." He sighs and looks off in the distance. "But he treated me okay. I was stubborn and he put up with it."

"Owen, supper!" Judy Montclair sticks her head out the door and calls sharply.

"I know one person who's going to thank whoever set that fire," he says.

"Maybe things will turn out better than you think," I say, and then instantly feel foolish for presuming to spout empty phrases to Owen Montclair.

But he takes it as intended and says, "Could be."

"I'll be on my way, but if you hear from George, will you let me know? I'd like to talk to him about the place that burned in the woods."

"Why don't you call him?"

"I did, and I only got his daddy. He told me he'd pass on the message, but I didn't get the impression it was high on his list."

CHAPTER 20

It's still daylight when I get home, and I can't wait for Jeanne to arrive. I stand in the kitchen weighing whether she'd rather cook or go out, but before I make up my mind, I hear her car pull into the driveway. For a second I freeze. I feel different than I did a couple of days ago. Will I seem strange to her? Is it the autopsy that made me feel different, or was it Truly being arrested? Or deciding to take my job seriously?

It doesn't matter. I rush out the door, grinning. She's getting out of the car, and I'm as stunned as I always am when I see her after we've been away from each other. How did I ever get so lucky? She stretches her arms over her head, and her pretty swish of hair falls across her shoulders. She wriggles all over, and her impish smile takes over her face. We move toward each other as if it has been weeks and not just two days since she left.

We both start talking at once, saying, "I have so much to tell you." Then we laugh and I pull her into my arms and kiss her. I suddenly want all I can get of her, right now. We pull back, breathless. "Let me help you get your things out of the car."

She gets on tiptoes and throws her arms around my neck, pulling my head down to meet hers. "We can do that later," she says. I swoop my arm down and pick her up, with her still clinging to my neck, and carry her inside. She's laughing. "What are the neighbors going to think?" she whispers.

"I don't know and I don't care." I don't care about much of anything. Let the house catch on fire, the telephone ring, somebody come banging on the front door. It will all have to wait. There's only one thing on my mind, and Jeanne is right with me. As we clamor onto the bed like a couple of newlyweds, I breathe in her scent and can hardly stop looking at her, losing myself in her dark eyes.

The last thing I hear her say is, "I'm so glad to be home with you."

Later, we lie in bed, and as the dusk closes in she chatters about her trip and I savor the sound of her voice. Suddenly she sits bolt upright. "I almost forgot. I have a surprise. Okay, I mean not really a surprise. Not for you anyway. It's for me, and you, too, of course. I hope you'll like it."

I know by the way she's talking, begging me to understand, that she has brought home another painting. Jeanne and her mother collect art the way some people collect knick-knacks. I try to act like I like the art, but it's all a mess to me. Give me a good picture of bluebonnets and cactus, and I'm satisfied. I did make her happy when we went to a museum and I really enjoyed looking at Frederick Remington. She was nice enough to admit that his art is important. But what she loves is modern art—things that look like a jumble of shapes and colors.

We go out to the car, and she opens the trunk. "This is the surprise," she says. "Mamma thinks you'll love it. I hope she's right." She's practically dancing with anticipation. I pull the well-wrapped painting out of the trunk and carry it into the house, with her tripping along beside me.

"Let's open it," she says when I lay it on the kitchen table.

"Let me bring in the rest of your stuff while there's still daylight."

She fetches her small cosmetics case while I carry the big suitcase. "I hope you had enough clothes for two days," I grumble.

"I had to have a lot of outfits. You know how Mamma is. We went out to dinner twice and I had to go to lunch with some of Mamma's friends. They're my friends, too, I guess. Anyway I've known most of them my whole life. I'm not like you and wear the same old thing every day."

If I didn't know her, I'd think she enjoyed all the social outings that her mamma drags her to. But in reality she goes to please her mamma, who is as friendly a person as you'd ever meet. The problem is, where her mamma is outgoing and can't get enough of social life, Jeanne likes a quieter life. When we first got out of school, we tried living in Fort Worth, but after a year Jeanne couldn't wait to get away from the city. I wasn't altogether excited when she suggested that we move back here, but she seems happy, and I'm learning to appreciate it.

"What are we going to do about dinner?" I ask. "I could eat a sixteen-ounce steak." I grin at her, knowing she's about to bust to show me the picture.

"Oh, you! Open it."

I tear off the brown paper, then the foam around the edges, and finally the cardboard covering the picture.

What I see surprises me. The background is a strong red, and in the foreground, boxes and stick-like shapes in bright colors seem to be tumbling from the top of the painting. I'm happy that I really do like it. I like the movement and the vibrant colors. I even like the size of it, which seems like an odd thing to notice. The proportion is perfect. "I don't know what to say. This is . . . I don't know how to describe it. I like it."

She raises her hands to the ceiling. "He likes it. Oh. He likes it. It's a Kandinsky!"

"In that case, I like it even better." I laugh. She knows I couldn't tell a Kandinsky from a coconut.

"I'm going to call Mamma right now and tell her she was right. She'll be so glad."

"No, we're going to dinner right now."

We go to a barbecue place out on the road to Bryan–College Station for brisket and potato salad. We order at the counter and bring our drinks to the table with us.

When we sit down, she says, "We've only been talking about me. What happened while I was gone?"

It's hard to pick the right details. I don't want to upset her with talk of the autopsy, and I'm reluctant to tell her that Truly was arrested, although she'll hear it soon enough from the grapevine. "There's a lot going on," I say.

She looks at me as if seeing me for the first time since she got home. "You look different."

"Different how?"

"Older or something."

"Well, you were gone for two whole days."

She smiles and speaks softly. "How was that autopsy? Was it awful?"

"Unpleasant. Informative." I take a swallow of beer.

"You know the Dallas newspapers made a big deal out of it. They said those people were murdered. Why didn't you tell me?"

"I didn't want to upset you."

"Did you know right away?"

"I did."

She squeezes lemon into her iced tea, and when she looks up at me her face is serious. "I know I said I didn't want you to be chief of police, but that doesn't mean I want you to keep secrets from me."

I put my hand out onto the table, palm up, and she lays her hand on top of it. "I didn't intend for it to be a secret. It was a shock, and I needed to get it straight in my mind. Here I was thinking being chief of police was easy, and then something like that happens."

"Just don't shut me out, that's all. Anyway, you told me the highway patrol or the Rangers would be in charge, so there's nothing for you to worry about."

I want to tell her the struggle I'm having with John Sutherland, but it's hard to put it into words. I squeeze her hand. "Did you happen to bring a Dallas paper with you?"

"No, why would I?"

"You said the papers made a big deal out of the murders, and I thought maybe you would have brought it."

"I'm sorry, I didn't think of it. Have they found out who did it yet?"

The moment I've been dreading. Even if I don't tell her, it will be all over town tomorrow and she'll wonder why I kept it from her. "They arrested somebody, but I don't think he's guilty."

She sits up taller and her eyes widen. "What do you mean you don't think he did it? Who is it?"

"They arrested Truly Bennett."

She claps a hand over her mouth. "Oh, that's terrible. Who would have suspected?"

"You know he couldn't have done it."

The waiter chooses that second to plop our barbecue platters down in front of us. "More iced tea?" he asks Jeanne.

"Yes, please." He pours it from the big pitcher, and she squeezes more lemon into it, not meeting my eyes. But I see the pink spots high on her cheeks. She takes a sip and says, "What do you mean I know he couldn't have done it? I don't know anything of the kind."

"Jeanne, I've known Truly my whole life. He's a good man. He's been at our house. He's worked for us."

"He's been at our house? He's done work outside, that's all. Other than that, we don't know a thing about him." She sounds frightened.

"He has never been in any trouble."

"Never got caught, you mean."

"He's a good, church-going man."

"Since when did you care whether somebody goes to church?" She doesn't like that she has to go to church without me.

"I think they're jumping the gun by arresting him, that's all," I say. "I'm pretty sure the highway patrolman investigating just wanted to make a quick arrest."

"He must have evidence, or they wouldn't have arrested him. Why don't you let him do his job? Why borrow trouble?"

"Because I don't like the idea that they can arrest somebody because it's convenient."

"You sound like somebody from an old western. *Shane*, or something." She takes a shuddering breath, and tears are standing in her eyes. "Samuel, I don't want you to get hurt."

She never said that before. "I won't get hurt. I'm going to be fine.

Hey, let's change the subject. Something you're going to like." I tell her that Horace asked if Tom could stay with us for a few days.

She lights up, as relieved as I am to move on to another topic, especially having Tom with us. "When is he coming?"

"Sometime tomorrow."

"Tomorrow? Why didn't you say so? That means I have to go to the grocery store in the morning. Maybe when I pick Tom up, I'll stop by and see your mamma, too. I'll call Horace and ask him what time he's planning to leave."

"Don't do that. You know how he is. He doesn't like to be pinned down. I have to go into work for a while tomorrow, so I'll have time to pick up Tom."

"It's Saturday. Why do you have to go to work?"

"Crime never sleeps," I say, trying to lighten things up. It hits me again how much I ignored Jeanne's resistance to my job. Not wanting to rock the boat made me lazy. I hear Bonnie Bedichek's voice, exhorting me either to be a chief of police or to forget it. "John Gilpin is after me to get to the bottom of the drug problem he's having at the high school."

She nods, picking at her food. She's used to having me make light of my job. "Isn't it going to be dangerous, poking around with drug dealers?"

"I don't think we're talking about hard-core criminals, Jeanne. The kids are getting hold of marijuana."

"I wish you'd figure out something else to do. You know my brother would take you on in a heartbeat."

"We've discussed this before. It means a lot of travel." Her brother runs her daddy's oil and gas exploration company and wants to hire me as a land man, someone who scouts out property for likely well prospects. He pointed out to me that it would make use of my geology degree. I like her brother, so it wouldn't be the end of the world if I took on the job. "If I did that, who would take care of my new herd of cattle?"

"I could learn to do it." She makes a face and I laugh. The tension between us eases.

"The cows are doing well," I say. I tell her some of the funny things I've already noticed about them, and how they seem to have their own personalities. "You come down to the pasture with me in the morning, and I'll point out some of the good ones. You'll like the calves."

"I know I will, but tomorrow I've got to get things ready for Tom."

By the time we get home, Jeanne is back in good cheer. She sees the answering-machine light blinking and runs to it. "That's probably Mamma. I told her I'd call when I got home."

She pushes the button to listen, and a man's voice comes on. "Leave the business with those colored people alone, if you know what's good for you."

She turns a stricken face to me. "Who was that? Was that a threat?"

CHAPTER 21

It took some doing to calm Jeanne down last night. She called her mamma, and they were on the phone for an hour in hushed conversation.

This morning, she's full of excitement at Tom's arrival, but when I tell her I'm going out, she balks. "After that phone call, I'd think you might want to back off."

"Jeanne, I took this job, and I'm going to do it. I'm not taking the phone call seriously. If you're worried, you can go back up to Dallas until this blows over. Take Tom with you. Your mamma would love it."

"I couldn't have a good time being worried half to death about you."

I take her in my arms and kiss her on the top of the head. "Do you think I'm so weak that I can't take care of myself? Is that it?"

She wiggles away. "Of course not. You're not weak. But you might be meddling into something bigger than a small-town cop ought to be handling."

"I'll be careful."

As soon as I get to headquarters, I call Horace. Donna answers the phone. "Donna, can you give me any idea when you and Horace are going to drop Tom off?"

"Whenever Horace gets back."

So she's not going to be pinned down either. "I'll come by and pick him up. That way y'all don't have to worry about timing and you can head straight out when you're ready."

"I guess that would be all right. When do you want to come?"

I tell her I'll be by in a couple of hours. Between now and then I want to check on Truly and maybe talk to a few more neighbors near Cato Woods to see if I can persuade somebody to tell me more about the folks living there.

Roland Newberry isn't in the office. "What do you need?" the duty officer asks.

"I want to know how Truly Bennett is doing this morning?"

"He's popular, for one thing. His daddy has been in here asking about him, and some Texas Ranger called and said he's coming by in a little while."

"Has anybody checked to make sure he's all right this morning?"

"Nobody saw the need. Sheriff Newberry put a special detail to watch him."

"That's good. Is he going to be in jail there in Bobtail all weekend?"

"As far as I know. Nobody has mentioned that they're going to move him anywhere."

He tells me he doesn't know the name of the Texas Ranger who called, but that he said he'd be by around noon. I intend to be there to greet him.

As I'm walking out the door to head to Darktown, the phone rings. "This is Chief Craddock."

I hear someone breathing on the line. I wonder if it's the same person who left the threat last night, and my heart rate shoots up. "Hello?"

"Talk to Beaumont Penny," a voice whispers, and the receiver clatters down. I'm certain the caller was Alva Bennett.

I remember Penny only vaguely. He's a dozen years older than me. But I do know he had a reputation for getting in trouble with the law regularly. Nothing big that I recall. I can't even remember if he ever spent time in jail, other than maybe an overnight for being drunk.

Johnny Pat Hruska comes in, apologizing for being late. He's always late, but he apologizes as if it's never happened before.

"Johnny Pat, do you remember Beaumont Penny?"

Johnny Pat scratches the back of his head. "Not much. He moved away at least ten years ago. You weren't living here then, isn't that right?"

I nod.

"The last I heard of Penny, he was in San Antonio."

"You know anything about his people?"

"I don't keep up much with those folks, but his mamma, Zerlene, cleans house for a few people in town. Maybe she can tell you where he's at."

"Who does she work for?"

"The Methodist preacher, for one."

I toss back the last of my coffee and head for the door. "I've got some things to do. Hold down the fort."

"Yessir, I can sure do that," he says.

The Methodist preacher, Rolly Hawkins, is a good-natured man. I catch him in the front yard of his modest little house next door to the church, watering his garden. When he sees me getting out of the car, he turns off the hose and comes over to greet me, wiping his hands on his khaki work pants. "Hello, Samuel, what brings you here?"

"I've got a question for you."

"Come on in the house and let me give you a glass of iced tea." It's said that Hawkins has become domestic since his wife died a year ago, but he's thinner than he was, which leads me to believe that his cooking might not suit him the way his wife's did.

We walk into the kitchen, where a tall, sturdy, gray-haired black woman is engaged in cleaning out the refrigerator. Hawkins introduces us.

"Good morning, Mr. Craddock." She has erect posture and a regal tilt to her head.

"Zerlene, you're just who I want to see. Rolly, I actually came to ask you when Zerlene would be here so I could track her down. Since she's here, do you mind if I ask her a couple of questions?"

"Go right ahead."

Zerlene closes the refrigerator door carefully and smoothes her apron. "What is it you want to ask me?"

I don't know whether it's better to question her in front of her employer or alone. I know she's not in danger of losing the job with the Methodist preacher because of my questions, but I don't know if she'll feel less or more inclined to answer me honestly in front of him.

"Would you rather we talk after you get off work?"

She glances at the preacher.

"It doesn't make me any difference," he says. "It's up to Zerlene."

"I don't know what you have to ask me that I can't say in front of Reverend Hawkins, so let's get it over with."

"It's about your son."

"Which one? I've got three."

"Beaumont."

Her lips come together in stern disapproval, and her shoulders slip from their rigid pose. "I was afraid you were going to say that."

"Why is that?"

"He's the only one of my boys who seems to invite trouble. What is it this time?"

"I'm not sure if it's anything at all. Where is he living? Is he still in San Antonio?"

She raises her eyebrows. "He wore out his welcome there and moved to Houston a few years ago."

"What does he do there?"

"If you find out, you tell me. He doesn't keep me informed on what he's up to."

"When was the last time you saw him?"

"He come around about two months ago. He don't stay long when he comes. He and his daddy don't get along. I guess I ought to appreciate that he comes by, but I always worry that they're going to have a set-to."

Hawkins poured me a glass of tea, and he's been hovering over us like a bird. "Why don't you two sit down, and I'll leave you to talk?"

"I don't know what more I have to say," Zerlene says. "I need to get on with my work. Mrs. Hall up the street is expecting me this afternoon."

"I can talk to you while you work," I say. "I just have a couple more things to ask."

"I'll leave you to it," Hawkins says. I appreciate his discretion, but Zerlene looks after his retreating back as if she's seeing her only hope disappear. She wrenches open the refrigerator and takes up a sponge and starts scrubbing vigorously.

"What do Beaumont and your husband fight about?"

Her voice comes back muffled. "What most daddies and their sons fight about. Why he doesn't have a visible means of employment, why he doesn't settle down with a good woman." She backs out and arches an eyebrow at me. "And I fuss at him because he dresses up like a river-boat gambler."

I smile. "I know he was rowdy and had a few run-ins with the law when he lived here, but has he gotten in any trouble since he moved on?"

She sticks her head back in the refrigerator. "I believe he has." I don't say anything and in a moment she backs out again. "Okay, yes he has. My husband had to go to San Anton' to bail him out. He got in a fight and the other man got cut." She glares at me like it's my fault. "But the charges were dropped and he never had to go to trial."

"Do you know what the fight was about?"

"I told my husband I didn't want to know."

"What's your husband's name?"

"His name is Alvin. Named after the town where he was raised. We named all our boys after towns, too. Beaumont, Tyler, and Carmine— places we lived where my husband found work before he found a steady job here."

"Where does Alvin work?"

"He's retired now. He worked for the tie plant until it closed down, and then he was a cook over at a barbecue place in Bobtail. He still cooks for parties and whatnot. He does a pretty fair brisket." Her eyes shine with pride in her husband.

"I'd like to try some of that barbecue one day," I say. "A couple more questions. When your son comes here, who does he spend time with?"

She walks over to the sink, rinses out the sponge, and lays it on the counter. "He goes over to see Wink Nelson, and sometimes he catches up with some of his friends over at the Ink Spot, but I don't keep up with that crowd. Now, if that's all you want to ask, I need to get out the vacuum cleaner."

"I do have one more question."

Her smile is patient. "I figured you might. All this beating around the bush has got to be for something."

"Do you know if he knew any of the people who were killed in that fire out in Cato Woods?"

She stands still as a statue. When she stirs, she says, "Why would he know any of those people? They ain't from around here."

"Really? Where are they from?"

"I don't know. You'll have to find that out from somebody else."

"Do you know any of their names?"

"I do not. Now, if you'll excuse me, I'll be gettin' back to work."

I thank her for her time. "If you think of anything you believe I ought to know about those people, will you get in touch?"

"I sure will." But I know from her tone of voice that it isn't likely.

Hawkins looks at me with great curiosity when I pass him still working in his garden, but he's too polite to quiz me.

I'm itching to go talk to Zerlene's husband, but I promised I'd pick up Tom.

Donna acts like she's surprised to see me. "I didn't know you were coming over so soon." Her bruises have eased into a hideous yellow with purple streaks.

"Is Tom here, or is he out with his buddies?"

"He's in his room. I told him to get packed to stay a few days. You'd think he was moving in with you. He's taking pretty much everything he owns."

"I'll go hurry him up," I say. I can hardly stand to look at her mass of yellowing bruises. I wonder where she told Tom they came from.

Tom's door is open. It's a two-bedroom apartment, but his bedroom is no bigger than our bathroom. A tiny little twin bed takes up most of the room, and a stack of crates serves as a chest of drawers. I once asked if he wanted me to buy him a real chest of drawers. He told me he liked the open crates. "Seems to me drawers are for hiding stuff," he said. "This way, if I'm in a hurry to find something, it's right out there where I can see it." I had to admit he had a point.

His old suitcase once belonged to my daddy. He has filled it with everything but clothes.

"You going to wear the same clothes all week?"

"If I could, I would."

"You know your aunt Jeanne isn't going to let that happen."

"I know." He grabs some random clothes and shoves them in on top of a shoebox. Below the box I see some books and a slingshot and a bunch of toy cars. He has Lincoln Logs at our house along with more cars. I always tease him that he's going to end up as an auto mechanic, which suits him fine.

"What's in the shoebox?"

"Rocks."

"That ought to come in handy."

"They're special kinds of rocks. Like some of the ones you showed me."

"We'll look them over. You ready?"

He closes the lid of the suitcase, but it won't snap shut. I hold it down while he presses the clasps. Then I pretend that it's too heavy for me to carry. "We're going to have to get a mule up here to carry this."

He giggles.

"You had any lunch?" I ask.

"Nope."

"Good. Me neither. We'll go get something to eat."

Donna is sitting in the living room, staring at the wall and smoking a cigarette. We've had words about her smoking around the boy, and her look is defiant.

"Horace still isn't back?" I ask.

"He called and said he'll be a while longer." She looks at Tom in a way that gives me an uncanny feeling like Donna is my mother all over again. "I want you to behave," she says.

"I will."

"He always does," I say. "You're raising him to be a good young man."

"He'll eat you out of house and home." She gets up and grabs him in a headlock. He squeals, but he likes it. I change my mind. She may be a little bit like Mamma, but not altogether. Thinking of Mamma, I realize I should have gone to see her before I picked up Tom.

Tom ducks out from under Donna's arms and grabs the suitcase and starts dragging it toward the front door.

"You going to run out of here without kissing me good-bye?"

"Aw, Mamma, I'm too big for that."

She looks at me and winks. "Let's shake hands then."

He sidles over to her and sticks out his hand. She grabs it and pulls him to her and plants a kiss on top of his head. "Now get on out of here. Have a good time."

She watches him go, and there's a strange, melancholy expression on her face.

"You okay?" I ask.

She shrugs. "Sometimes I don't think I'm a good mother," she says.

"You're doing something right. He's a good boy."

We hear him thumping the suitcase down the steps. "I better go before he busts the suitcase open," I say.

When I get the suitcase into the car, I ask him if we ought to go say good-bye to his grandmother, too.

He winces. "I guess we should, but she'll talk and talk, and I'm hungry. We can come back later."

"You're right. Let's get on with it."

We turn the corner onto the highway, and down the street I see Horace's car turn onto another road.

"Look, there's Daddy," Tom says.

"You want to chase him down and say good-bye?"

"Nah, he said 'bye this morning."

"Did he say where he was off to?"

"He said he was going out to Roundtop, but I don't know why."

Wherever he said he was going, he's back in town and he has me curious.

"Shall we go pick up your aunt Jeanne to have lunch with us?"

He's all for that. We drive out to the house and unload his suitcase. Jeanne is back from the store with enough food for a small army, and we help her put it away.

"Where do you want to go to eat?" I ask them.

"The Dairy Queen," Tom says, jumping up and down.

"Oh, you always want to go there," Jeanne says in a pretend whiney voice. "I'd like to get dressed up and drive over to San Antonio and get a fancy meal. You could wear a suit. You'd be so good-lookin' the girls would swarm all over you."

"Ewww."

"All right, I guess if you don't want girls making a fuss, maybe we should go to the DQ," I say. "We can get you a burger. I heard they started making them with armadillo, and they're pretty good."

CHAPTER 22

As soon as we're done eating, I tell Jeanne that I need to go up to Bobtail.

"What for?"

"I need to meet with a Texas Ranger there."

"Oh boy!" Tom's eyes are wide. "A real Texas Ranger? Can I go?"

"No, honey, your uncle Samuel has work to do." Her emphasis on the word "work" gives me some idea what she thinks of it.

He whines a little bit until Jeanne asks him if he'd like to have a friend over to the house. "You can tell him your uncle is off helping the Rangers," she says.

I arrive at Bobtail PD to find the parking lot full of media vehicles. Apparently the press has found out that an arrest has been made. There's even a TV news truck from Houston. I recognize a couple of the reporters from the fire site, but clearly no one recognizes me because they barely glance my way as I walk up the steps. At least there's some advantage to being a small-town cop.

Inside, Curren Wills and his partner, Luke Schoppe, are standing with John Sutherland. I see from their posture that the two senior men are having an argument. "It's not enough to go on," Wills says. His arms are folded tight across his chest.

"We'll let the district attorney make that decision," Sutherland says. His face is bright red.

"You know as well as I do that that boy is in danger staying in jail over the weekend."

"You saying you think Newberry can't keep him safe? That's not my problem."

"Newberry needs manpower, and that costs money."

"I'm not backing down on this. If you're so all-fired worried, lend Newberry a couple of your men. You've got the resources to do that."

Wills takes his hat off and runs his hand across his balding head. "I guess that's what I'll have to do," he says.

They both look my way, and I feel like fresh meat. "What are you doing here?" Sutherland asks. Before I can reply, he grins a nasty grin and says, "I hope you liked that autopsy."

"I can't say I liked it. But it was informative."

"Humph. It was a waste of time. We've got our man." Sutherland must have asked how I behaved during the autopsy, and he doesn't like it that I managed to get through it without making a fool of myself.

"You asked what I'm doing here. I'd like to talk to the two of you," I say.

"Sorry, I've got somewhere to be. Maybe Officer Wills has time on his hands."

He follows up on his words by heading out the door.

"Don't let the door hit you on the backside," Wills mutters. He gives me a bland look. I feel pretty good hearing those words, since they echo my sentiments.

I tell Wills I have something I'd like to run by him. We go down the street to a coffee shop to confer. There, I tell Wills and Schoppe about the feud between the two Cato brothers, the fire out at the farm, and about coming upon Blue Dudley and Freddie Carmichael at the burned house. Then I tell them I had a threatening phone call. Wills sits up straight. "That I don't care for. Have you ever had a call like that before?"

"No, sir. But the caller wasn't specific. There's a chance this is concerning something else."

He tilts his hat back. "And what might that be?"

"We've got a drug problem in town. Everything has been kind of quiet on that front for a while, but all of a sudden the high school principal called me in to light a fire under me."

"What kind of drugs? Hard drugs? Marijuana?"

"I think it's marijuana. That and kids stealing pills out of their parents' medicine cabinets."

"We're seeing a lot of that in small towns. Used to just be the cities." He rubs his hand along the side of his jaw. "I expect if you've kept a low profile and suddenly somebody thinks you're investigating where the drugs are coming from, that might be enough to warrant a warning call." He looks directly at me. "But you said the caller mentioned 'colored people,' so I doubt the call was about the drug problem, am I right?"

"I suppose."

"You watch your backside. Now what about this man they've got in custody? Why don't you think he's guilty?"

"I wish I had something smart to say, but all I know is I don't believe he is. I've known Truly my whole life. He's not the kind of person to do something like that."

Wills grunts. "Unfortunately, that's not much to go on. I'm with you on thinking that Sutherland has jumped the gun, but unless a better suspect is found, I fear that your man Bennett is going to be charged."

"Is there anything the Rangers can do?"

Wills sighs. "Craddock, this is a jurisdictional problem. The highway patrol has to ask for us to step in. We can't just take over."

I start to reply, but he holds his hand up. "There's more to it than that, but I can't go into with you. What I can say is that if whoever really murdered those people is going to be found, it has to be done by somebody other than the THP." He raises he eyebrows at me.

"And that somebody could be me."

He nods his head slowly. "That phone call tells me somebody doesn't want you nosing around."

I swallow. "The problem is, I don't have the resources to investigate the people involved. I asked Bobtail PD to get me information about Dudley and Carmichael, but they didn't get much. And if I'm going to look into the Cato family, I doubt Bobtail PD will want to go after that. And there are a couple of other people I'd like to get a line on."

"Who?"

"Man by the name of Beaumont Penny."

Wills laughs. "Who is Beaumont Penny?"

I tell him about Zerlene's son.

"You've already been busy. How did you get a line on him?"

"I'd rather not say. It's a confidential informer."

"Well, well. A CI. Like the big-city cops have." He laughs harder and exchanges a look with Schoppe. "Told you Craddock had some brains."

I look over to see Schoppe grinning at me. Schoppe is lucky to have Wills to help him learn specifics.

"I'll tell you what," Wills says. "When you need information, you call Schoppe and he'll find it for you. He needs the experience anyway." He turns to his junior partner. "Is that going to be a problem for you?"

"No, sir," Schoppe says. "Whatever needs to be done."

Wills gets up. "Best get back to work. And let me tell you something. I think you're going to do okay."

"I appreciate that," I say. "One more thing. Can you tell me what evidence Sutherland thinks he has?"

"I don't suppose it will hurt for you to know. In one of the dead girls' pockets they found a note."

I nod.

"You knew that?"

"Found out at the coroner's office, but they didn't say what was in the note."

"It was a name and phone number."

"Whose?"

"Truly Bennett's sister. Sutherland's idea is that the occupants of the house were whores. He thinks they were trying to recruit Bennett's sister, and when he found out, he murdered the whole bunch."

Looks like I'm going to have to talk to Alva Bennett again and ask why a note with her name and phone number was in a dead girl's pocket.

When we walk back to the jail, Wills and Schoppe take off. I see Ezekiel Bennett pacing in the parking lot. I ask him if he has seen Truly today.

"Yes sir, they let me in to see him. He seems all right, except not able to get much sleep. The other man in there makes a lot of racket."

"I expect that's going to last the weekend. Not much to be done. I'm going in to see Truly now."

"Chief Craddock, I want you to know I appreciate your help."

I hope my shoulders are wide enough to bear his trust.

Once inside, I ask the duty officer if I can go talk to Truly and he says, "Be my guest."

When I get there, the desk outside the room with the cells is empty and the door is open. I step inside and find the officer leaning against the bars of Carl Rooney's cell, chatting with him. So much for security. He frowns and straightens up. "Can I help you?"

"I'm here to talk to your other prisoner." I nod toward Truly's cell.

"You have authorization?"

"I'm chief of police in Jarrett Creek." I hold out my hand to shake.

He looks at it for a couple of seconds before he snakes his hand out for a quick shake. "Marvin King." He looks me up and down and grins. "Have at it." He turns back and whispers something to Rooney.

Truly is sitting on the edge of his bunk with his hands folded in front of him, watching. He stands up as if his bones hurt and walks over to the bars. His voice is low. "You don't have to keep coming here, you know." He tips a nod in the direction of Rooney and his cop buddy.

"Listen, I'd like to try to get Bonnie Bedichek in here to do an interview with you. Would you talk to her?"

He shoves his hands in his pockets. His eyes are dull and there are purple circles under his eyes. "I don't know if I ought to."

"Have you got a lawyer?"

"They told me the state would get me a defense lawyer sometime next week. My daddy's trying to raise money for a private lawyer, but it's expensive."

"Maybe I can help out."

"No. Daddy wouldn't want you to. He's proud like that. He'll try to get help from the church congregation."

"I don't know what a lawyer would say, but I don't think it would hurt to talk to Bonnie. The big newspapers don't care who you are, and they'll just give you a name. Bonnie will make people see you as a person. You'll be better off."

"I suppose that's true."

Rooney and King break out in raucous laughter. I wonder how long it will take for Wills to get someone here to keep an eye on things, if he even remembers he said he would. I leave with an idea in mind that makes me queasy. Not only could it jeopardize my job, but it could get me hounded out of town if anyone finds out.

CHAPTER 23

Back at headquarters, I phone Bonnie Bedichek. "Can you come over here? We need to talk."

While I wait for Bonnie, I think a little more about my germ of a plan. I have no idea what Bonnie may think of it. She has never given me the slightest idea of her politics. Not that I wear mine on my sleeve either.

Bonnie comes rushing in the way she always does, hair flying back like she's running a race. She plops down like we're old friends. "Okay, have you found out what they have on Truly Bennett?"

"Whoa! Let's back up a little. First of all, would you consider going over to the jail to interview Truly?"

She shakes her head as if I'm a naughty child. "Samuel, they're not going to let me in there. You saw that the other day. If they let any reporter in at all, it would be one of the big ones."

I should have thought of that. "I might be able to persuade New-berry. Let me give it a try." I pause, staring at her. There's no turning back if I ask for her help. If she doesn't keep quiet, I may be sorry. "There's something else."

"What?" She narrows her eyes.

"You have to promise me you won't blab what I'm about to say."

She sighs. "I'm a newspaper reporter, not a priest. It's my job to blab. All I can promise is that I'll only publish it if it's real news."

"All right, never mind."

She shakes her head. "I'm a fool. Okay, spill it. I promise I won't tell."

"I want to let Albert Lamond know that Truly has been arrested."

"Oh, my Lord. Samuel, you're playing with fire. If people find out you did that, they'll never let you forget it."

"That's why I want you to keep it quiet."

"Why did you even tell me?"

I look at her with my eyebrows raised, a silent question.

"Now wait a minute. I know what you're thinking. I can't do that. It' a violation of journalist ethics because it would involve me in something I'm writing about. And besides, Lamond is going to find out soon enough."

"Suppose he doesn't? Suppose something happens to Truly over the weekend?" I tell her what I found when I was at the jail—Rooney and Officer King laughing it up. "Bonnie, even if somebody found out you made the call, they'd just think you were trying to stir things up for news. If they find out I did it . . ." I throw my hands up.

"I don't even know how to get in touch with somebody like that." She bites the knuckles of one hand. As big as she talks, like me she's a small fry in a big situation.

"I can get the number."

"If I'm going to make a call to those rabble-rousers, I need something in return. Tell me what the evidence is against Truly."

I don't want Truly's sister dragged into this, so I tell her half the truth, that a note in one of the victims' pockets pointed in Truly's direction.

"What was on the note?"

"I didn't see it. All I know is that Sutherland jumped to conclusions from whatever it said."

"Maybe you're right. The press needs to shine a light on Truly's situation. I better get on up there to Bobtail and see if I can talk my way in." She jumps up and then remembers. "I guess I owe it to you to make that call. Tell me when you can get me the number."

"I've changed my mind. I'm going to do it myself."

"Why?"

I wave her away. She leaves and I stare after her, wondering what it takes for someone to become a reporter. It's more than being nosy. It's like she's on a mission.

I pull the phone toward me and open my desk drawer where I stuck the card from Albert Lamond's aide. "Juno Williams, Assistant," the card says. I'm not foisting this off on Bonnie because I figure if she has the gumption to push her way into the jail, I can have the guts to call Albert Lamond.

I reach an answering machine and identify myself. "Mr. Lamond might be interested to know that someone has been arrested in the murder and arson case here in Jarrett Creek. His name is Truly Bennett, and I believe he's innocent and could use Mr. Lamond's help. He's in the county jail in Bobtail." I hesitate, trying to decide if I should ask them to keep it quiet that I alerted him, but then I hang up. What I did was impulsive, but I'm either committed or I'm not.

I know I ought to go home, but I also know that Jeanne is perfectly happy with Tom.

Zerlene Penny told me vaguely where she and her husband live, but I have to stop and inquire at two places before I find the house.

Alvin Penny is a wiry man, probably a head shorter than his wife. The muscles in his arms are like ropes. His face is light-skinned, and when he speaks there's a hint of some accent I can't quite identify. "Mr. Penny, I'd like to ask you a couple of questions about your son Beaumont."

"Zerlene told me you'd be poking around. Come on in."

I step into a comfortable living room, and it's obvious that Zerlene uses her mop and cleaning rags here as vigorously as she does at Reverend Hawkins's place.

"Sit down. I can offer you some coffee, but I'm afraid you won't care for it. It's chicory." Now I get the accent. He's from somewhere in Louisiana and came out with a bit of a Cajun lilt.

"That's all right. I won't stay long. I need to get the names of some of your son Beaumont's friends."

"Daddy? Did I hear somebody at the door?" A striking-looking man a few years older than me enters. He's darker than his daddy, but his eyes are electric blue. I wonder why I've never seen him in town.

I stand up and offer my hand. "I don't believe we've met."

He takes my hand easily. "I'm Tyler Penny. I remember you. You were a few years behind me in school. I left here as soon as I graduated."

"Got him a degree in biology from SMU, and he's teaching up there in Dallas." If Alvin Penny was any more proud of his son, he'd glow in the dark.

"Now, Daddy . . ."

"Not like that brother of his."

"Here we go," the son says.

"If you don't mind," I say, "you might be more able to answer my question than your daddy. Do you know any of your brother Beaumont's friends?"

"You mind telling me what this is about?"

"Your brother was mentioned to me as someone who might be able to tell me the names of the people who were living in the house that burned down."

Penny looks blank. "You mean Duchess Wortham and her family?"

Alvin Penny clears his throat, and his son looks at him. "What's the trouble? Oh, don't tell me. You all closed ranks. I'm sorry to spoil your fun, but I don't get the point."

"You never did," Penny says. He sighs. "I suppose you're right. It's just that it never did us any good to get mixed up with the law."

I jump in. "Mr. Penny, when those people were killed, I promised that I'd get to the bottom of what happened. How the hell am I supposed to do that if nobody will talk?"

They look startled at my outburst. Alvin tilts his chin up. "As I understand it, you're not the man in charge of the investigation."

"The man in charge has arrested Truly Bennett for the murders."

"Truly?" Tyler Penny's eyes widen. "You've got to be joking."

"I'm not joking. Do you think he's guilty?" I ask Alvin.

"Of course I don't," he says, "but I don't see that's going to help him. I expect now they've got him in their clutches, neither you nor I can do a dadgummed thing to fix it."

"Daddy, now stop it."

We both look at Tyler. "You stay out of this," Alvin says to his son. "Me and him are having it out, and he's holding his own. He doesn't need some city dude helping him out."

I can't help grinning. "I might need a little help."

Tyler grins, too.

"Mr. Penny, I don't intend to let Truly pay for a crime he didn't commit. But the only way to fix that is to find out who really did it."

"It's going to get you into a pack of trouble. You know that, don't you?"

"Maybe."

"Then why are you going out on a limb like that for a black man?"

"I've been asking myself the same question, especially since I'm trying to get help from people as stubborn as you."

The son laughs. "I'm glad somebody said it."

"Look who's stubborn," Alvin says to me. "You're the lawman trying to buck the system. All right," he says to his son, "I'm outnumbered. Tell the man what he wants to know."

Tyler knows three of the names. "Duchess is the mother of two of the girls, Lily and Alice, and the boy. I don't know her son's name, and I don't know who the other girl was."

"How do you know them?"

"I don't. I just remember somebody telling me they had been to some kind of party at their house."

"When was this?"

"Sometime earlier in the summer. I got the impression it was like a housewarming party, but I don't know why I thought so."

"I have to ask this. The girls were sexually active. Do you know if they were . . ."

"What, prostitutes? Daddy?"

Alvin shakes his head. "I can't tell you anything about that."

If they haven't been here long, maybe no one knew what they were up to. "Do either of you know anybody who might have been better acquainted with them?"

The two men exchange glances. "I guess we're back to the beginning," the older man says. "That would be my son Beaumont. He came home especially to go to that party."

Tyler raises an eyebrow. "Must have been some party."

"How can I get in touch with Beaumont?"

"I might have his number in Houston," Alvin says, "but I have to ask you not to tell him how you got the information. Me and him are not on good terms, and I'd as soon not feed the flames."

I agree and he goes out of the room to get the phone number.

As soon as we're alone, Tyler says, "My brother is not a good man. Daddy and Mamma have three sons. Two of us are regular people. Why Beaumont went off and became a troublemaker, I'll never know. The fact is, as crooked as he is, I can't imagine him being involved with killing women and children. He's a crook, but not a killer. At least I don't think so. If you find out different, I'd appreciate it if you can find a way to spare Mamma and Daddy."

I tell him I'll do my best. When Alvin comes back with a phone number and address in hand, I shake his hand and tell him I hope to use the information to clear Truly Bennett's name. I just hope I don't have to arrest this man's son in his place.

CHAPTER 24

Sunday, Jeanne has arranged a picnic with Marilyn Beffort, a friend she plays cards with and who has kids Tom's age. Marilyn's husband, Jake, is a friendly man who owns a hardware store in Bobtail but grew up in Jarrett Creek and refuses to move his family to the big city of Bobtail.

Jeanne has kept an eagle eye out that I won't get caught up in police business on Sunday, so it's midmorning before I have a chance to call the station in Bobtail to find out if Truly Bennett has survived another night. I speak with a deputy who sounds even younger than me.

"Your friend Bennett is fine, but all hell has broken loose here," he says.

"What do you mean?" I think I know what he means, but I'm trying to maintain innocence.

"You know that upstart troublemaker from Houston, Albert Lamond? He showed up here with a mob around seven o'clock last night, and they've been raising hell ever since."

"Raising hell how?"

He pauses. "You know the way they do, the head man standing on a soapbox and inciting everybody to get riled up."

"Has anybody gotten hurt?"

"Not yet. Sheriff Newberry has kept a tight watch on the situation."

When I hang up, I'm itching to get over to Bobtail to see exactly how Lamond is playing it, but Jeanne would pitch a fit, and it isn't really necessary for me to be there anyway.

We finally get the food, beach towels, water toys, and blankets loaded into the car. "We have enough to feed everybody in the park," I say, as I load the last cooler into the bed of the pickup.

Jeanne acts like she's offended by my remark, but she can't stop grinning.

She loves to feed me, but she loves feeding Tom even more. He's dancing around as if we were going to the World's Fair instead of Lakeside Park.

We meet the Befforts right where we're supposed to, and the three boys take off for the lake like they were shot out of a cannon. It's hot, and before we eat, Jeanne, Marilyn, and I decide to go for a swim, too. Jake Beffort says he doesn't much take to the water, so he stays behind to watch the food. "I have to guard Marilyn's chocolate cake. If anybody knew how tasty it was, they'd be willing to take it at gunpoint," he says.

The cool lake water feels good on this hot day, and I'm glad for a day off after a hard week. It seems like a long time since I was in Austin for the autopsy, although it was only a few days ago. Jeanne and Marilyn stay close to shore, but I swim out to the raft with the boys and we compete to see who can make the biggest splash when we jump in. When the boys start hollering that they're starving, we race back to shore. Jeanne and the Befforts have already got the picnic set out.

An hour later, the Befforts have gone off on a walk, and the rest of us are dozing in the shade. Jeanne and I are sharing a quilt. She's stretched out with her head on my shoulder. Suddenly she sits up. "What is that smell?"

As soon as she mentions it, I smell it too. It smells like tobacco, only sweeter, and I know exactly what it is. There's a breeze coming from the south, and I sit up and search for the source. Several yards away, a handful of teenagers are huddled in a circle on a blanket, smoking marijuana. I expect they think they're invisible.

I wonder if I should confront them, or pretend I don't notice what's going on? If I ignore them, I'm wasting an opportunity to warn them that they can no longer get away with thumbing their nose at the law. But what if they were drinking beer? It's illegal for them to drink, too, but when I was their age I sneaked plenty of beer. Am I joining the ranks of fuddy-duddies who can't stand for kids to experiment?

Tom is asleep on a blanket with the other two boys. Suddenly Tom says, "Daddy?" He raises onto his elbows and peers around, blinking.

146

"Your daddy isn't here," I say.

He frowns and sniffs the air, then yawns and lies back.

Jeanne is watching him, too, and we both look up at the same time. She raises an eyebrow. "What was that all about?"

"Dreaming," I say. But I know that the smell is what triggered his dream. I know my brother smokes pot at times.

The teenagers are getting louder. Two of them have fallen onto their backs and are giggling. "I have to go talk to those kids."

"Samuel, can't you let it go for today?"

"Is that what you want?"

My question creates a problem for Jeanne. She has strong opinions about drug use. Her adored oldest brother has drug and alcohol problems. He has been in and out of rehab. I've met him only a few times, and I don't give him much chance of recovering. I sometimes wonder if one reason Jeanne doesn't like the idea of me being a lawman is that her brother has been arrested and spent time in jail, and the connection is too close for comfort.

"Whatever you have to do," she says. "I wish I hadn't said anything." She lies back down and crosses her arms over her eyes.

I sit there a minute longer, but another strong whiff comes to me and I get up and put a shirt on. The group of half a dozen kids doesn't pay any attention to me until I'm standing over them. The boy holding the joint looks up at me and his mouth falls open. He hides the joint in his palm, even though there's no way I could have avoided seeing it. I hunker down next to them. "You know, marijuana is an illegal substance," I say.

One of the girls, a baby-faced blond, giggles. "I don't know what you're talking about." She's wearing a tiny bathing suit, and she repositions herself so that her breasts thrust in my direction. The boy sitting next to her throws a hooded glance at me.

"You kids go to JC High School?"

Nobody answers.

"I haven't introduced myself. I'm Samuel Craddock, chief of police in Jarrett Creek. Where did you get the marijuana?"

"What if we don't tell you?" the boy holding the marijuana asks.

"I don't want to have to arrest anybody, but if I can't get your cooperation, I may have to take all of you down to the station."

"You won't stand a chance by yourself," the girl's boyfriend says.

"A chance of what? A chance of getting all of you down to the jail?"
I let my gaze scan the surroundings. "Good number of people here, and
I expect some of them would be glad to help out if I called on them. But
like I said, I don't really want to go that far. So I'm asking politely if you
are students at Jarrett Creek High School."

One of the teens, a skinny girl with freckles and a scared expression, says, "All of us do except him." She nods toward the defiant kid.
"He goes to school in Bobtail."

"That means all the rest of you have parents here in town?"

They all exchange horrified glances. The skinny girl's lower lip
starts to quiver. "Please don't tell my mom."

The busty girl gives me a stink-eye. "Go ahead and tell. What are
they going to do to me? Ground me? Whoopee."

"I need to know where you got the stuff," I say.

A couple of the kids sneak glances at the boy who originally had the
joint. "You," I say, pointing at him. "I want to talk to you." I stand up.

"Why me?"

"Do you know who his daddy is?" one of the other boys asks.

"I don't care if his daddy is the governor," I say. I gesture to the kid.
"Come on."

I glance over to see that Jeanne and the boys have not moved, but
the Befforts have returned from their walk and are sitting on the picnic
bench, watching me.

The boy gets up and ambles toward me, full of bravado. His eyes
are red, and up close he reeks of marijuana.

I steer him down toward the lake. "What's your name?"

"Uh . . ."

"Your first name."

"Charlie. Charles, I mean."

"Charlie, it seems that you are the one who brought the weed. If you'll give me the name of whoever supplied you with the product, you get to walk out of here. But if you don't, we've got a problem."

"Why are you picking on me?"

"What kind of a question is that? You sound like you're in first grade. Listen, everybody was looking to you, and that tells me you were the one who supplied this little outing. Are you telling me it was one of the other kids?"

"I don't have to tell you anything."

"You're right. Go get your stuff and I'll run you down to the station, and you can call your folks; then we'll deal with it in front of them."

The kid finally looks nervous. "I don't know his name."

"What does he look like?"

"I've never seen him."

"How do you get it, then?"

He squirms. His shoulders are skinny and I see goose bumps scattered along his arm. "It's a drop-off. I let him know what I need, and he picks up the money and leaves the order. That's all I know."

"How often does this drop-off happen?"

His answers are coming slower and slower. "It varies. Depends on what we want."

"How does he know when you want to buy?"

"I've told you everything I'm going to tell you."

"Not quite." With more poking and prodding, I find out that anybody who wants to buy some grass leaves a note and money in a particular spot at the stadium. "The drill is that you leave the note and come back the next day and the stuff is there." He tells me that the supplier sells pills as well as marijuana, but no cocaine or heroin. He seems outraged at the very idea that the dealer would supply harder drugs. I fear that whoever is selling to him will ease into it sooner or later.

"You make some good spending money as part of the deal?"

He crosses his arms over his skinny chest and narrows his eyes. "I do it to help kids out. I don't make any money."

"Right." If I believed that, I'd believe anything. "Aren't you afraid somebody else will pick up the package and walk away with it?"

"Are you kidding? He said if he ever found out that somebody pimped his product, he'd kill them."

"You said you'd never met him. So how did he tell you that?"

"I talked to him on the phone."

"You called him?"

"Hell no, he called me."

"How did you get hooked up with him in the first place?"

He shrugs. "I met a guy in Bobtail, and he said he could hook me up with some weed and he'd have the guy contact me."

"How long has this been going on?"

"Not that long. A year, maybe a little longer."

"Charlie, I'm going to let you walk away from this because you cooperated with me. But I don't think I have to tell you to keep your mouth shut. If I find out you warned your connection, you'll be in trouble you can't talk your way out of. Do you understand me?"

"I guess."

"No guessing to it. You either understand or you don't," I say, looking him in the eye.

He blinks first.

We turn around to walk back, and I burst out laughing. His bosom buddies have cleared out, leaving his clothes lying in a heap.

"That bastard Leo! How am I going to get back to town?"

"Tough problem," I say. "Maybe you ought to choose a better grade of friends. Or at least braver ones."

I leave him cursing quietly while he gets dressed.

By now the boys are awake and have taken off to swim again. Jeanne and the Befforts are sitting at the picnic bench. Jake Beffort is drinking a beer, and I accept his offer of one.

"What was going on?" he asks.

"Just getting some information."

CHAPTER 25

Back home I tell Jeanne I need to go check on something and I'll be back in a while. She barely notices when I leave because she's busy persuading Tom that swimming in the lake isn't the same as having a bath. She is holding out a bribe of chocolate-chip cookies if he'll get in the tub.

I head straight for Ezekiel Bennett's place. I don't expect him to be home, because he's most likely up at the jail in Bobtail. But I hope to find Alva home. Sure enough, she opens the door.

"You can't be here," she says, flinging her hands up like she's surrendering.

"I have to talk to you."

"I don't have to talk to you. I already did my talking. You're going to get me in trouble."

"Would you rather meet me somewhere? We have to talk here or somewhere else."

"I don't know. Okay, I'll meet you at the house. The burned house." She's practically shivering.

"Ten minutes," I say.

It's late afternoon, but it seems darker than it ought to be. Clouds have sneaked up and gathered into a low ceiling. I'm glad it waited until after our picnic to rain.

It's only been a few days since the fire, but the burned house looks like it could have been months ago. Desolation and ruin hang over the place. The front porch that was sagging has now collapsed. Most likely the embers of the fire continued to eat away at the pillars. The yellow crime-scene tape is broken and lies limp on the ground. I wonder who has been in here. Have vandals made off with the things remaining in the house? Someone should have been posted to keep out trouble-makers and curiosity seekers. Was that my job, or Sutherland's? Even if it was his, I should have known he wouldn't do it, and I don't have the manpower for it.

I go around back and into the kitchen. Nothing here has been touched as far as I can tell. Flies and maggots have settled in to do their work of cleaning up the food left on the dirty dishes. I walk carefully into the hallway and the front room. Seeing as the front porch collapsed, any of the floorboards could be weakened.

In the front room I see that people have been in here. All the photos have been removed. I don't remember particular furnishings, but the room seems barer than it was.

Out the front window I see Alva creep into view. She sneaks a look over her shoulder as if she's scared someone followed her. I go back outside and call out so as not to startle her.

She rushes toward me. "Oh, Mr. Craddock, I wish I hadn't said to come here. I'm scared."

"What are you afraid of?"

She gestures toward the house. "It looks like spirits in there. Those poor folks that got killed."

She's right—between the lowering sky and the gloom of the house, it isn't inviting to be here. "Let's walk. I won't keep you long." We head toward the road. "I have some things to ask you. One of the dead girls had a note in her pocket with your name on it. Why would she have that?"

She stops in her tracks, her mouth open. "I don't know."

"Don't lie to me. You must have known Duchess Wortham or one of her kids."

"I swear I didn't know them."

It occurs to me that it might not have been one of the Wortham females with the note. It might have been the unknown girl. "Did you know anybody who might be visiting them? There was one girl nobody seems to know the name of."

She doesn't say anything, so I keep quiet. We're walking along the deserted road. The air is heavy and still. I expect the heavens to open up any minute and douse us. Finally she sighs. "Cathy. She was a nice girl."

"Did you know her last name?"

"No, sir."

"How did you know her?"

"Met her when I went to the house once."

"How about the boy? You know his name?"

Her head is lowered, watching her feet while we walk, so I can't see her face. "Bobby. Poor little man. I don't know why they had to kill him." She begins to weep softly.

"Do you know why they killed the girls?"

She slows and turns her tearstained face to me. "How would I know that? I just meant he was so little it hardly seems like he could have deserved getting killed."

"What might the girls have done to deserve it?"

"You know, they was teenagers. They get up to a lot more than a little boy. No telling what they saw or heard that might get them in trouble."

"Like what?"

"I understand that you want me to know something, but I don't."

"You said you had been out to the house?"

She digs a toe into the dirt. "I guess I had. Just the one time, though."

"When was that?"

"Sometime in July."

"Why were you there?"

The first drops start to spatter on the leaves with a plopping sound. We're walking under a thick bunch of trees that line the road, so it can't get to us yet. She doesn't seem to notice. "Duchess came by and asked us all if we'd like to come over one afternoon, maybe it was the Fourth of July. Said they were having a cookout and some firecrackers and wanted to invite neighbors."

"Had you met Duchess or any of the others before that?"

"No, sir, they ain't been around here that long."

"Did your daddy or Truly go to the party?"

"No, sir. Truly was gone somewhere and Daddy said I could go if I wanted to, but he needed to go over and help with something at the church. He doesn't like parties anyway."

"Do you know if Truly ever met any of them?"

"You'd have to ask him."

"At the party, did you see Beaumont Penny?"

"Ohhh." The word comes out low.

"What?"

"He was there all right. I didn't talk to him, though. My daddy would have had a fit if he found out I talked to somebody like that. He wouldn't like knowing I was even at a party where he was at."

"Your daddy's got sense."

I ask her more questions about the party, but she doesn't have anything useful to say. She was a young girl having a good time. No reason for her to think anybody there was going to come to such harm. I thank her for her help.

She answers back, "Only reason I'm talking to you is to get my brother cleared."

Suddenly there's a great clap of thunder and the rain comes sloshing down. We run back toward my truck, "Let me take you home." I have to yell to make myself heard above the rain.

"No!" She takes off running in the direction of her house. I jump into the truck and wait until she's had time to get home before I start up and head back to Jeanne and Tom.

All the way home my mind is in turmoil, but when I walk in, it all falls away. Laughter greets me and I go into the kitchen to find the two of them giggling over a jigsaw puzzle. The remains of cookies and milk are on the table.

"How did you get all wet?" Jeanne asks.

"If you hadn't noticed, it's raining hard out there."

Tom laughs. "Raining cats and dogs. Meow! Arf!"

Jeanne looks up from a puzzle piece. "I know it's raining, smarty. I mean, what were you doing out in it?"

"I was talking to somebody and we weren't near the truck."

"You better go change clothes, or you're going to catch a cold." She jumps up. "Come on, Tom, help me clear the table so we can have supper." They carefully move the puzzle down to the other end of the table. I grab a cookie and go change into dry clothes.

After a supper of chili and cornbread, Tom watches TV, and we go out on the porch to watch the rain. It's let up a good bit and there's a nice breeze.

"You look worried," I say. "Everything all right?"

"I was wondering if your mamma is okay without Horace and Donna there. If anything happened, she'd be on her own."

"She'll be fine. I don't imagine they check on her as often as you think."

"I'm going to call her. Maybe she knows where they are."

"Wait. I wouldn't ask that. She'll make out that we're complaining that they left Tom with us."

She sighs. "I suppose you're right. I am going to call, though, to make sure she's okay. I'll take her some groceries tomorrow."

"I'll call her," I say.

"Or see her?"

What she means is that I ought to go over there. By now the rain has let up, so I don't have a good excuse not to go.

It turns out that I've interrupted her favorite TV show, so I have to sit and finish watching *CHiPs* with her. She talks to the TV as if she's in the middle of the action, and I feel a twinge of guilt that she must be

155

lonely. But there are people her age she could do things with. She could play cards at the American Legion Hall or go to church. But she doesn't like people in real life and doesn't put herself out to be friendly. She does have a couple of people she likes to gossip on the phone with, though.

When the program is done, she's in a good mood for a few minutes, going back over some of the crime scenes. But then she remembers that I'm here in the flesh, and she sinks into her usual sour mood.

She tells me she has no idea where Horace and Donna are. "I could die right here in my bed and no one would know."

"You're not fixing to die in your bed," I say. "You're in fine health."

"You don't know a thing about my health," she says. "I've got problems I don't tell you about."

I know how this will go, but I give it a try anyway. "Why don't you tell me?"

"You don't really want to hear it."

This could go on and on. "Something I want to ask you. You ever heard of someone named Duchess Wortham?"

"I might have."

"What do you know about her?"

"Who's asking?"

"She was one of the people killed in that house fire."

"I heard that."

"You what?" I can't believe it. All the trouble I had finding out who the woman was, and all the time my mamma knew.

"Donna told me."

"How did Donna know?"

"I have no idea. She just told me it was Duchess Wortham and her family that got murdered." She peers at me with a satisfied smirk.

"Did she know the woman?"

"What is this? The third degree? You have to ask Donna yourself."

"Can you tell me anything else about the family?"

"I thought you was the law and you was supposed to know everything."

My fists clench. Sometimes when I talk to Mamma, it comes clear to me how men can get violent. "I'd appreciate it if you tell me anything you know."

"If you'll pour me a sip of whiskey, I'll tell you, but don't get your hopes up. It's not much."

After the years of dealing with my daddy's alcohol problem, I'm surprised that lately Mamma has gotten in the habit of sipping a couple of fingers of bourbon before bedtime. I go in the kitchen and pour her some. I pour myself a little, too. If I don't, she'll complain that I'm too stuck-up to drink with her.

I hand her the glass and sit down. She eyes my glass. "Glad you helped yourself," she says. "I'm made out of money, so I can afford to keep you in liquor."

"I'll bring you a bottle the next time I come."

"If you don't forget."

"You promised to tell me what you know about the Worthams."

She takes a sip and hunches forward, eyes alight with gossip. "I heard Duchess was married to a man who got into a little trouble and moved her out there to the woods to keep her safe. But I have my own ideas. I bet she was running around on him and he wanted to keep her to himself." She always likes to add something salacious to the gossip she hears.

"Did he build that illegal house?" I ask.

"Way I heard it, it wasn't illegal. The owner of the property let him build there."

"Why would he do that?"

"You'd have to ask him."

"Where was she from?"

"Houston, the way I heard it. But you know all them coloreds lie. They could be from anywhere."

"Were the kids enrolled in school for the fall?"

"You'll have to ask the school." She sips her whiskey and licks her lips.

"Did you ever hear rumors that there was prostitution going on out there?"

"I wondered when you were going to sneak around to that matter."

"So you did?"

"The men are the ones who know that kind of thing. It's not fit for ladies to talk about, and I should take offense that you asked me, your own mamma."

Meaning she hasn't heard such a rumor, but she wishes she had.

That night, lying in bed, I can sense that Jeanne is not asleep. "Something's on your mind," I say. "Tell me."

She turns to me and props her head up on her elbow. "It's silly, but I don't understand something."

I brace for her to complain that I was away all afternoon, but instead she says, "Why haven't Donna and Horace telephoned to check on Tom? You'd think they would want to know how he's getting on."

"Maybe they're . . ." I stop. I can't think of any excuse.

"They're what?"

"I don't know. Busy, I guess. Did Tom seem upset?"

"That's the other thing I wonder. He hasn't said a word about them except when he half woke up this afternoon. He doesn't seem to wonder where they are, or anything."

"You manage to keep him pretty entertained."

"I know, but it seems odd. Do you think they treat him all right?"

"I do." I tell her how it was with Donna; how she fussed over him. "He knows us pretty well. I'm sure he feels safe here with us, and he knows we love him."

She sighs. "Life doesn't seem fair sometimes."

I know she's talking about Horace and Donna not appreciating the boy they have when the two of us would cherish a child. We fall asleep with our arms around each other.

CHAPTER 26

I'm beginning to wonder if it was a good idea to buy a herd of cattle. I barely have time to feed them before I'm off. When I arrive at headquarters, I take one look at the parking lot and wish I had lingered with the cows. There are five cars I don't recognize, and a van with a Houston TV station logo on the side. The doors of the vehicles open as soon as I park. Several men rush to my pickup and flashbulbs go off in my face.

I put my hand up to shield my eyes. "What in the world is going on?" I ask the nearest reporter.

"Are you one of the deputies?"

"No, I'm Chief Craddock. You mind telling what's going on?"

"You're the chief?"

Seeing the thundercloud on my face, he quickly continues, "Are you aware that Albert Lamond has set up camp outside the Bobtail jailhouse to protest the arrest of Truly Bennett?"

"I heard a rumor to that effect."

"Chief! Chief!" someone yells. "Do you have a statement to make about it?"

"Mr. Lamond has every right to protest, as long as it's peaceful."

"How did he know Mr. Bennett had been arrested?"

"You'll have to ask him that. Now, if you don't mind, I've got work to do."

I try to walk forward, but the reporters block my way. "Do you think Mr. Bennett is guilty?"

I may not be seasoned, but I know enough not to answer that. "If he is, the evidence will come out," I say. That's a line I heard from one of the instructors at the academy. Not much else I learned there has been useful to me. "Now, if you'll excuse me . . ."

"One question," one of them calls out. "Would you care to comment on the suggestion that he killed those people because they wanted to prostitute his sister?"

I've held onto my temper pretty well, but that makes me want to put a fist in the man's face. I feel like steam is about to come out my ears, but I know that if they see any reaction, they'll know there's something to dig for. "Sounds like a rumor to me, and I don't deal in rumors. Now let me pass."

I shove my way into the building and feel like I've escaped from a pack of hounds.

First thing I do is call Tilley, who is due to arrive soon, and tell him to keep his mouth shut when he gets here.

"I don't know anything anyway," he says.

"Well, don't let them suck you into making a comment."

The message machine is lit up, and I dread what I'm going to hear.

A muffled male voice that came in at midnight says, "I understand that killer's daddy was involved with those dead folks, too. We can't have people like that living here in Jarrett Creek. I'm for running them all out of town." I delete the message.

The next one is a woman who called at two a.m. to say she couldn't sleep because she was pretty sure she was going to be murdered in her bed. Another delete.

There's another of the same type at four a.m.

Then at seven o'clock there's a man who says, "This is Raymond Ostrand. We haven't met. I'm with the law offices of Metcalf and Ostrand in Bobtail. My son, Charles, tells me you were giving him some trouble yesterday out at the park. I think we need to have a sit-down. He's an upstanding boy, and I don't appreciate him being hassled." He leaves a phone number.

Thank goodness the next are routine calls. Somebody's dog got into a garden and tore it up, and somebody else had the hubcaps stolen off his car. I never thought I'd be glad to get calls about those minor annoyances.

There's a grim-sounding call from Sheriff Newberry asking me to get back to him, and finally one from George Cato. "My father said you needed to talk to me. I'll be coming in to town tomorrow to assess the damage to our property. I'll contact you when I get there." He sounds relaxed, not like someone riddled with guilt.

When I get in touch with Sheriff Newberry, he does not sound relaxed. "I want to know how Albert Lamond knew Truly Bennett had been arrested. I've been cooperative with you, but if you are responsible for him finding out we had Bennett in jail, we're going to have words."

Discretion being the better part of bravery, I tell him that I didn't get in touch with Lamond, which isn't exactly the same as telling the truth, since it was his answering machine I talked to. "Now, for my part, I want to know why reporters are here on my doorstep asking me if Bennett killed those people because they were trying to recruit his sister."

"Goddamn that Sutherland. It's either him or one of his people that leaked that."

He asks me to come up to Bobtail to see for myself what Lamond has organized.

"I'm glad to come up there because I have something to tell you. I know the names of the people who got killed."

"How did you get those folks to open up?"

"I'll tell you when I get there."

Before I go, I call Luke Schoppe.

"Sounds like things have gotten pretty wild out there," he says.

"You heard that Lamond set himself up in Bobtail?"

"Oh, yes. We keep a pretty good eye on him. He's caused a good bit of trouble. My boss wondered if you had sicced them on the Bobtail PD to keep things honest."

I laugh as if it's a ludicrous idea. "Listen, I've got to ask you to look up a couple of names for me."

"Let me get my pen. . . . All right, shoot."

"The guy I mentioned the other day, Beaumont Penny. And then a woman named Duchess Wortham." I remind him that I asked the Bobtail PD to look into Blue Dudley and Freddie Carmichael. "They didn't come back with anything, but you all might have more resources for digging into people's background." As an afterthought, I give him the names of George and Ronald Cato.

"Cato. Where have I heard that?"

"Cato Woods. That's the land where the house burned."

He whistles. "Big landowners. I imagine they've got a little clout, being a good part of the county tax base. You're dancing close to the edge on that one."

"They may be totally on the up and up, but it won't hurt to find out."

When I arrive at the Bobtail police station, I see what got Newberry so flustered. The parking lot is taken over with people sitting on crates or on blankets on the ground, and some are standing. A few have set up portable barbecue cookers, making it look like a carnival. A half dozen highway patrol cars are double-parked in front of the building, and officers are standing vigil at strategic spots around the area.

I have to park a couple of blocks away. When I return to the parking lot on foot, I spot Albert Lamond strutting among his followers, in his element. He notices me walking up the sidewalk to the front door. Cool as ice, he nods ever so slightly. I didn't need to worry that he'd tattle that I was the one who called him here. I expect it works to his advantage for folks to think he's part wizard when it comes to sniffing out discrimination issues.

Inside, the station is crowded with officers. It looks like extra manpower has been called in, and most of them look serious. When I identify myself, I'm immediately taken to Newberry's office, where he's in conference with my buddy John Sutherland. They're sitting across from each other at Newberry's desk, each on the edge of their chair and looking like he might lunge at the other across the desk.

"I guess you're pretty satisfied," Sutherland says to me when I walk in.

"What's makes you think so?"

"You were worried about your boy Bennett, and now he's got half the colored people in the state of Texas gathered out there." He makes a sweeping gesture toward the windows.

"Quite a crowd," I say. I don't want to goad Sutherland, but I also don't intend to let him bully me.

"Craddock, take a seat," Newberry says. "With Sutherland here, I think you need to tell both of us what you were going to tell me. You said you had the identification of the people who got killed."

Even though it doesn't make me happy to include Sutherland, I tell them the names and what I've learned about them. I never thought I'd want to hoard information, but I feel jealous that I got it on my own and Sutherland will no doubt claim credit.

"Who did you get this information from?" It's a demand, not a request from Sutherland.

"I'm going to keep that to myself."

"Oh no you're not. This is my investigation and I need to question the source myself."

"You can question the sources you find."

"Now you tell me who you got it from, or I'll have you thrown in jail for withholding evidence, right next to your friend Bennett."

"You afraid it'll be too hard finding your own sources? I haven't noticed you putting yourself out much."

Sutherland gets up so fast, his chair almost tips backward. "By God, at least I made an arrest."

I have to look up to talk to him. "Just any arrest? Is that what satisfied you? Do you care whether Truly Bennett is guilty, or do you just want to strut the fact that you have an arrest to your credit?"

"Whoa now." Newberry is also still seated. "Let's dial it back. The important thing is we've got names of the victims. Craddock, you say they were from Houston. You know why they moved to Jarrett Creek?"

"I heard a rumor that they moved to get away from a jealous husband, but I don't know whether that's true," I say.

"That's the kind of thing an amateur would take at face value," Sutherland says with a sneer. "I'd have pushed to find out more."

I've had enough. I jump to my feet. "It's more information than you bothered to get, even though you're the one with all the manpower. I haven't had time to look into why they are there. I only found this out yesterday. If it was me in charge, I'd find out where they lived in Houston, who they knew, and what their acquaintances had to say about why they pulled up stakes and moved to a small town." My voice is raised, and I don't care. "I'd also talk to the owners of the property where the house was located. But of course, I'm an amateur. What do I know? And the landowners are wealthy big shots, and you probably don't want to poke that bear, so it's a lot easier to hassle the people in my town."

"Who the hell do you think you are?" Sutherland moves chest to chest with me.

I'd like nothing better than to get into it with him, fists and all, but Newberry says sharply, "Stop. I mean it. Stop. Both of you. Sit down. We have bigger things to deal with. What are we going to do with that crowd outside, for one thing?"

I come back to my chair and sit down, knowing that the last man standing looks like the bigger fool. Sutherland looks like he could easily send me straight to hell, but he sits, too.

"I told you, I'm going to move Bennett to the jail in San Antonio," Sutherland says. "I doubt all those folks out there are inclined to follow him all the way there."

"So you really think you've got enough to prosecute him?" Newberry asks.

"Damn right, I do."

"What all do you have?" I know full well he's not going to give me the time of day, but I'm still feeling the glow from asserting myself and trying not to think of it as showing off.

Sure enough, he stares at me.

"It's a legitimate question, John," Newberry says.

"It's legitimate for the district attorney, not for some hick cop."

The comment should aggravate me, but I understand that it means I've gotten to him, so instead I feel cocky. I've scored more points than I ever thought possible. I sit forward and address Newberry. "If you don't have any further need of me, I'm going to be on my way. You've heard my information."

Newberry sits back and pokes his lips with his thumb, thinking. "Keep me informed of what you find. I don't want you biting off too much."

I nod to him and get up. "Sutherland, did you take a bunch of photos out of the house where those people were killed?"

"Why would I do that?"

"I don't know. To investigate the crime, maybe?"

Sutherland turns his head to look at me, and his eyes could be the eyes of a big old rattler. "If you think you're going to keep information from me, you've got another think coming. I'm going to tear your little town apart until I get to the source."

"Be my guest," I say. And then I point to him. "But be advised, I'm going to be doing my own investigation, and when I find out who really killed those people, it's not going to be Truly Bennett."

I walk out to the sound of Sutherland yelling, "By God, you keep your nose out of my investigation." I don't give him the satisfaction of slamming the door behind me. I close it softly and I walk softly, but my heart is pounding and my knees are wobbly. How the hell am I going to follow through with what I said?

CHAPTER 27

When I get back to Jarrett Creek, the reporters are gone, which is a relief. There's a note from Tilley saying he's off doing what used to be the normal work of a small-town cop, pursuing the case of the stolen hubcaps.

With a few moments of quiet, I come face-to-face with the promise I've made not only to myself, but to others: to find out what really happened out there in Cato Woods. My mamma dwelled so seriously on my shortcomings that I've never felt the need to do the same. But right now I feel the weight of my lack of experience. I did well enough in school, not because I'm smarter than average, but because I persisted. I know how to make lists and to work my way through them. I haven't had to do that much lately, but now I fall back on that old habit.

I write down the names of every person related to the case. Those connected with the Cato property: Ronald Cato, his son, George, and his stepson, Owen Montclair. The squatters: Duchess, Lily, Alice, and Bobby Wortham; and Cathy, the girl with them, whose last name I still don't know. The strangers on the sideline: Blue Dudley, Freddie Carmichael, and Beaumont Penny. At that I'm stuck. "One foot in front of the other," I mutter to myself. I'm going to see George Cato tomorrow, and I've asked for information from the Texas Rangers on most of the people on the list.

I don't know what Sutherland intends, but I feel like it's only fair to warn Alvin Penny that Sutherland may get onto him. As I get up to go over there, the phone rings. It's Charlie Ostrand's daddy. I forgot to call him back.

"I was afraid you were going to ignore my call." There's an edge to his voice, which I recognize as someone who thinks he's entitled to special treatment.

"I've had a busy morning. You're on the list."

"I imagine you have had a busy time, considering what happened last week in your town."

"I assume you called to discuss my encounter with your son?"

"Tell you what, I can take a little time off. How about if you drive up here and we can meet."

I laugh. He wants me to come to him. "I'm in Bobtail sometime Wednesday. Maybe we can have a minute then."

Silence greets my suggestion. "You understand your predecessor didn't seem to have any trouble finding time for me."

It takes me a second to parse what that means. "What was the nature of your meetings with him?"

"I don't see that that's of any importance."

"Might be, if it concerned your son."

"I don't care for your implication."

"No implication intended. I'm asking flat out if your son has been in trouble before."

"Charlie is a good kid. I don't know if you're aware, but he's the quarterback on the varsity football team, and that puts him under a lot of pressure. He might let off a little steam every now and then."

"Surely you aren't suggesting I should overlook the fact that your son was in possession of an illegal substance?"

"Do you have proof of that?"

"I do. The only proof I need—I saw him with my own eyes. I thought a word to your son was enough to settle the matter between us. Apparently he didn't think so, and he brought you into this. The next time I have an encounter with your son and his friends, a warning might not be sufficient."

"Is that a threat?"

"It's an appeal to your fatherly duty to see to it that your son stays out of trouble."

"I don't know who you think you are, but this conversation is ended. And if I were you, I'd be looking for another job." He hangs up.

At that moment, Tilley comes through the door, grinning. The grin dies when he sees the look on my face. "What happened?"

"Tilley, do I look any different than I did last Friday?"

He looks confused. "Not that I can see. What do you mean?"

"I've had two different people today ask me who I think I am. I'm checking to see if I got lost somewhere."

He laughs and goes over to pour himself a cup of coffee. "You been stepping out of line?"

"What line would that be?"

He peers over his cup at me. "Usually, when somebody asks a question like that, they're not happy—because a small-town cop is supposed to be Officer Friendly and they think you've gotten all official on them."

"Sounds about right. You came in here with a big grin on your face. What's going on?"

"Those hubcaps?"

"Tell me something good."

"Clinton Walls had his tires rotated last week, and the station forgot to put the hubcaps back on when they finished the job. Took him five days to notice."

I sigh. "Maybe that's all we're good for."

"Could be."

I leave and go over to talk to Alvin Penny, but he isn't home. I leave my card with a note on the back to call me.

It's lunchtime, and I usually go home for a bite, but I stop by the café for a bowl of chili. I'm halfway through when I look up to see that a man I went to high school with is approaching my table, his straw hat in his hand. "Can I talk to you?" he asks.

I gesture to the chair across the table, and he sits down stiffly. His face is bright red, and he seems struck speechless.

"Haven't seen you in a while," I say.

He clears his throat. "I don't come to town much. I'm working my daddy's farm over in Burton. He had a heart attack last year, and my wife and I moved onto the homeplace to help out."

"I'm sure he appreciates that. Something I can do for you?"

"I heard Truly Bennett got arrested for murdering them people and burning the house down."

"He is a suspect," I say.

He looks around us and leans forward with his voice lowered. "I don't want to stir anything up, and I'm no n . . . I mean I'm not partial to black people or anything like that." He pauses and swallows.

"I understand."

He chews on his lower lip like he's screwing up his courage. "I've had to hire Truly a few times to help out, and to be downright honest with you, I don't see how he could have done nothing like that. I've tried to work it out in my mind, and I don't see it."

"Thank you for coming forward. I believe a mistake has been made, but it might take some time to undo it."

He lets his breath out in a rush, like he was afraid I was going to argue with him. "All right, then. Like I said, I didn't want to stir things up, but I think sometimes you have to speak up. He's a hard worker is all I'm saying." He stumbles to his feet.

I get to my feet to shake his hand. Clearly it wasn't easy for him to say his piece, and I appreciate it.

Back at work, I call Luke Schoppe to see if he's gotten anywhere with his inquiries, but he hasn't. I'm too restless to stay in, and the call from Charlie Ostrand has given me an idea. I drive slowly past the high school. It's midafternoon, early in the school year, so school is quiet— no groups of kids hanging out, looking bored, as there will be in a few months. The football field is one block past the high school. It's a fine old structure of local stone that looks indestructible.

I ease by, checking out the site Charlie described as the drop point for the drugs, seeing if there's a good surveillance position. Ostrand said Charlie is on the football team. He didn't look like he had the physique for it, and if he smokes a lot of marijuana, he probably doesn't have the temperament for it either. So how did he get on the team, and as a quarterback, no less?

I may be wasting my time. My guess is that if Charlie ran to his daddy complaining of being picked on, he'd also complain to whoever is selling the weed, so the drop off will be changed.

I wonder what kind of person sells drugs to high school kids. The kind that wants money, that's who. I picture myself doing a stakeout, but now I realize I can't be hanging around here all night, watching for a drug dealer. It's time to delegate something more than looking for lost hubcaps.

Since I'm at the high school, I go into the principal's office and ask if Gilpin is around. His secretary talks to him on the intercom and says, "Go on in. He can spare a few minutes."

He doesn't bother to get up, but waves a hand for me to sit down. I tell him I put the fear of God into kids smoking weed at the park yesterday.

"Did you take names?"

"Only one. Kid by the name of Charlie Ostrand."

He blanches. "Oh, I'm so sorry to hear that."

"His daddy called this morning and tried to bully me."

"I, uh, hope you didn't give him a lot of trouble about Charlie."

"I'm not sure what you mean."

"Mr. Ostrand is a big sports booster. I'd hate to have him upset. He buys the uniforms and helps pay for transportation to away games. Without him, we'd have money trouble." Which might account for why his scrawny kid is the quarterback.

"You're telling me you want me to back off the Ostrand boy?"

"No, no . . . well, maybe a little."

"Gilpin, either you want this drug problem handled or you don't. Which is it?"

He shifts his bulk so that his chair squeaks in protest. "Of course I want it handled. But I want it done with some delicacy."

"You mean it depends on who is involved."

He pulls a big handkerchief out of his back pocket and wipes his forehead. "I'm trying to give you a dose of reality. It's a matter of balance."

"You know, when I took this job, it never occurred to me that it was political in nature."

He smiles. "I never thought being a high school principal would be either, but it sure is. Mr. Ostrand is one of those people the school calls on when we need funds that the state doesn't see fit to give us. His son won't be here forever. He's a senior. But if we handle this right, Mr. Ostrand's good will could last for years."

I should be annoyed, but I appreciate Gilpin's honesty. I leave him with the promise to do my best to tiptoe around Charlie Ostrand and his daddy.

CHAPTER 28

I thought George Cato would look like a businessman, wearing a suit and tie and carrying a briefcase. So when he walks in at ten o'clock Tuesday morning, I think he's some farmer I haven't met before. He's dressed in blue jeans and a blue denim work shirt and work boots. His hair is longish, and his face is tanned, like he spends a lot of time in the sun.

"Excuse the way I look," he says after he introduces himself. "I figured as long as I was down here, I might as well hire a couple of men and start cleaning up that house. We'll have to tear it down."

"Not so fast," I say. "That's a crime scene, and we may need to get more evidence out of it."

His smile reaches his eyes, and the skin around them crinkles in a merry way. "I called the highway patrol, and they said they were done with the building. Same with the fire department." He sits back in his chair and folds his hands across his flat belly. "But I'll tell you what, I'll work around whatever you want to do. Why don't we go on out there, and you can point out any areas you want us to keep away from."

"I appreciate that. Can I ask you a couple of questions?"

"Shoot."

"Do you have any information about the people who lived there?"

"No."

"Were you aware that a house had been built there?"

He squirms around and resettles in his chair. "I admit I did know. I realize I should have made the old boy who built it get permits, but he said it was going to be up to code and I didn't have time to deal with it. I was working on a big office-building project in Dallas. I kind of blew it off. I suppose I ought to go to the city and pay whatever fines they want to assess."

"How did they get water and utilities out to the house without a permit?"

"It's on a septic system, so they didn't have to do a sewer hookup. As for water and electricity, I'm afraid I wasn't a party to that."

"Who built the house?"

"I don't know the name of the builder, but it was arranged by a real-estate man I'm acquainted with by the name of Blue Dudley. He said he had a business partner who wanted to put up a small house."

"Did he say who was going to live there?"

He screws up his face and runs a palm across his forehead. "That's what I get for having too many irons in the fire. He said the man he was building it for had a wife and some kids, and he wanted to move them out of Houston because he thought they'd be safer in a small town than in the city."

"You can see how that worked out."

He grimaces. "Something went wrong, that's for sure. But my point is I didn't have anything to do with the building. I was careless and didn't obtain permits. That's all it amounts to."

"You know the name of the family that moved in?"

"Naw. After I told them to go ahead, I didn't think any more about it. But I can call Mr. Dudley and ask him."

"Why don't you do that? You can use my phone."

For the first time, I see a crack in his cheerful demeanor. "I'm afraid I don't have his phone number with me."

I open my desk drawer. "I have his number. I ran into Mr. Dudley and a friend of his right after the fire." I pull out Dudley's card and hand it to Cato with a big smile.

He stares at the card. "I need to have a private conversation with him."

"Just to get the name of the family that moved in?" I couldn't act any more innocent. Clearly he doesn't want to talk to Dudley in front of me, and I'd like to know why.

He licks his lips. "I haven't talked to him for a while, and I have a couple of other sensitive matters to discuss with him."

"Why don't you stick to the one subject on this call and tell him you'll be in touch later about your other matters?" Now I'm really eager to find out why he's reluctant. "I tell you what, why don't I step outside and give you some privacy. First, let me dial the number, and we'll make sure he's in his office."

He looks down at the card in his hand as if he'd give anything if it disappeared into thin air. I keep on smiling.

"Okay, but let me dial the call," he says.

"That's okay. The phone is right in front me." I hold out my hand for the card, which he hands over with reluctance.

Blue Dudley answers his own phone, a nice, old-fashioned touch. "Mr. Dudley, this is Chief Craddock over in Jarrett Creek."

We exchange hearty pleasantries while Cato drums his fingers on the desk. "Listen, the reason I'm calling, I have a fellow here who wants to have a few words with you, name of George Cato."

"Who?" Dudley asks.

"Cato. Owns the property where that house was built, where those people got killed?"

"Uh . . . oh, yes. Sure, put him on."

I hand the phone to Cato, who says, "Hello there, Mr. Dudley. Nice to talk to you again." He widens his eyes and nods his head toward the door, wanting me to live up to my promise to give him some privacy. I look a question at him. "Hold on." He puts his hand over the receiver. "A little privacy?" he whispers.

"Oh, right." I walk slowly out the door and close it behind me. If I'm not very much mistaken, Mr. Dudley had no idea who George Cato is.

I cool my heels for several minutes, during which time the sound of

Cato's voice comes through the door a couple of times, although I can't hear any particular words. That's all right. I keep a tape recorder in my desk drawer in the event that I need to record somebody being questioned. I've never had occasion to use it, but when I took Blue Dudley's card out, I turned it on. If it's working, it will pick up Cato's side of the conversation. I'm ready to barge back in when the door opens and a decidedly nervous George Cato beckons me back inside.

"I've got myself into an uncomfortable situation," he says when we are seated.

"What's that?"

"Turns out that Mr. Dudley never found out the name of the people who moved in."

"I wonder who the contractor is who built the place?"

"That I can tell you." His grin returns. "Man by the name of Carmichael. Freddie Carmichael."

"Was Carmichael building the house for his own family?"

"Tsk. I didn't get that information."

"Don't worry. I'll follow up. Why don't we head on over to the place. Did you ever see it after it was completed?"

"I didn't. I hardly ever get down this way."

Interesting, since his half brother, Owen Montclair, said Cato comes once a month to collect his rent in person.

Before Cato arrived this morning, I phoned the Bobtail PD to ask them to let me know when Truly arrived at the jail in San Antonio, and when the phone rings, I tell Cato I need to take the call. But instead of the Bobtail PD, it's Principal Gilpin on the line. "We've got a problem."

I listen to what he has to say, and as soon as I hang up, I say to Cato, "I'm sorry, I'm going to have to postpone going to the place with you. In fact, I'd as soon you didn't go out there. I can meet you back here in a couple of hours."

"That's all right. I've got things I can do in town. I'll see you back here at one."

As soon as he's out the door, I turn off the hidden recorder and put in a call to Tilley. He's not home, so I try Eldridge. He's surprised when I tell him what I need him to do.

"Suppose Cato shows up? What am I supposed to do? It's his property."

"Eldridge, it's a crime scene. Tell him he'll have to take it up with me if he wants to do anything with the house."

"I don't know if we have that authority."

"I'm giving you that authority. Something has come up over at the high school, and I have to get over there."

"Why don't you get Tilley to do this?"

I hang up. He'll either confront Cato or he won't. But one thing is for sure—once this is all over, I'm going to seriously consider whether the police deputies I'm stuck with are capable. I call Tilley once more and leave a message telling him if he gets home soon, to get over to the site of the fire.

When I arrive at the high school, the ambulance is pulling away. Gilpin is standing on the curb next to a green Chevrolet with the doors open and a couple ready to get in. They are a few years older than me. The man is dressed in slacks and a golf shirt, and the woman in jogging shorts and a T-shirt. Her eyes are red; and her face, puffy.

"Here's the chief," Gilpin says. "Craddock, this is Mr. and Mrs. Blackman. Their daughter is the young girl who was, uh, taken ill." The girl apparently overdosed on some kind of drug.

I've seen Blackman around town. He owns the flower shop. I shake his hand. "I'm sorry about your daughter. I hope she'll be all right."

The woman lunges forward, a fierce scowl blazing across her face. "I want to know what you're going to do to punish this boy who poisoned my daughter. He's a menace!"

"Now, Julia, you have to calm down. The chief just got here. He doesn't know what happened."

She puts her hands over her face and starts to sob. Blackman puts his arm around her shoulders and says, "We need to get on to the hospital. But my wife is right. I want this boy prosecuted." He tucks her into the passenger side, and then without another word he gets in the car and they roar away.

"What boy are we talking about?" I ask Gilpin.

"I think you know. Let's get on inside, and I'll tell you what happened."

The building is strangely quiet. There are a dozen people in the reception area outside Gilpin's office. In the corner, three teenaged girls huddle in a circle, clutching each other's shoulders and sobbing. The secretary is standing near them, murmuring softly to them. Girls of their age can be pretty dramatic, so it's hard to tell how much of their grief is real, and how much is nerves.

A teenaged boy is sitting on a bench next to a wall, hunched over with his head in his hands, while an adult leans over, talking to him. He looks up as I walk in, and I see that it's Charlie Ostrand. When he spots me, he looks away and then down at the floor. Another boy sits near him, arms crossed, not looking at anybody, just staring off into space.

"All right, Gilpin," I say, "I'd appreciate it if you explain what happened."

Gilpin shoots a look of venom toward Charlie Ostrand. "Second period had just ended when a couple of those girls came running into the office and said Eileen Blackman was in the bathroom having convulsions."

"What time was this?"

"Second period starts at nine thirty, so it was about ten o'clock."

I glance at my watch. It's 11:15. "That's over an hour ago. What took you so long to call me?"

"This place was pure chaos. The girls were hysterical. I had Mrs. Clayton here stay and call the ambulance and notify the school nurse while I ran down to see if there was anything I could do."

I look my question, and he says, "I was a medic in Vietnam. Not for long, but I do have some training."

"Okay, go on."

"Anyway, at least the girls had sense enough to leave Eileen with the only one of them who has a head on her shoulders, Judy Boyd. She had Eileen rolled onto her side. Eileen had thrown up and was moaning and thrashing around. I asked Judy what happened. She didn't want to tell me at first, but I wasn't about to put up with that, and I got her to talk. She said Eileen took some pills she got from Charlie Ostrand. That son-of-a-gun!" He looks another dagger in that direction.

"Who is the other boy?"

"That's Mike Damon."

"What's he doing here?"

He beckons to the woman who has been standing watch over the two boys.

"This is Mary Verdeen. She's the social studies teacher. Mary, tell Chief Craddock what you told me."

She's a plain woman, and although she's young, she wears her hair in a bun and she's got on sensible shoes. "When I heard all the commotion in the hallway, I went out to see what was going on, and I found Charlie in the hall talking to Mike. I thought Mike looked a little out of it, but he does half the time anyway. I sent the two of them into class, and then I went down to the bathroom to find out what was going on. Mr. Gilpin told me that Eileen had gotten sick from some pills she got from Charlie, so I took him and Mike out of class and brought them down here."

"Did they say anything to you?"

"Not a word. But that's not unusual for boys their age."

"Have you ever had any sign that these two have been high on anything?"

"Mr. Craddock, they act like that half the time. That's all I know about this business. If you don't need me, I'd better get back to my class. I gave them a reading assignment, but they're bound to be getting rowdy by now."

When she leaves, I ask Gilpin to hold on a minute. I look over to Charlie Ostrand. "Get over here," I say.

He looks up at me, and I have the distinct feeling he's going to give me some lip, and I shortcut it. "Don't say a word to aggravate me."

The other kid on the bench turns his head in our direction, but he doesn't seem anymore with it than he did before.

Charlie ambles over to me and Gilpin, and I have to hold back from reaching out and snatching him by the arm to hurry him along. "What kind of pills did you give her?"

"Pills?" All innocence.

"Don't even think about bullshitting me," I say. "You're in more trouble than you're going to know what to do with."

"You can't prove anything."

"Really? There's a girl on the way to the hospital, and you're going to take that line?"

"Charlie, the girl said you gave her pills that made her sick," Gilpin says.

Suddenly, a burly man in a sharp business suit comes striding into the office. "What are you doing with my son?"

"Hey, Daddy," he says. His face goes into a smirk. "These guys are hassling me again. I didn't do anything."

"I hope you kept your mouth shut."

"'Course I did. There's nothing to tell."

I look over at Gilpin and see him wavering.

"I'm Chief Craddock. I assume you're Raymond Ostrand."

"I'm a little tired of you harassing my son."

"Mr. Ostrand, a girl is in the hospital. She said she took some pills she got from your son."

"I'm sorry for the girl, but it's her word against his."

"Maybe so. But based on the accusation, I'd like your permission to search your son's locker."

"Absolutely not."

"That's fine. I'm going to have to put the locker off-limits, and I'll talk to a judge and get a search warrant issued."

"Wait a minute," Charlie says. "I've got to get my football cleats out of the locker."

"Sorry," I say. "It's a potential crime scene."

"Dad!"

"You could let the boy get his cleats."

"I could if you'd consent to a search. Otherwise, not going to happen."

Gilpin clears his throat. "No need for the cleats. There's not going to be any football for Charlie until this is cleared up." He's barely speaking above a whisper.

Ostrand turns on him. "You know what this means?" It's obviously a threat.

"He may know what it means," I say, "but I don't. I'd like to have it explained to me." I know exactly what it means, but I want to make him say it.

Ostrand looks at me like he's looking at something he'd find on his shoe. "If my son isn't on the football team, I may find better use for my limited funds than paying for a bus for the team to travel to games."

"I can't help it," Gilpin says. "It's out of my hands. It's state rules. An accusation like this requires follow-up, and until it's cleared up the athlete can't participate in sports."

"It's not so bad," I say. "When I went to school here, the parents had to drive the kids to games, so I don't think it will kill them if they have to do it again." Not that I ever had a chance to play a sport. I was always too busy working after school.

CHAPTER 29

Since my house is close to the school, I stop by to get a sandwich. Jeanne is on the phone in the kitchen when I walk in. She waves to me and says, "He's here now. I'll find out what's going on."

I'm looking in the refrigerator when she hangs up.

"What are you looking for?"

"I'm going to grab a quick bite of lunch."

She comes over and puts her arms around me and kisses me. "Let me fix you a sandwich."

When she has the mayo, pickles, and lunch meat on the counter, she reaches for the bread and says, "I heard the ambulance over near the school. You know anything about that?"

Gilpin and I agreed that the less said, the better. I'm of two minds. I know Jeanne isn't a big gossip, but I also know she talks to a lot of other women during the day. If I don't tell her what's going on, she'll wonder why I didn't confide in her. I tell her the bare bones—that a girl took some unidentified pills and had to be hospitalized.

"Was she trying to kill herself?"

"It looks more like she was experimenting."

She pauses from plastering the bread with mayonnaise. "I thought the kids were into marijuana?"

"It's not just that. Gilpin tells me that kids steal from their folks' medicine cabinets."

A look passes between us. Jeanne's brother used to do that. Her mother broke her wrist and had to lock up her pain medication. She walks toward me with the mayonnaise knife raised. "Samuel, I don't understand what's going on. Jarrett Creek is a small town. I expect that sort of thing in Dallas or Houston, but not here. That's one reason I wanted to settle in Jarrett Creek. Where are the kids getting drugs?"

"I'm working on the answer to that. I told you when they hired me—Hazel said they thought that because I'm young, I'd have an appreciation for the problem."

She lifts an eyebrow. "Did they think you were into drugs?"

I grin. "Don't you remember I was always stoned in college?"

"Oh, you!" She walks back and finishes making the sandwich. I hope the conversation has run its course, but when she hands the plate to me with the sandwich, she says, "Isn't it dangerous for you to investigate this? Drug dealers target lawmen."

"I don't think we've got hard-core criminals in town. More like somebody trying to make a buck."

She props her arms on the counter and watches me eat standing up. "I don't like it. You don't have the experience to be going after drug dealers, even if they are small-time."

I walk over and tear off some paper towels and wrap the sandwich in it. I don't want to argue with her, and part of me worries that she's right. "I'm going to take this with me."

"Samuel! Really. How are you supposed to deal with this?"

I kiss her on the lips. "Sweetheart, don't worry about me. If it gets too big, I'll bring in the Texas Rangers. But I really think I'm dealing with nothing more than somebody who is out to make some money and who found a kid to sell for him."

"What?"

"I'll tell you later. I have to go."

I want to get to the burned-out house in case George Cato went there after all, but first I need to go by the station to listen to the tape I made of him on the phone with Blue Dudley. Taping it was illegal, and it would have no place in court. I did it because I hoped it would give me a clue about the murders. But when I listen to the tape, I'm disappointed. Cato tells Dudley that I've asked him for the names of the people who lived there. And then the conversation is all on the other side, with Cato interjecting the occasional "hmm."

I wait for the "other topics" that Cato mentioned he wanted to discuss with Dudley, but there's no such thing. The only deviation from the subject of the murder victims is, "Dudley, when you talk to Freddie Carmichael, will you remind him that he still owes me five hundred bucks?" No mention of why.

Two cars are parked on the road near the crime scene. One I recognize as Eldridge's old Ford, and the other is a black Lincoln Town Car that looks brand-new.

Cato and Eldridge are standing back from the house, having what looks like a relaxed conversation.

"Here he is now," Cato says. "I just got here," he says, giving me his friendly smile. "I thought I'd swing by and take a look at it before I met you at the station. This was quite a house. I didn't realize it was going to be so big."

"You never saw it?"

The smile tightens, and a look of calculation comes into his eyes. "I saw it when it was being framed out. You know how buildings look smaller when they're nothing but frame."

Eldridge says he'll be on his way, looking at me like he's annoyed that I called him out for nothing. When he's gone, I say, "What was the occasion for you to see the house when it was in the early stages of being built?"

"No occasion. I stopped by to see if they were serious about building something here."

George Cato may be crooked in some way, may be hiding something, but nothing I've heard so far gives me any indication that he is. I'm beginning to doubt he had any involvement with the family that lived here.

"Shall we take a look inside so you can assess the damage?"

He shakes his head. "I changed my mind. I'm not going to tear the place down. Looks like it was built pretty well, and a good bit of it could be saved. I'll go over to city hall and find out what I have to do to bring it into compliance with building codes."

When we get to his car, he turns and extends his hand. "Sorry I couldn't be of more help to you." He starts to open his car door.

"You planning to visit Owen Montclair while you're here? I guess you heard about the fire that took out one of his fields."

He shakes his head. "Poor devil. He's tried to make a go of the farm, but I think that fire was the last straw."

"You wouldn't have any idea how it started, would you?"

He looks startled. "Of course not. I hope you're not suggesting I had anything to do with that. Why would I?"

"Montclair told me you wanted him to give up farming so you could get money from the federal government to let the land lie fallow."

He crosses his arms and leans against his car. "He's right, I did want that. But I sure as hell didn't want it bad enough to burn the man out."

"He also told me you're his half brother."

"I'm surprised he admitted it. I guess he told you we kind of had a bet about whether he could make a farm work."

"He did."

He shakes his head and looks down at the ground. "I'm sorry for him. He's always been sort of a sucker for a bad idea. He's the stubbornest man I ever knew."

Back at the station, a familiar car is waiting for me in the parking lot. Bonnie Bedichek is inside sharing a cup of coffee with Tilley.

"I need to catch up with you," she says. "My deadline is tonight for the next edition."

I pour a cup of coffee and sit down. "What is it you need to know?"

"I understand they transferred Truly Bennett to San Antonio. Was that to get rid of Albert Lamond and his followers?"

"Newberry is interested in keeping Truly safe, and I think he persuaded Sutherland to make the transfer." I meet her eyes. She raises her eyebrows. "There might have been some desire to scatter Lamond's followers."

She jots something in her notebook.

"If you're printing that, I didn't say it."

She barks a laugh. "For the record, have you got a lead on who committed the murders?"

"No, but at least I found out the names of the victims."

Tilley has been worrying a paperclip, and he drops it and stares at me. "When did that happen?"

"Saturday."

"Why didn't you tell me?" Bonnie asks.

I don't want to tell her that I forgot to keep her up to date. "I only have their names—not even all the victims' full names—but not who they are or why they were living here. I'm trying to find out more. In fact, it might be helpful if you print their names and ask anybody who knows anything about them to get in touch with me."

She likes the idea, so I give her the information.

"You sure that's a good idea?" Tilley is frowning.

Bonnie and I look at him. "Why wouldn't it be?"

"I just wonder if you're asking for more trouble. Until we know something about them, we ought to be cautious." I never thought of Tilley as a coward, but he sounds nervous.

"Cautious? Why?" I ask.

"We don't know what kind of people they are. They did get themselves murdered, so they may not have been good people."

"Too late," Bonnie says. "I'm printing it."

"It's your funeral," Tilley says.

Bonnie snorts and swings her attention back to me. "I saw George Cato in town this morning. Was he here to see you?"

"How do you know George?"

"Samuel, I'm in the newspaper business. I know everybody."

"Then you know Owen Montclair?"

"Of course I do. He's the man who had a fire on his farm a few days ago."

"Did you also know he's George Cato's half brother?"

I can tell by the look on her face that she didn't know that.

"Does that have anything to do with the people who got murdered?" she asks.

"Off the record?"

"Yes." She sits up, eagerly.

"I don't know." I laugh.

"Very funny. There's something else I need to ask you about. Did you know some girl had a drug overdose this morning at the high school and had to be taken to the hospital?"

I nod.

"What the hell!" Tilley lurches forward in his chair. "You never tell me a damn thing."

Bonnie ignores him. "The principal clammed up on me. Are you going to do the same?"

"What do you mean he clammed up?" I ask.

"Wouldn't tell me anything. Not the name of the girl or the type of drugs, where she got them, nothing."

"Then in that case the answer is yes, I am going to clam up. The girl is a minor, so her information is off-limits."

"At least I know that it wasn't marijuana."

"How do you know that?"

"Because you can't get an overdose from that. It's probably pills." She watches me for a reaction.

"I couldn't say. Now, Bonnie, you're going to have to excuse me. I've got a lot to do. Seems like you've got plenty to put in the newspaper."

"Hints and rumors, that's what I've got."

"And the names of the people who died in the fire. That's something."

She eyes me, speculating. "Seems like the only way you're going to get Truly Bennett out of jail is if you find somebody to put in his place."

"Spending all my time talking to you isn't going to get that done."

That sends her on her way. After she leaves, Tilley says, "She's right, you know. You planning to investigate, or are you leaving it to the THP? If it was me, I'd leave it alone."

"I'm waiting to hear back from Luke Schoppe. You met him the day of the fire. He's the junior Texas Ranger."

"Hear back for what?"

"I asked him to look into some people to see if they have criminal records."

"Wait a minute." He picks up a piece of paper. "He called a while ago. I have the message right here. I forgot about it when me and Bonnie were talking."

I call the number on the message, and when I reach Schoppe, he says, "Hold on to your hat."

"What's going on?"

"I found out some things about Duchess Wortham and her family."

"That's great."

"You may not think it's so great when you hear it. Her husband was some kind of big shot in the drug trade. Rumor has it that he sent his wife and family out of Houston to keep them safe. There was a drug dispute going on with one of the suppliers."

My heart starts to pound. "Big shot in the drug trade" sounds ominous. "Have you talked to the woman's husband?"

"No, and I'm not likely to."

"Why's that?"

"He was gunned down in broad daylight in Houston—two days after Truly Bennett was arrested."

"Do they know who did it?"

"Not yet, but looks like it's part of the drug war he was trying to protect his family from."

"At least that's good news for Truly Bennett," I say.

"Why is that?"

"Nobody can connect him with drug dealers in Houston. When Sutherland hears about the drug war, he'll have to release Bennett."

Schoppe sighs. "The problem is finding evidence."

"There ought to be plenty of evidence. If the dealer's family moved here to get away from a drug dispute, and then ended up dead, clearly the two things are tied together. Any evidence they get in the Houston murder is relevant to this case as well."

"I'm not disputing that. The problem is that when I called John Sutherland and told him all this, he dug in his heels. He said he was holding Bennett until somebody finds real evidence."

"That won't take long, though."

He's quiet for a moment. "I'm afraid it might take longer than you think. There are other aspects to the case."

"What aspects?"

"Craddock, I'm not at liberty to say."

CHAPTER 30

Ten minutes later, I'm pounding on Ezekiel Bennett's door. It's a little before five. He probably spent the day in San Antonio, holding vigil for Truly, and may not be back yet, but I thought I'd try anyway. He answers the door right away.

"We need to talk," I say.

He holds the door wider so I can step in.

In his tiny, cramped living room lighted only by a small lamp, we sit down and I lay out for him the problem I'm facing. "Unless I can lay my hands on evidence of who killed that family, Truly stays in jail."

He nods. "I figured something like that. It's hard for a black man to get a break from the law. Present company excepted."

"Don't give up."

"What can I do?"

"Help me. Or tell me who can. Somebody around here knows more than they're saying. That family had only lived here for a short while, but people knew them. Your daughter told me she went to a party there. She couldn't help me. She's young and her concern was with the other youngsters. But an adult who was out there must know more about them."

"Chief, that may be, but I don't have a clue who it is."

"Maybe you don't, but somebody does. Why did the family choose Jarrett Creek to settle in? Did they have friends here? Or relatives? Apparently one of the girls was visiting. Where was she from? What was she doing here? Somebody has to know."

He rubs his hands along his thighs. "That's a pack of questions."

"I'm asking for help in identifying who might know answers. The black community is close here, isn't it?"

"Not exactly. Folks stick to themselves and their families, and their church friends."

I look at his bewildered, care-lined face, and I'm sorry I demanded things he can't provide. He'd do anything to help his son. He's not keeping things from me deliberately. The people who were killed were not Bennett's kind of people.

"Just keep your ears open, and if you hear anything at all that you think would help me, please let me know."

"I promise I'll do that."

I'm drawn back yet again to the burned-out house. It has become a symbol for me of all that I don't know about these murders. I walk around the clearing again, back to where at one time they had a cookout. Maybe it was even during the party they threw. I picture men sitting around on aluminum folding chairs, tipping back beers and laughing. Who was here? Was it all local people, or were they mostly strangers? I saw the shoeprints of women, and I imagine them flirting, gossiping with each other, serving food, dealing with the children. The teenagers huddling together, thinking up mischief.

I walk back to the house. It's early in the evening and it's still stifling hot inside. The night of the murders, two more people ate dinner at the table. Who were they? And where are they now? Who came in and took down the photos of all those people? In the kitchen, I open the cabinets, something I didn't do before. If looters took the family pictures, they probably took other things. But the cabinets haven't been looted. They are full of mismatched dishes and one nice little teapot with a sugar and creamer set that looks like it would have been somebody's treasure. There is a decent stock of food in the larder—a bag of cornmeal, dried beans, potatoes, and canned goods.

I go back to the gaudy-looking bedroom, and it appears to be untouched. Nothing seems to be missing from the previous time I was here. I pull out one drawer after another in the little chest of drawers, rummaging through the contents and looking for anything that seems out of place. I'm hoping to find photos missed by whoever took the ones in the living room.

In the girls' bedroom, I locate a little hole-in-the-wall of a closet and find a shoebox with mementos, including a few photos. Most of them are taken so far away from the subjects that you can't really see their faces. But there is one that looks like a school photograph, with that nervous look that kids have in school pictures. The girl in the picture is probably twelve. On the back is stamped HISD—Houston Independent School District. I have a moment of satisfaction from finding what I was after, but then I think, "What is it you planned to do with it?" The picture is likely four or five years old. Who would recognize her? And what difference would it make anyway? It's not like I can go to Houston and find people who knew her.

The next photo I find features a man who looks to be around forty, and he looks vaguely familiar. He's stylish-looking in the way of about five years ago, with a big, puffy hairdo and a silky-looking yellow shirt with deep-pointed collar tips. I tuck the two photos in my shirt pocket and go on to the next rooms.

An hour later, I've got two more photos in my possession, found abandoned in a drawer in the living room. One photo is of a woman. She's grinning into the camera with mischief on her face. The other is a picture of a family, including a man whom I assume is the daddy, since the children favor him. The kids are grinning, but the parents look grim. The woman is the same one whose single photo I found. It's a few years old. The kids look like preteens and the boy is a baby. I thought the man's photo I had found in the shoebox might the daddy, but he's not the same man as in the family photo. So who is he?

I leave with two thoughts. One, that this family had more money than most of the black people who live in Jarrett Creek. Two, that John Sutherland should have found these photos if he had any interest in really investigating this case. He told me he didn't take the ones from the wall, and when I asked Schoppe, he said they didn't either. So who did take them?

I head back to headquarters to ponder what to do next with these photos. Fewer than one hundred black people live in Darktown. I suppose I could go door to door asking if anybody recognizes the man in the photo. But when I walk into headquarters, I see that I've got bigger problems. Hazel Baker, the city administrator who persuaded me to take the job as chief, is sitting in the chair next to my desk, wearing an unhappy expression. She's a substantial woman with an ample figure and eyes that look like they're about to pop out of her head. She's wearing a tight black skirt and a sleeveless white blouse with a bow at the neck. I remember Jeanne remarking at one time that Hazel's arms were not made for sleeveless blouses. I have to agree, although I would not have thought of it on my own.

"Hello, Hazel, what brings you to my neck of the woods?" I sit down behind my desk.

"I think you know the answer to that."

"I could think of more than one reason, so how about if you enlighten me as to the specifics?"

"You have upset one of our biggest school boosters." Her mouth snaps shut after that pronouncement.

"You mean Raymond Ostrand, whose son not only smokes marijuana out in the open but also apparently was responsible for supplying pills to a young girl who had to be taken to the hospital. Is that who you mean?"

Her eyes bug out farther. "What evidence do you have of this?"

"The first part? Evidence of my own eyes and nose." I sketch out the incident in the park. "And regarding the pills, I'm relying on the word of friends of the girl who went to the hospital."

"That isn't evidence that will stand up in court," she says with a crisp tone.

"As I recall, when you came to me asking me to take up drug problems in Jarrett Creek, you didn't tell me certain people were off-limits."

"You upset a man that the football team depends on for funds. I thought you had more sense than that."

I sigh. "Hazel, the time for me to show that I had any sense would have been if I had turned down the job. But I didn't do that, and now you're stuck with me."

She points a finger at me and her expression has grown hostile. "We can fire you."

"No, actually, you can't. That would be up to Sheriff Newberry."

"If I get enough votes together, he'll do as we say."

"Until then, I'm going to do the job I'm paid to do."

"You are a young . . . upstart." She has to struggle to her feet, which takes some of the wind out of what she said. She stomps across the floor. "We'll see how long you last."

I settle back in my chair after she leaves, feeling pretty good about the exchange. Worse things could happen than losing this job.

It's been a long day and I have two options. The most appealing one is to go home, but this is Jeanne's afternoon to play bridge. Tom stays after school to play ball of one kind or another until it's too dark to see the ball, and he isn't likely to welcome me interrupting him. So I'm left with the other option.

CHAPTER 31

George Cato's car is parked in front of his half brother's farmhouse, which I more or less expected. The surprise is that the two men are sitting out on the porch in rocking chairs, drinking what looks to be glasses of iced tea.

Montclair gets up from his chair and walks down the steps to meet me. "What brings you out here?" He looks uneasy, as if I've interrupted them plotting something illegal.

"Wanted to see how you were getting along. No more fires at your place?"

His neck flushes red. "No. No more fires."

"I talked to George earlier today. Everything all right between the two of you?" The relaxed air between the two of them seems odd, given what Owen and Judy told me.

"Yeah, it's fine. I guess there's no reason to keep it a secret from you. George made a generous offer, and I've decided to pack it in. Now all I have to do is think of some other way to make a living." He scratches his neck and gazes off into the distance. "Don't know what exactly."

George walks down the steps to join us. "I finally talked some sense into this mule."

"What does your wife have to say about this turn of events?" I ask Montclair.

His flush deepens. "She's happy about it."

At that moment, the screen door opens and Judy Montclair pokes her head out. Her eyes are red-rimmed and swollen. If she's happy to leave the farm, I wonder why she has been crying. "You all come on in." Her voice is subdued. "Supper is ready. Mr. Craddock, you're welcome to join us."

"I appreciate the offer, but my wife expects me for supper. Owen, could I have a quick word with you before I go?"

He tells his brother and wife to go ahead and he'll be there soon.

"I want to check out something with you," I say when we're alone. "Is there any need for me to think you all are in any danger from any more fires?"

Montclair crosses his arms over his chest and lowers his head. "I don't have to worry about that anymore."

"You think George was responsible? That he did it to drive you out?"

He shakes his head. "I know he didn't. Let's leave it at that."

For a second I think he means that he set the fire himself, but it doesn't make sense. Suddenly I think I know what accounts for Owen Montclair's change of heart and his wife's tears. It was clear the first time I set foot on this farm that Judy Montclair was bitterly unhappy, and that her husband either didn't understand how deeply unhappy she was or didn't care. I suspect Judy set the fire to force the issue. Maybe the fire down the hill gave her the idea.

"People may say you're stubborn," I say. "But you gave it a good shot. You've got nothing to regret here."

"That may be," he says. His voice is low, and he gazes out over the property "But I lost track of why I was doing it to begin with. I wanted a nice life for my family."

"You're young. You'll have another chance," I say.

He turns toward the house, and I say, "One more thing."

I pull the pictures from the burned house out of my pocket. "You ever see this man before?"

"No, who is he?"

"Someone I'm looking for. Would you ask your brother to step out here?"

When George Cato comes back out, I show him the picture.

If I hadn't been watching him, I wouldn't have seen the little jerk of recognition before he said, "No, he doesn't look familiar."

"Are you sure?"

He makes a show of looking closely at the picture, but then he shakes his head and hands it back. "Who is he?"

"I don't know," I say. "But I'm going to find out."

It's getting dark, and Jeanne probably has supper ready, but I stop back at the station with the idea of making a copy of the photo and sending it to Luke Schoppe. When I arrive, I see Eldridge's car in the lot, which is a surprise since he was supposed to be off duty now.

Inside, he's talking to a woman. She turns around when she hears me come in, and I see that her face is battered the way Donna's was last week. I don't recognize her. Eldridge says, "This is Molly Gundersand."

"What happened to you?"

She sniffs, and a tear leaks down her check. Eldridge says, "Somebody gave her a ride and beat up on her."

"Where are you from?"

"Bobtail." Although she's got to be over thirty, her voice is like a little girl's.

"Do you know the man who did this to you?"

She shakes her head.

I pull up a chair near her. "You say he gave you a ride. Where were you going?"

She shakes her head again and stays quiet. I glance at Eldridge, and he raises his eyebrows. That's when I take a mental step back and notice what she looks like. Without the bruises, she would probably be attractive. She has a swirl of long brown hair and a fine figure. She's wearing a short white skirt and, despite the heat, white knee-high boots. Her blouse is sheer and low-cut, showing off an ample bust. There's a big bruise above her right breast. She sees me notice it and covers it with her hand.

"Did he do that?"

"Yes."

"Miss Gundersand, why were you getting a ride?"

"I needed to get to town."

"You mean to Bobtail? But he brought you here instead?"

She nods.

"Did he bring you straight here after he picked you up?"

She swallows. "No, we . . . uh . . . drove around a little bit."

"Did you go somewhere to have sex?"

Her eyes spark fire. "What if we did? We're both adults."

"I expect he drove off without paying you."

She crosses her arms and clamps her mouth closed.

"And he beat you up. You're lucky he didn't kill you. How did you get away from him?"

"He dumped me here in Jarrett Creek. I didn't know what to do, so I asked somebody where the police station was, and I walked over here."

I ask her for a description of the man and the vehicle, but her answers are as vague as Donna's were. I don't know if they're protecting him or themselves.

"You live in Bobtail?"

"Yes."

"I'll take you back there, and we're going to stop by the police department."

I tell Eldridge he can go home, and before I leave I call Jeanne and tell her I've got to run up to Bobtail.

"It's suppertime."

"You and Tom go ahead and eat. I've got some police business."

"Is it more about Truly?"

"No, it has nothing to do with him."

She's quiet for a second. "Can't somebody else do it?"

"I'll be back in forty-five minutes."

When we get to the city limits of Bobtail, Molly says, "If you don't mind, I don't feel so good and I'd like to go on home."

"This won't take long. You need to report this man. Somebody else might get a worse beating than you did."

"I really don't want to," she says in her little-girl voice. She scoots toward me and runs her hand over the bruised area on her chest, sliding her blouse down a few inches until it barely covers her breast. "I need to go put something on this bruise. Maybe you could help me." She takes my hand and lays it on the swell of her breast. There's not a man alive who wouldn't be tempted, but I snatch my hand away.

When I pull into the police parking lot, she whines, "No, don't stop here. Take me home? We could have a little fun." She sticks out her lower lip.

"Come on in. You need to file a report."

I practically have to pull her out of the car, and as we walk up to the station, she starts to walk away. I grab her by the arm. "You're coming with me."

"I don't like you," she says. "You won't cut a girl some slack."

Inside, the man at the desk barely glances up and then does a double-take. "Molly, what the hell happened to you?"

"You know this woman?"

He snickers. "In a manner of speaking. Molly is one of our working girls."

"You get a lot of that here in Bobtail?"

"Not a lot. But out there on the edge of town where the roadhouse is you get a few."

"As you can see, somebody beat her up. Same thing happened to a woman in Jarrett Creek last week."

"Uh oh. We got a bad man on the loose." He asks the same things I asked, and he gets the same vague answers.

"What did this woman say who got hurt last week?"

I don't tell him she was my sister-in-law. "She said some man was passing through, and she was hitching a ride to the grocery store because her husband was gone."

"Ha! Sounds like BS to me," Molly says. Her little-girl voice is gone. "Who the hell hitches a ride to the grocery store?"

I leave Molly in the care of the Bobtail PD and head home, but all the way her words echo in my head. She's right. Who hitches a ride to the grocery store in the middle of the night? I don't like where my thoughts are going. Not that I didn't have a suspicion before, but I didn't want to believe that Donna was soliciting. Does Horace know what she's up to? Do they need money that badly? And most important, how will it affect Tom if kids find out?

I pass the football stadium on the way home, and I slow down. After what happened to the Blackman girl, I'm determined to put a stop to the drug sales. Charlie Ostrand said he got his supply by putting cash and a note with his order under a specific stone. I could try a trap, putting my own note there, but I don't have the manpower to stake out the place. I'm still tempted, but I don't even know what a note should say, or how much money to leave. It's another one of those ways in which I feel over my head in this job. I should have asked the boy for more information.

CHAPTER 32

I usually fall right to sleep, but I lie awake for some time, questions circling like wolves. How am I going to find evidence of who killed those five people when it was apparently a revenge killing that had its roots far from here? Without evidence, Truly Bennett is stuck in jail. Is the photograph I found really of any importance? The only thing that makes me cling to the possibility that it is came from George Cato's startled reaction this afternoon. But if he knows who the man is, why didn't he say so? How is he connected? And what does Beaumont Penny have to do with any of it? My impulse is to go tearing off to Houston to investigate. But investigate what? I wouldn't even know where to begin.

Closer to home, how am I going to get to the bottom of the drug problem here in town? I don't know how the girl who was taken to the hospital is doing. I should have called to check on her progress. I'll call first thing in the morning. If she's well enough, I'll find out if it really was Charlie Ostrand who provided the drugs that felled her.

Finally, why am I uneasy that my sister-in-law was lying when she told me the circumstances under which she was attacked? And where are she and Horace? Why haven't they called to check on Tom? It's been a few days since they brought him. You'd think they'd check on him every day. At least Jeanne and I would.

I circle back to the people who were murdered. Why did they move here? People don't pick a place to move out of thin air, but I haven't discovered their connection with Jarrett Creek. Freddie Carmichael and Blue Dudley acted like they were familiar with this town, and George Cato claimed he knew them. Is that the connection I'm looking for?

I resolve that first thing tomorrow I'm going to Darktown to rattle a few cages. Somebody has to know something about those people. But it does nothing to solve my sleep problem. Finally, I roll out of bed. There is one thing I can do. The football field is a few short blocks from here. I can try putting a note in the place Charlie told me about. If the drugs get dropped off, then at least I know we won't be wasting our time if I put together a surveillance team. The deputies may complain, but they will have to put up with doing some real police work for a change.

At the kitchen table I make out a request for one hundred dollars' worth of marijuana and sign it with an unintelligible signature. I have no idea if a hundred is a reasonable amount. I slip the note and the money into an envelope and seal it with tape.

It's cool outside, or at least cooler than it is during the day. A breeze has sprung up, and the trees shiver as I walk. I'm almost never out alone at night. Jeanne and I sometimes go dancing on weekends if there's a good band in Bryan or Bobtail, and we don't get back until late. But I like the feel of the night air, or at least I think I would if I weren't on such a dodgy mission.

The gate to the football field is closed with a lock on it, but the lock is hanging open. There's a half-moon out, and the stadium's stone grandstands glow in the light. It's hotter inside the stadium. The stone absorbs the heat during the day and hasn't had time to cool down. I'm sweating. The drug drop-off area is in shadow. I pause, look around, and square my shoulders. I'm not a fearful man, but the play of shadow and light makes me feel edgy.

In the shadowed area, I shine my flashlight from one stone to the next until I find the one Charlie mentioned that has a crack in the mortar. I crouch down next to the loose stone and tug it out. I take the envelope out of my pocket, but when I go to slip it into the hollow space, I find that there is already something there.

The envelope I pull out is sealed. I rip it open, and by the light from the flashlight I see that what I had written is a joke. This envelope contains three hundred dollars in cash and asks for both pills (ten reds and ten yellows) and two hundred dollars in marijuana.

Whoever put this here must be expecting to have it picked up tonight. I decide to put the stone back and wait to see who gets it. Before I have a chance to replace the stone, though, I hear a noise close behind me. I start to jump to my feet, but a blow to the back of my head sends me sprawling. I struggle to get to my knees. Someone says, "No, don't." I almost recognize the voice, but another blow makes everything go dark.

When I wake, I'm confused. It's dark and I should be in my bed, but something feels wrong. My face is pressed against something rough and hard. The back of my head aches, and my jaw feels like it has been scraped with sandpaper. I smell something earthy. I grope around to feel the surface near my face, and I realize I'm facedown on rock. I move gingerly, gradually remembering where I am. I don't hear any sound, so it seems like I've been left alone. When I try to lift my head, pain shoots through my eyeballs.

I take a deep breath and force myself up to my hands and knees. The knife of pain sends nausea through me, and I hunch over, waiting for it to pass. I take a few deep breaths, and then ease back so I'm sitting upright with my ass on my heels. After a few seconds like that, I look around me. I'm in dark shadows, but the moon has the field bathed in light.

After the pain in my head and the nausea eases, I struggle to my feet, fighting dizziness. I take a couple of steps toward the light, and my foot hits something hard, sending it skittering away. It slides to a stop, and in the moonlight I see that it's my flashlight. I lean over and pick it up, gritting my teeth against the nausea that seizes me.

I shine the light around and see that the loose stone has been replaced. I dig it back out, and the indentation is empty. The note I had planned to use for bait is gone, as well as the money I found before I was attacked.

All I want to do now is get home and lie down. On my walk back,

I think about what happened and wonder if someone followed me. But that means they had to be watching my house, and that seems unlikely. I come to the conclusion that I was in the wrong place at the wrong time.

In the bathroom mirror I see that my face is scraped where I hit the stone deck of the stadium seats, and my cheekbone is puffed up. I'm going to have a nice bruise. I feel the back of my head. It's sticky, and my hand comes away with blood on it. That brings on another wave of nausea that I dispel by sticking my head under the faucet and letting the cold water wash over it. The water stings, but I keep it flowing over the wound until the pain subsides. I feel around and find it's nothing but a small gash. More blood than the damage would warrant.

After that, I go into the kitchen and turn on the light over the sink, pull out a glass, and throw back two fingers of bourbon.

I'm opening my bedroom door when Tom comes out of his room, headed for the bathroom. The sight of him makes me freeze momentarily, but he doesn't look at me. He mumbles something and goes into the bathroom. I stare after him. The sight of him stirred up a memory of the last thing I heard before I lost consciousness. Someone said, "No, don't." A familiar voice, I believe, but my head is throbbing, and the memory is too fleeting to catch hold of.

I file the thought for tomorrow and slip into the room, where Jeanne hasn't stirred. When I ease into bed, it isn't long before weariness takes over.

I wake to find Jeanne lying on her side, her head propped on her arm, gazing at me. "What in the world did you do to yourself?"

I reach to my chin and cheekbone, which feel bruised and sore. "Fell down."

"Fell down where? I heard you leave, but I didn't hear you come in. Where did you go?"

I reach out and pull her to me. She lies down with her head on my chest and her arm around me. "I had something I meant to do, and I couldn't sleep so I went off to do it."

"What time was it?"

"I don't exactly know." I turn onto my side so I can lean down and kiss her. Her lips are soft and open to me in invitation. The movement stirs up my headache, but there's something more stirred up, more important than the headache. I kiss her harder, and she falls onto her back, her hand against my chest. Maybe because of the danger I confronted last night, I feel a sense of urgency that transmits to Jeanne. She grabs me around the waist and pulls me to her, breathing hard. We are usually more languid in our lovemaking, but this time we go at it hard and fast.

Afterward, she giggles softly. "I hope we didn't wake Tom." Which reminds me of Tom and of the voice I heard.

I ease off the bed. "I'm going to get a shower. Long day ahead."

In the shower, I try to remember my plan for the day, but after last night's fiasco everything is a jumble. First I'll see to the cows and try to shake the headache, and then maybe I'll get my plan straight.

CHAPTER 33

The hospital tells me that the girl, Eileen Blackman, will be released to her parents this morning. I find her in a private hospital room in the company of her mother, Julia, who is calmer than she was yesterday. Eileen is sitting in a chair next to the hospital bed, dressed in a hospital gown and with a pink, fluffy robe around her shoulders. She's slouched in the chair, her long hair falling to the sides of her face so it's impossible to see her expression.

Julia Blackman is overdressed in a pleated black skirt and blue blouse with a bow at the neck. Her intense blue eyes are red-rimmed. "Her daddy has gone to sign the papers to get her out of here." Her voice is sharp.

"Do you mind if I ask Eileen a few questions?"

She doesn't look at her daughter. "Sure, go ahead, see if you can get any more out of her than we can. This one thinks she's tough."

I hunker down next to the chair. "Hey, Eileen. You feeling better?"

She doesn't move her head. "I guess."

"Look at Chief Craddock when he speaks to you." Julia Blackman's tone is knife-edged.

Eileen gradually lifts her head and looks daggers at me. Her eyes are the same intense blue as her mother's. I recognize her. She was one of the teenagers at the park Sunday. I remember that when I told them I might have to contact their parents, she was the one who was scornful of the threat.

"What happened to your face?" she asks.

"Eileen!"

"It's all right. I probably shouldn't tell you, but I was investigating what happened to you and somebody attacked me. The only reason I'm telling you is so you understand that people who sell drugs to minors aren't the best kind of people."

She stares at me. "I can take care of myself."

"What is *wrong* with you?" her mother wails.

"Eileen, what happened to you was scary for a lot of people. I need to find out what led up to it, and I need your help."

"What help?" She glares at me as if she hates me. Her mother hisses through her teeth. I look back over my shoulder and meet her eyes and try to convey that she should cool it, but I can tell she isn't going to. Fear for her daughter has given way to fury.

"First off, I want to know what kind of drugs you took."

"I don't know," she mutters. Her eyes flick from me to her mother and back again.

Even though I took aspirin this morning, my head is pounding and I have to tamp down my impatience. "You told your friends you got the pills from Charlie Ostrand. Is that right?"

She presses her lips together firmly.

"I need to know."

"I'm not ratting on anybody," she says.

"Eileen!" Her mother says sharply.

I'd like to speak to the girl alone, but that won't be possible. Her parents wouldn't allow it even if the state of Texas would. "Let me tell you something," I say. "You were lucky. The next person Charlie Ostrand gives drugs to may not be so lucky. Do you want that on your conscience?"

"He didn't *give* me anything," she says.

"You're saying he sold the drugs to you? Did he tell you what they were?"

She pauses for a long time, staring down at her lap. I wait it out, hoping her mother will keep quiet. Eventually she says, "He told me they would make me feel good."

"Feel good!" Julia Blackman's voice quivers. "What do you have to feel bad about? You have everything you could possibly want. You've got friends, a family that loves you."

Eileen's lips tremble. "It's not as easy as you think."

"Look. You two probably have a lot to talk over, but I need to get some answers here."

Both of them look at me with outrage, which is probably a good sign. At least they are united in something.

"Did Charlie tell you what kind of the pills you bought from him?"

"No, he didn't." She's picking at the arm of the chair and won't look at me. "I don't feel so good," she says.

"Oh, baby." Her mother rushes to her side and puts her arms around her.

I tell them good-bye and head out. I've got the information I came for, which is that Charlie Ostrand is the culprit. In the hallway I pass the girl's father. He has a stricken look on his face and is so intent on getting to his daughter's room that he doesn't even see me.

I get to headquarters at nine. In the parking lot there's a Texas Ranger vehicle. Curren Wills and Luke Schoppe are inside talking to Tilley.

When I walk in the door, Tilley opens his mouth to say something and then he does a double take. "What the hell happened to you?"

I had forgotten the abrasion on my face. Although it stings, the pain doesn't compare to the pain in my head. I tell the men about my failed attempt to set a trap.

"Lucky they didn't kill you," Wills says.

"You didn't get a look at anybody?" Tilley asks.

"No, they came at me from behind."

"You shouldn't have gone out there on your own."

"He's right," Wills says.

"I was pissed off." I tell them about the girl who overdosed and the budding drug dealer who sold her the pills. "A kid named Charlie

Ostrand sold her the drugs. His daddy is a lawyer, and I'm sure he has a dozen ways he can get the kid out of trouble."

"I've met Ostrand," Tilley says. "I expect you're right."

"I hope you take a lesson to be more careful, and don't run off acting like a cowboy," Wills says. "To take on something like that you need backup."

"True words," Tilley says, which annoys me more than Wills's lecture.

"What brings you here?" I ask Wills.

"Luke found some information we thought you'd be interested in." He nods to Schoppe, who has been holding a folder in his hand. He thrusts it at me.

Inside the folder are a few sheets of paper. The top one contains a summary of information about Blue Dudley, and the second is about Freddie Carmichael. Dudley has a substantial record of shady real-estate dealings in the Houston area, but only two arrests, one for a mortgage scheme and one for fraudulent sales.

"No trials or convictions?" I look from Wills to Schoppe.

"No. Every complaint was dropped."

"What exactly is a fraudulent sale?"

"Means he sold property he didn't have a right to sell."

I nod, remembering that Freddie Carmichael originally said he was the owner of the house where the people were killed, and that Blue Dudley hedged on the claim when Sheriff Newberry showed up.

"Mind if I take a look?" Tilley asks. I pass the sheet to him.

"Read Carmichael's record," Wills says to me.

Carmichael has a history of assault charges, everything from barroom brawls to intimidation of a trial witness. He was dressed like a smooth operator the day I met him. The last thing I expected is that he would be a strong-arm man. He also has only arrests and no convictions. Tilley reaches for the sheet and I pass it over.

"What's going on here? Why haven't there been any convictions?"

Wills smiles and looks at me sharply. He wants me to work it out.

"These guys have some kind of protection," I say.

Wills forms a pistol with his fingers and mock-shoots me. "Got it in one. I thought you seemed pretty clever."

I'm thinking hard, which increases the pounding in my head. I walk around to my desk drawer, shake a couple of aspirins out of a bottle, and wash them down with coffee. "So if these guys are connected with the killings here, they aren't likely to be arrested for it. Is that what you're telling me?"

"I wouldn't make that leap too fast. Their records don't show any history of homicide. It's likely they weren't involved with the murders, just arranging housing for the people who lived there."

I get the distinct impression that Wills is leading me to a conclusion, and he wants me to draw it for myself. "I'm thinking out loud here. Whoever actually did it might have the same kind of protection?"

"Seems likely."

"Same for the woman's husband who was killed in Houston?"

"Same."

"So you're saying that all these people involved in the drug trade aren't likely to be arrested for the murders or the drug trafficking."

"That's the way it looks."

"The question is, who's doing the protecting? Are we talking police corruption?"

"That's probably the case, but that's not something you need to concern yourself with."

"Except that it's not good news for Truly Bennett," I say. "If no one gets arrested for the crimes, Sutherland has no reason to release Bennett."

"You could be right." Wills is watching me so closely that I feel nervous. He expects a lot of me. "I think you have to look closer to home to help your boy Bennett."

"You mean like why did those people choose to move here?"

"That would be a good start."

I'm still holding a third sheet of paper. Now I look at it and see that the subject is Beaumont Penny. It says the reason he left San Antonio is that he was in deep trouble with a drug dealer there. It seems that he tried to compete with the dealer, but he didn't have the backup to make it work. Investigators speculated that Penny got run out of town and left rather than get himself killed. In Houston he had better luck. In Houston there had been no arrests on drug charges, just a minor conviction for auto theft that got him a six-month suspended sentence.

I put the sheet back in the folder and throw the folder on my desk. "Looks to me like the criminals are having a fine time in the big city of Houston."

"Does look that way."

I pull out the photo I've been showing around. "So this is likely to be useless." I hand him the photo.

Will studies it and then passes it to Schoppe. When he looks back at me, his expression has changed subtly; he looks angry. "Where did you get that?"

I tell him that I searched the burned-out house again and found the two photos. I hand him the one of the family.

He nods, but I get the feeling his mind is elsewhere. He glances over at Tilley, who looks a little pale. "We're going to have to get on the road. Why don't you walk us out to the car?" he says to me.

When we close the door behind us, I say, "Something else is going on. You want to tell me what it is?"

Wills puts his hands on his hips. He speaks quietly. "I didn't have the authority to pass this information on to you the last time we talked, but my boss has since given me the go-ahead. There's an investigation going on, not only of Dudley, Carmichael, and Penny, but the whole drug operation in Houston and the kind of protection they're getting."

My mind is racing. I feel like I'm one step behind. "So what are you telling me?"

"For one thing, eventually your boy Bennett should be in the clear."

"How long is eventually?"

"That's the problem. This investigation has been going on for two years, and my guess is it will take another year before we wrap it up."

"We? You mean the Texas Rangers?"

We've reached his car, and he turns to face me. "Not only the Rangers. We're working with the FBI. But, Craddock, that isn't for anyone else to know."

I'm stunned. I thought I was in over my head, but being on the edge of a big-city corruption scandal that may have touched our little town never crossed my mind.

"I figured I owed it to you to let you know personally what you're up against trying to get Bennett freed."

"The photo I showed you. You recognized him. Who is he?"

Wills sighs. "More like 'who *was* he?' He's an undercover agent. We haven't heard from him in a while, and I wouldn't be surprised if the same people who took care of Duchess Wortham and her family got rid of him, too. Now do you understand why I want you to be careful?"

For the first time, my one-man crusade to free Bennett seems utterly impossible. What kind of hubris made me think I could do something to help Truly on my own? "So you don't think, knowing about the corruption investigation, John Sutherland will drop the charges against Bennett?"

He raises his eyebrows. "John Sutherland isn't privy to the information I just gave you."

This can't be good. There can only be one reason why he isn't in on the investigation. "Do I want to know why not?"

"Don't jump to conclusions too fast. We're not looking at Sutherland specifically, but we have an idea that members of the THP might be part of the problem. Seems better not to tip any of them off."

CHAPTER 34

When I go back inside, Tilley says, "I need to talk to you."

I sit down at my desk and wheel my chair around to face him "About what?" I'm still buzzing with the news I've heard and don't have much attention for Tilley. He has turned out to be more timid than I thought he'd be. We've never had to tackle anything as serious as the murders, so I've never seen him tested.

He hunches over his desk, trying to move closer to me. "I know you want to help that boy in jail, but Wills was talking about some dangerous people. These are people who didn't think twice about murdering a woman and four young people. If I was you, I'd let the Rangers and the highway patrol deal with all this. I'm sorry for Truly, but it sounds like he'll be out sooner or later anyway."

"Later," I say.

He shrugs. "We aren't set up to help him, and that's a plain fact. You've got to consider the safety of your wife and brother and his family. Whoever killed Duchess Wortham and her family won't hesitate to go after you and yours."

I'm not paying attention as he drones on with his reasonable-sounding words, because his mention of my brother Horace has sent a shock through me. I get up abruptly. "I've got something I have to do," I say.

Before I leave, I telephone Jeanne. I'm relieved when she answers the phone. "I'm coming right home," I say. "We have to talk."

"What about?"

I hang up and head out the door. I'm almost to my truck when I hear the door slam and Tilley's voice shouting. "Samuel, don't ignore me!" He grabs my arm and wheels me around. "Listen, you think you're so goddam smart, but you're asking for trouble. I have a lot more experience than you. You've got to back off, and I mean it."

I yank my arm away. "Tilley, you had your chance to take this job, and you passed. I'm going to do it my way."

"You're going to get yourself killed." His face is purple.

"If that happens, then you'll have another chance at the job. Now I've got to be somewhere."

Jeanne is waiting for me on the porch with her arms crossed and an angry look on her face. "What's gotten into you? You sounded so serious. You scared me to death."

"I didn't mean to scare you, but what I have to say is serious."

"Has something happened to Horace and Donna?"

I'm momentarily startled by what seems like ESP, but of course she thought of it because they are on the road. "Let's go inside and sit down for a minute." When we're settled on the sofa, I take both her hands in mine. "I want you to pack your bags and Tom's and go stay with your mamma for a few days. Maybe as much as a week."

She pulls her hands away. "Why? What are you going to be doing?"

"I'm going to stay right here. This case has taken a turn I don't care for, and I'll feel a lot better knowing the two of you are out of here."

"Tom's in school. We can't just take off."

"He's smart. It won't hurt him to be out of school for a few days."

"Why do you have to stay?"

"It's my job." Because I can see that she's ready to protest, I say, "Please, just do this for me."

"I won't leave here without you. You've poked a stick into a bed of snakes, and now you're worried somebody's going to get bitten. And you know what?" Her eyes are blazing. "It's going to be you." She jumps up. "When you took that job as chief of police I thought it was a bad idea, but, oh no, you had to be a hero. I know you don't like it that your family never had anything when you were a boy. Maybe you got teased or were embarrassed at the way you had to live, but I thought you had left all that behind. You went to college and made something of yourself, and now you can't seem to enjoy it. You're putting yourself in harm's way for nothing." She's trembling and almost in tears.

"Jeanne." I stand up and rest my hands on her shoulders. "Whether it's my fault or not, I'm worried about you and I want you to be safe. Why don't you and your mamma take Tom out to Disneyland? I bet all of you would love it."

A tear spills down her cheek, and she swipes at it. "I've never seen you like this. Why did you have to get involved? Why couldn't you leave it to the Texas Rangers? What is it about that . . . about Truly Bennett that makes him more important than your family?"

All the air goes out of me. It's like she punched me in the gut. "Not more important than you. Nothing is more important than you." We stand at a face-off. I've never told her that I have a debt I don't know how to repay. It's a debt that causes me pain.

"Then why do you have to stir this up?"

I walk to the screen door and look out, trying to find a way to talk to her. "You're right. Truly is important. I don't mean him in particular, but what he represents."

"I don't understand."

"Come into the bedroom and pack your bag, and I'll tell you what I mean. But you have to promise you'll go then."

In the bedroom, I take her suitcase down from the high shelf in the closet and lay it on the bed. I sit down on the bed and watch her open a drawer and take out some items. She walks to the suitcase and stops. "Start talking."

I don't know why the story is so hard for me to tell, but maybe I'll feel better getting it out. "There are things I haven't told you about how I grew up. You know Daddy drank and had a hard time holding down a job, but what I didn't tell you is that for a time we lived in a trailer on a lot in Darktown. It was the only place we could get somebody to let us stay. Horace was eight and I was six."

I pause, not wanting to tell the story, but when I stop talking, she stops packing. My throat is dry.

"Eventually Daddy found a job at the railroad tie plant. But for that year he was out of work, my brother and I never had enough to eat. To this day, I don't understand how my mamma thought it was okay for us to go without meals."

She leans against the chest of drawers and watches me.

"I was always hungry. One day, Horace and I were walking along and I was crying, and this old black woman came by." I snort. "I thought she was old, but she was probably no more than forty." I sigh. "She asked Horace what was wrong. Horace wouldn't talk to her, but I was little and I told her I was hungry. So she took us to her house and fed us."

"Samuel." Jeanne sits down and puts her arm around me, and only then do I realize that I've barely been talking above a whisper.

"Here's the thing. She fed us every day after that. Horace and I got to depend on it. It got to where we stopped by there after school every day, and she was waiting with a meal."

She lays her head on my shoulder. "That's not so bad, honey. It wasn't your fault."

"That's not the bad part. Horace talked behind her back like she was dirt. Horace would tell me she was filthy and that her house smelled bad and that she was stupid. Oh, he was awful. And I bought it." I bow my head. "He had sense enough not to say those things to her face, but I suspect I didn't hide my scorn."

Jeanne puts her arms around me and kisses my check. "You were a little boy," she says. "You didn't know any better."

"When my family moved out of there and into a house, Horace and I never went back to see her, never thanked her. When I got older and thought about it, I knew it was wrong for him to say those things and for us to take her for granted. I kept thinking one of these days I was going to go back and tell her I appreciated what she did for us. And then one day it was too late. I heard she had died."

Jeanne pulls back and stares at me. "Let me ask you something. Where did she get the money for the food?"

"I wondered the same thing. She probably got help from her church congregation."

She lays her head back on my shoulder. "Then it wasn't just her."

"Maybe not, but she's the one who went out of her way. I still owe her, and I'm going to see to it that Truly Bennett is exonerated. It's the only way I know to pay the debt." I pull her arms away and stand up. "Now I don't want to talk about it anymore. Finish packing. I'm going to the school to pick up Tom." I've spoken harshly, so I walk over and put my hands on her shoulders. "Please."

She walks to the closet and takes out some blouses and throws them into the suitcase. Usually she's a meticulous packer, but she hardly seems to notice what she's doing. "Do you think somebody is coming to kill you?"

I realize that she's picturing something out of an old cowboy movie, like *High Noon*. I smile and hug her tight. "No, it's not that bad. I'll feel better if I don't have to worry about you, that's all."

"All right. I'll go, but I don't have to be happy about it. I can't imagine going to Disneyland and playing like I don't have a care in the world while you're here in danger."

"You don't have to go to Disneyland. Your mamma has always wanted to get to some art galleries and museums out there in California. You can do that."

"Maybe." Her eyes get a faraway look, like she's already planning what she'll say to her mamma. "If you're sure you're okay."

"Absolutely. I'm going to school to get Tom. I'll be back soon."

When I arrive at the school, I see a familiar car pulling to the curb ahead of me. My heart starts pounding in time with the pounding in my head. I get out and walk over to my brother's car just as he's opening the door. Donna isn't with him.

"Look who's here! Hey, Samuel, you're saving me a trip. I was going to pick up Tom and then head over to your place to get his things."

Anger surges up in me so hard I could knock my brother down without a second thought. "Why are you taking him out of school?"

"Me and Donna have rented a place in Houston, and we're going to move there."

"You're not taking Tom with you."

He laughs. "Sure we are. He's our boy."

"You're going nowhere, except maybe to jail."

His eyes harden. "Have you lost your mind?"

"No, but I think you've lost yours. At least you've lost your way. How long have you been back in town?"

"Now listen here, little brother, you have no right to question me."

"Horace, I've been hearing you say that ever since I moved back here. And now I know why."

He sneers. "You came back here full of yourself because you got a college education. You think you're pretty smart, but you don't know as much as you think you do. There are a lot of things you don't know about . . . the way the world works."

"I know you're getting yourself in big trouble."

"Who are you to judge me? I protected you from hard knocks the whole time we were kids. You owe me." He's referring to how he protected me from our folks—from our daddy's drunken rages and our mamma's sharp tongue.

"And I'm grateful. But that doesn't give you a license to break the law. I want you to go back to your place and wait for me. I'll be there in twenty minutes. We need to talk."

"By God, you can't tell me what to do. I'm getting my boy."

"You're not. If I have to, I'll arrest you."

"Arrest me for what?"

We glare at each other. The school bell rings, and kids spill out on the schoolyard for recess. The happy shouts of the children are a sharp contrast to the tension between us.

"I heard your voice last night, telling whoever hit me not to do it again."

He's startled, but he recovers and says, "I don't know what you mean. That wasn't me."

"Yes, it was. We can talk about it in a little while at your place."

"I don't know what you think is going on, but you're dead wrong. But I don't want to create any more problems than we already have, so I'll go home and wait for you." He climbs into his car and revs the engine. I watch him drive away, hoping that Tom is not one of the children out at recess.

My hope was in vain. I spy Tom standing in a corner of the school-yard away from other children, watching me intently. As I walk into the yard, he runs to me and throws his arms around my waist. He's trembling. "Was that Daddy?"

"He was here to pick you up, but then he remembered he had something to do, so I'm going to take you instead."

I gather him up in my arms. He looks off to watch his daddy's car disappear down the road. "Are you taking me to him?"

"No, you're going away for a few days with your Aunt Jeanne."

He nods. His face looks like a wise old man's. "I don't really want to go with him."

"Why is that?"

"I just don't."

"Did he hurt you?"

He shakes his head. "I don't think he likes me."

"Tom, listen, your daddy loves you a lot. I know he does. He doesn't always have good judgment, but I assure you he loves you, and your mamma does, too."

He sighs and relaxes, a little. I set him down, and together we walk into the school so I can find his teacher to tell her he's going to miss classes for a few days.

Jeanne keeps up a good front for Tom. If she didn't have his welfare in mind, she'd probably refuse to leave my side. But when she tells him they are going to fly to California to see Disneyland with Jeanne's mother, his excitement is contagious.

She sends Tom to change clothes and says, "I talked to Mamma. She's making arrangements. I hope you're sure about this."

I hug her and tell her I am. A half hour later, they are gone; the house has never felt so empty.

Horace's car is not in front of his place. I'm torn between being annoyed and being relieved. The idea of hauling my brother and sister-in-law off to jail doesn't appeal to me. But neither does letting them get away. I bang on their door in case Donna is there, and the door swings open. I walk inside. "Donna? Horace?" The living room is bare of everything but the shabby furniture.

In the bedroom, drawers hang open and empty. The bed has been stripped of linens. A few ragged bits of clothing have been left on hangers, and a few pairs of worn shoes remain on the floor of the closet. They can't have been gone more than a few minutes, but already the place has a stale feel.

I walk into Tom's room with dread in my heart, and, sure enough, they haven't bothered to take any of his belongings. I sit on the edge of his little bed and wonder what to do. Jeanne will know. Until then, I'll call the man who owns these apartments and make sure the rent is paid up so I don't have to make a decision right away.

They didn't bother with the kitchen, either. They have left unwashed dishes in the sink, and clean dishes in the cabinets. A motley assortment of pots and pans remain in the lower shelves. There's not a lot of food—a few cans of soup, a box of saltines, oatmeal, and noodles—but Donna never kept food on hand for more than a day or two.

I wander through the rooms again in a daze. If I hadn't met Jeanne, would I have ended up the same as my brother? No, I mustered the gumption to go to college, while he didn't even bother to get through his last year of high school. I blame the woman upstairs, but I can't leave here without telling her they're gone. I lock the door behind me.

My heart trips double-time as I trudge up the stairs to the second floor. I'm going to bear the brunt of her anger and disappointment; and as disgusted as I am with Horace, I'm not sure I can hold my temper. I wish I could harden my heart to her and walk away, but Jeanne would be disappointed in me, and truthfully I'd be disappointed in myself, too.

"A person can't get a bit of peace and quiet around here," Mamma says when she comes to the door, cigarette dangling from her hand. The TV is blaring, so I'm not sure what kind of peace and quiet she expects.

"There's been a lot of noise?"

She takes a deep drag off the cigarette. Makes my lungs ache just to watch her. "I don't know what in tarnation was going on downstairs, but it sounded like Horace and Donna were tearing the place apart."

"In a manner of speaking, they were," I say. "They've cleared out."

"You mean for good?"

"That I can't tell you." It unnerves me to see that she has a look of glee in her eyes.

"How soon will you know? Not that you'd ever tell me."

"Mamma, let me ask you something. Did you ever get an idea that Horace or Donna was doing things that weren't on the up and up?"

"You mean like some kind of criminal thing? I wouldn't put it past Donna one bit, but I don't think Horace has the brains to be a criminal."

"You ever get any idea that Donna was prostituting herself?"

I don't know what Mamma had in mind, but it clearly wasn't that. Her mouth falls open. "I never. And if I was you, I'd get my mind out of the gutter. That's what comes from getting all those ideas in college and the military." She glares at me and then gets a funny look on her face. "What made you think she was doing that?"

"There was a woman in Bobtail who got beaten up the same way Donna did. She was a working girl."

That and Donna's flimsy excuse that she went out late at night to get milk, plus my history with her, all add up to a tawdry picture. But no way am I going to bring up any of that.

She stares over at the television, and I realize for once she's speechless.

"Horace didn't give you any idea he might be leaving town?"

"Neither of you boys ever give me the time of day. Did they take Tom with them?"

"No, as it happens, Tom was spending a few days at our house."

"You mean they just up and left him behind? I never did figure out why they had a child to begin with. I guess they found out it wasn't always fun and games when you have children. I should know. There was never any end of trouble with you boys. And your daddy wouldn't lift a finger to help. If anything, he was worse than you two." Although she is rattling on in her usual way, she looks scared and sad.

"Mamma, I worry that you aren't going to be all right here by yourself."

"Of course I am. You really think Horace and Donna ever worried one bit about me? It's going to be the same with them gone as it was with them here. They wouldn't have known whether I died until I started to stink up the place. Neither would you, for that matter."

I don't even bother to protest. It wouldn't make any difference. "I've got to go. Some things have come up." I start toward the door, but a thought stops me. If Tilley is right and the Houston drug dealers want to get at me by attacking my family, they might go after her. The problem is, even if she is in danger, I don't know where she could go to hide. I can't have her at my place for more reasons than I can count. She has a sister in Brownsville, but I don't think they talk to each other except to exchange birthday and Christmas cards. "Mamma, when was the last time you saw Aunt Judy?"

Her interest has gone back to her TV program, and I'm not sure she heard me, but after a minute she says, "It was at Daddy's funeral. Let's see, that would be fifteen, no, sixteen years. Why?"

"Would you like to go visit her?"

"Why would I want to do that?" She looks at me with a sneer. "She has snippy ideas that I can't put up with."

"I thought you might want to see her."

"You're lying. You always was a terrible liar. What kind of bee have you got in your hat?"

"I don't want to scare you, but there may be some trouble in town. My family might be targeted. I sent Jeanne and Tom off to Dallas an hour ago."

She snorts. "Scared? Me? You know better than that. If anybody thinks they're going to mess with me, they're just plain wrong. I'm not going nowhere."

I don't like to leave it at that, but persuading her otherwise is beyond my capacity. Truth is, I have pity on anybody who runs cross-wise of her. "All right, if that's the way you feel."

"I do. Who are these people anyhow?"

"Not anybody from around here." Although George Cato is from around here and seems to know something about them. "You ever hear anything in town suggesting that George Cato was into any shady deals?"

"All I know is that George Cato is another one of them with big ideas. That silly woman that writes the newspaper, Bonnie Bedichek? She's the one to ask about him."

That makes sense. Bonnie knows everybody. "I'll be on my way. Mamma, I'm serious now, call me if you need anything."

"I'll tell you what I need. I need to know if Horace is gone for good. If he is, I want to get his apartment. It's on the ground floor, and I wouldn't have to walk up and down stairs."

Now I understand why she seemed so chipper at the idea of Horace and Donna leaving. I tell her I'll let the landlord know. What I don't tell her is that I'll do it in my own good time.

"Be sure you do, and don't take no for an answer. You always were something of a cowardly boy, not standing your ground."

CHAPTER 35

After I leave Mamma's place, I go back to the office and get on the phone. I track Bonnie Bedichek down at her home. "Can I come by? I need to ask you something."

She tells me I'm welcome as long as I don't tattle to anybody what a mess her house is. When I walk in, I see what she means. It looks only slightly less chaotic than my brother's apartment.

"Sorry, I don't have time to keep house." She picks up a stack of magazines off a saggy chair and plops it on the floor so I can sit down.

She brings me a mug of coffee. The cup is chipped, but at least it looks clean.

I can't reveal what Wills told me about the corruption investigation, but I tell her that there's a good chance the murders were committed by people connected with the drug trade in Houston. I also mention my confrontation with Tilley, and his warning that I should reconsider messing with people involved in the drug dealings. "He was pretty heated up. I wouldn't want you to broadcast it, but I think he's scared. Anyway, I sent Jeanne and Tom off to Dallas to keep them out of harm's way."

"You don't plan to follow his advice, I take it?"

"I don't like the idea of Truly Bennett sitting in jail for a crime he had nothing to do with."

"I do admire you, but I don't see how you're going to get anywhere unless you plan to go to Houston and lay waste to the drug dealers there."

"I'll leave the big drug people to the big lawmen. All I want is to get my little corner cleaned up and get Truly out of jail."

"You really think you can stop people from selling drugs around here?"

"I'll do my best. I remember hearing somebody say that if a burglar hears a dog in somebody's house, he'll move on to a house with no dog. I intend to be the dog in town. Let the dealers move on to a town that they don't have to fuss with."

Bonnie chuckles. "I hope you can make that happen, and I'll be glad to get the scoop when you do. But you might want to listen to Tilley."

"I'm not ready to do that yet. Bonnie, what do you know about George Cato?"

I've never known Bonnie not to have a quick reply, but now she looks startled. Color rises in her usually sallow cheeks. "Why are you asking me?"

"You seem to know pretty much everything that happens around here, so you're a natural person to ask. What is it I don't know?"

"I'm surprised you don't know. Twenty years ago, George came to Jarrett Creek and lived here for a while. The two of us had a . . . a thing."

"A thing?" I realize now that Mamma must have heard gossip about the two of them. That's why she told me to ask Bonnie.

"Affair? Courtship? Whatever you call it, we went at it pretty hot and heavy for over a year. I thought something was going to come of it. Then, all of a sudden, he upped and went back to Dallas." She bites her lower lip.

"I'm sorry. I didn't mean to bring up an old wound." If anyone had asked me, I would have thought Bonnie was too independent to let a man into her life.

She cocks her head. "Why did you ask me about him?"

"He comes back here once a month. Do you ever see him?"

Her color deepens. "I don't know that it's anybody's business, but he occasionally drops by." I've never known her to be a bitter woman, but her mouth twists. "Once a fool, always a fool."

She's in love with him. "Then I'm not sure you're the one I should be asking."

"Samuel, I'll tell you the truth. I may be a fool for him, but my life has taken a different turn. The truth means more to me than any man could. Ask your question."

"Cato has connections with a couple of men I think had something to do with Duchess Wortham's family being killed. The Texas Ranger I'm getting help from said he didn't think they were directly responsible, but that they may have something to do with it."

"What men?" Bonnie gets up and begins to walk around as if she can't sit still.

"A real-estate developer by the name of Barton Dudley, who goes by the nickname 'Blue,' and his sidekick, Freddie Carmichael."

She comes to a stop in front of me with her arms crossed. "I've never heard of them."

"There's one more you probably *have* heard of: Beaumont Penny."

"He's like a bad penny. Turns up in all the wrong places. I never knew him to be violent, though. Just crooked."

I don't tell her that he is connected with the drug trade in Houston. "Does it come as any surprise to you that George Cato might be involved in something that turned shady?"

She takes a long time answering, during which she paces, staring at the floor. "I won't say I'm surprised, but I don't know anything specific. I know that George likes money, and if he thought he could make a killing by doing something a little shady, he wouldn't hesitate." She realizes what she has said. "I don't mean a *killing* killing. I mean a get-rich-quick scheme."

When I leave, I think about the get-rich-quick aspect of what she told me, and for the life of me I can't figure out how George Cato was going to turn letting Duchess Wortham live in a house on his property into a money-making proposition. Even if she was a prostitute and he got a cut, Jarrett Creek is not a place where anybody is going to find big money. More likely, he was doing somebody a favor. But why?

It's dusk, and I run by the house to make sure the cattle are okay. I wish Truly Bennett was here to look in on them, too. I don't know much more than the bare minimum about how to keep cows. With that in mind, I resolve to drive over to San Antonio tomorrow to see Truly. But tonight I've got one more stop to make.

It's dark by the time I pull up in front of the Montclair farm. I'm relieved to see that George Cato's car is here. He's the man I want to see, and I was worried that he might have gone back to Dallas. The front of the house is dark, but there are lights on in the back.

A youngster's head appears at the window, looking to see who has come calling. I get out of the car as the front door opens, and the dog comes roaring out. I speak to him, and he quiets immediately and trots over for a scratch behind the ears.

Owen Montclair comes out onto the porch. Even though the house is on a hill, there is no trace of a breeze. The norther that came through last week is a long-gone memory, and I'm sweating by the time I walk up the steps.

"What brings you out here this time?" he asks.

"I need to talk to your brother."

"You might as well come on in. We're in the kitchen." His voice sounds funny, and as he walks in front of me, he staggers. I smell alcohol on him.

George is sitting at the kitchen table. There's no sign of Judy or the children, but from somewhere I hear the sound of a TV. As sparse as their lives are, I'm surprised that they have one. There's a bottle of Jack Daniels on the table and two glasses.

Without asking, Montclair gets a glass out of the cabinet and pours me a healthy shot and then sags into his chair. He waves his hand airily. "Wife and kids are watching the TV that George brought in today, and I'm drinking the whiskey he brought."

Cato picks up his glass and turns it around and around with a pained look on his face.

I take a sip of the whiskey and shudder. It goes straight to my head since I haven't eaten for many hours. My headache had gone down to a dull throb, but the whiskey wakes it back up. I set the glass down. "George, I need to have a few words with you in private. You want to come out on the porch?"

"Oh, hell no," Montclair says. "This farm won't be mine much longer, but while it is, I can show some hospitality. Make yourself at home. I'll be watching the TV with my family." He pours himself a half glass of whiskey and lurches out of the room.

George watches the door long after Montclair leaves.

"He's going to regret the whiskey in the morning," he says. Then he turns to me. "Why are you here?"

I've become aware of the gulf of age and experience between Cato and me. Some things you can't know from just observing, you have to live them, and I dread that Cato's deal with Dudley and Carmichael is in that vast land of experience. "Tell me about your relationship with Blue Dudley and Freddie Carmichael."

Cato's eyes are full of melancholy. Although I never saw any war action in my years in the air force, I was around men who had. They had that kind of look, like the world they looked at was different from the world other men saw. "I wouldn't exactly call it a relationship. More like an understanding."

"What kind of understanding?"

"About what I owe and how to pay it off."

I don't have any training in psychology, but something tells me that Cato wants to talk, so I say the simplest thing I can think of. "Tell me about it."

He knocks back his bourbon, and I take a sip to show some kind of comradeship, even though I suspect I don't really want to be his comrade.

"It all comes down to family. When I was a kid, I lost my mamma and for a while it was just me and Daddy. When he remarried and he and his wife had Owen, I thought I would be pushed to the side. But my daddy held fast to me. He told me that no matter what happened, the two of us were joined forever. His wife's people were from Dallas, so we all moved back there. She was a nice-enough lady, treated me okay, but of course she favored Owen, and then they also had a daughter." His voice wobbles when he mentions the daughter.

"When I got older, I decided to come back here and settle down. I liked it here. It's a good town, and I knew a lot of people." He pauses and looks off in the distance and takes another swig. "One in particular. I kind of thought I had everything going fine, but then all hell broke loose. Owen's mamma ran off with another man, and a month later Daddy hit a tree coming home from work and was busted up real bad. And you know what?"

"What?"

"I called that bitch to tell her what happened, and she didn't even bother to come see him. I couldn't leave Daddy at home like that by himself, and Owen was in college and I couldn't ask him to give up his education, so it was up to me to go home and take care of him."

"Did you think of bringing him back here?"

"Of course I did. But I had my little half sister, June, to take into consideration. She was in high school and pitched a fit not to be taken away from her friends."

"Her mamma didn't take her along when she left?"

"She wanted to, but Junebug wouldn't think of leaving Daddy. I decided I'd go back and take care of the two of them. I figured when Junie went off to college, I'd move Daddy down here and take up where I left off with my lady friend."

"Why didn't you?"

He looks tired. "Oh, you know how it is. One thing led to another. I met a girl and we got married, had a couple of kids." His voice trails off.

"And you didn't want to bring them here?"

"It wasn't that. It was June. She got into some trouble. Took up with a kid who was up to no good. She didn't go to college, just . . ." He rubs his face. "Why am I telling you all this?"

"Somewhere along the line, it's going to lead to Blue Dudley."

His smile is tight. "And Freddie Carmichael."

I make the connection. "The boyfriend."

"Yep. Anyway, June got into trouble, and Freddie said he could make it go away, but it would cost me. Not right away, but somewhere down the line."

A deal with the devil. "June's trouble was drug-related?"

"In spades." Suddenly he starts laughing. "Spades. Get it?"

He doesn't seem to want an answer. "What happened to June?"

"Died of an overdose couple of years back." He wipes his eyes with the back of his hand. "She was the cutest thing you ever saw." He coughs a couple of times. "Now do you understand?"

"Not completely. When she died, that didn't cancel out the debt?"

"No, sir, not by a long shot. Right after her funeral, Carmichael talked to me and said a debt is a debt and when he called on me for help, he expected me to follow up."

"What did he ask you to do?"

"I don't suppose it will hurt to tell you. Last fall, he came and told me he needed a place to stash the family of this man he did business with. I didn't ask him what kind of business, but he told me anyway. Said it was June's drug dealer, man by the name of Clyde Wortham. He told me it wouldn't cause me any trouble, all I had to do was provide the land."

CHAPTER 36

There's a light on in the Bennett house. Alva Bennett comes to the door, peeking around it when she answers it, as if she's terrified of who might be coming to the door so late at night.

"Alva, I was hoping to talk to your daddy," I say.

"He's not back from San Anton' yet. He stays there most days, keeping vigil."

"How is Truly? I'm sorry I haven't gotten over there to see him."

"He's passable. At least nobody has beaten up on him, but Daddy says his spirits are low." She's hanging onto the door, obviously reluctant to invite me in. "Alva, I need to ask you something, and it seems too silly to do it with you half in and half out of the door. Come outside, and we'll sit on the steps."

She scoots out the door, but before she sits down she says, "Can I get you a Coke?"

"No, I'm fine." She probably smells the alcohol on my breath, but there's nothing I can do to fix that.

As soon as we sit, a mosquito lands on my arm, and I swat it. The air is so sultry, this could be the Gulf Coast.

"Alva, tell me what you know about Beaumont Penny." Since she's the one who put me on his trail, I'm sure she knows something.

She makes a humming noise deep in her throat. "Everybody knows Bee."

"Then you know he's involved in the drug trade? Does he sell drugs?"

She hugs her legs up to her chest. "I don't know nothin' about that. I know he got in some trouble over in San Anton' and he left in a kind of hurry."

"Does he come back here often?"

"You know, Chief Craddock, I don't keep up with people like him. I'm trying to make enough money to get to college next year at Bobtail JC, and I work two jobs. I don't have time to fool around much."

"Two jobs?"

"Yes sir, I work over at the motel in the mornings; and then on the weekends I work at the barbecue place over in Bobtail where Beaumont's daddy cooks sometimes."

"Has Beaumont ever come around there?"

"I ain't never seen him, but like I said, I work weekends."

Ezekiel's pickup drives up, and Alva jumps to her feet. "I got to get inside and warm up some supper for Daddy. He's hungry when he gets back at night."

I step down to greet Ezekiel. "I'm glad you came home before I left. How's Truly?"

He takes his hat off, gets out a big handkerchief, and mops his head. "About like you'd think. He's looking at hard time and he's in despair. He feels like the Lord has deserted him."

I never was much for religion, so I don't know about whether God has deserted Truly, but I know the law has.

"I'm going by tomorrow to see him. It might help him to know that I'm working hard to get him out of jail."

Bennett grunts. "I'm sure he'll appreciate that," he says. But he's being polite. I doubt he sees much possibility in my efforts.

"Is Albert Lamond still leading protests?"

He chuckles. "You know as well as I do that wasn't going to last. That man has no real interest in Truly. He only wants to get his name in the paper."

"At least he was of use in getting Truly transferred to San Antonio."

"Yessir. I suppose I should be thankful for that."

I head home to my solitary state. I don't have the heart for a big meal, so I heat up a TV dinner, feeling sorry for myself. Finally I call Jeanne. She comes to the phone laughing, which helps my spirits.

"Mamma and I were playing gin rummy," she says. "For money. She owes me $8.25." I hear her mamma laugh in the background.

"I'm glad you're having fun. Are you all set to go to Disneyland?"

"We leave tomorrow at noon. Tom is so excited that I almost never got him to sleep." She lets silence stretch for a minute and then says, "You would tell me if you are in danger, wouldn't you?"

"Probably not. What good would it do?"

"Does this have anything to do with Horace?"

"What makes you ask that?"

She sighs. "I was trying to talk to you the other night. Remember when I asked why Tom didn't seem to miss his folks, and I wondered how they could just take off without him?"

"I remember." Of course she doesn't know the half of it; that Horace and Donna have disappeared.

"I mentioned to Mary Lee that I thought it was odd. Samuel, she told me there have been rumors for some time that Horace and Donna have been involved in something illegal. And I think she meant drugs."

"When did she tell you this?"

"A few days ago," Mary Lee Bosco is her best friend. She's the doctor's wife, our only GP in town. "You know that friend of hers, Loretta Singletary? She's the one who ought to run a newspaper. She knows everything that goes on in the whole county. Anyway, she told Mary Lee that the reason the city council hired you to be police chief was so you could do something about Horace and make it go away without a lot of fuss. Did you know that? Have you been keeping all that from me?"

"No, it's news to me." I sigh. I'm glad she can't see me. My cheeks are most likely fire-red, not out of embarrassment, but because I'm furious at my brother for putting me in this position, and furious at Hazel Baker for neglecting to tell me the real reason I was hired. "Or at least I didn't when I took on the job. I guess I ought to tell you, I recently discovered what he was up to."

"You sound mad. Don't be mad long-distance, Sammie. You know I can't stand that."

"I'm not mad. Frustrated, that's all. How could Horace be so stupid? . . . Don't answer that."

"You know what I think?"

"What?"

"I think the reason you wanted me to take Tom out of town is so you could deal with Horace without involving us."

"That's part of it."

"Are you going to arrest him?"

"I haven't decided what to do."

"Be careful."

"Jeanne, Horace won't hurt me. At least not physically."

"I wish I could be there."

I wish she was here, too. Before I hang up, I tell her I love her, but it's not the same as being able to pull her close physically.

I walk to the fireplace and look at the painting she brought back last week. It has grown on me. When all this is over, I'm going to take her to Houston to look at art galleries there.

In college we dated for several months before I even knew she had more money than most of the people I went to school with. Before we went to Dallas to meet her family, she warned me, as if it were a guilty secret.

Her folks live a bit grander than we do, but as her father pointed out to me, "As you get older, you get to enjoy the fruits of your labor more. We raised Jeanne and her brothers to understand that they were fortunate to have nice things, but not to feel like they're something special just because my daddy and I were lucky in business."

I've had some worries along the line about not being able to provide for her in the same way, but she always swears that she only wants a regular life with me.

CHAPTER 37

As soon as I get to work the next morning, I call Curren Wills.

"You're up and at 'em mighty early," he says. "I was going to call and check to see if you're still alive."

"Check back tomorrow."

"Have you made any plans based on what we talked about yesterday?"

"I'd like to tell you that I have a plan, but all I have is a vague idea of shaking bushes until something jumps out."

"Just be sure that whatever jumps out isn't carrying a gun."

"I got some interesting information last night." I describe my conversation with George Cato, and his connection with Freddie Carmichael.

"That's of interest," he says, "but I don't know what good it's going to do your boy Bennett."

"A couple of things have been bothering me," I say. "I never heard what kind of gun was used in those murders. I know they recovered bullets at the autopsy, because I was there. Did Sutherland ever follow up on that?"

"You know, I haven't heard a word about that, but even if you know what kind of gun it is, I don't know what you're going to do with the information if the murders were committed by drug dealers from Houston."

"If the bullets that killed those people came from the same gun as the bullets that gunned down Clyde Wortham, Truly Bennett couldn't possibly have done it. Sutherland knows that, too. Of course, they might not match. But it's up to Sutherland to check the ballistics."

"I suppose I could call Sutherland and nudge him." He doesn't sound enthusiastic. "You said there were two things bothering you. What else?"

"Were there fingerprints taken from the dishes at the location of the murders? There were seven plates and five victims. Is it possible that undercover man in the photo might have been one of them?"

Wills sighs. "I was wondering the same thing. I'll call Sutherland and get back to you, but I seriously doubt anything was done with either."

"Why not? How can he justify letting evidence slip away?"

"Could be several reasons, but as I warned you, we may not be able to press him at this particular time. And I'm not sure anything will come of either for your friend Bennett."

"Maybe not, but I don't like loose ends."

After we hang up, I think over one of the biggest challenges I have to deal with: what to do about my brother. Now that I know he has been involved in drug dealing, I have to decide whether to track him down and arrest him, or let him escape to Houston, where he'll be someone else's problem. From what Jeanne told me on the phone, the town hired me to make the problem of my brother disappear, not necessarily to arrest him. I'm not yet clear on how I stand on the issue.

I hear a car outside, and Ezekiel Bennett comes in, hat in hand, looking grave. I freeze, wondering if something has happened to Truly in the night. "Mr. Bennett, I thought you'd be in San Antonio."

"I need to talk to you."

"Let me get you some coffee."

When we sit down, he says, "Chief Craddock, I was awake half the night, thinking. I want you to stop worrying about Truly and go back to your everyday business."

"You mean catching boys speeding on the dam road? Finding lost dogs? Straightening out bar fights?"

"Yes, sir."

I'm startled by his request. Does he think Truly is guilty? "Why would you want me to do that?"

"I appreciate what you've been trying to do for Truly. I do. But, Chief Craddock, people in this town aren't going to put up with you going on a crusade for a black man. I have lived with prejudice my whole life because of the color of my skin. I don't like it, but I'm used to it. And here you are, choosing to bear a burden you wasn't born to bear. I don't want that, and I believe my son wouldn't either. So let it alone, and we'll hope the Lord will see fit to work his wonders."

He sits back like a man satisfied with what is probably the longest speech he ever made to a white man.

Bonnie was right. I have to decide what kind of man I am. I don't have any idea whether Truly Bennett is worth getting myself in trouble for—maybe even killed. But I know that someone connected with the drug trade in Houston committed those murders. John Sutherland knows it, too, and yet he isn't willing to let Truly go. It would hurt his pride and maybe smear his arrest record. If I don't work to free Truly, I'm no better than Sutherland.

And I also know that as generous as Wills is with his time and his information, he hasn't been willing to stick his neck out by pushing Sutherland to drop the charges. I'm not going to say any of this to Bennett. I'm not a hero. I'm not taking on the whole issue of black versus white. I'm just working to free one man I know is innocent.

"I appreciate your coming by. I'll give it some thought."

He sighs and gets to his feet. "I figured you'd say something like that. I've taken your measure, and I know what kind of man you are. You won't let go."

I stand. "I'm the chief of police. And that means chief of the whole town, not only the white part."

He shakes his head and starts toward the door.

"I told you I was going to visit Truly today," I say, "but I don't think I'm going to get to it. My time will be better spent working to free him. Tell him I sent my regards."

I get another cup of coffee and sit down with the list I made yesterday of all the people involved in the case. It's as if now that I'm fully committed to seeing Truly Bennett released—whatever it takes—I finally see a pattern that leads to one man. My brother wouldn't have had the initiative to approach drug dealers about selling drugs to high school kids in Jarrett Creek by himself. Somebody had to approach him. Clyde Wortham brought his family from Houston to Jarrett Creek because he knew somebody from here. He was a drug dealer, and the person he knew was surely someone involved with drugs, too. Both point to the same man: Beaumont Penny. I doubt he killed the people in that house, but he brought drugs and violence to this town. He's the key. It's time I tracked him down. I fish out the phone number that Alvin Penny gave me, but when I dial it, I find that it has been disconnected. I sit and think how I'm going to find him, and my first stop has to be his folks'. If they don't know where he is, I expect they can find out.

Before I leave, the phone rings. It's Curren Wills. "I've been thinking, and I'm going to lend you my deputy, Luke Schoppe. The two of you are young enough to have fire in your belly, and maybe between you, you have enough sense not to get killed."

"How soon can he get here?"

"He can be there in an hour. We're over in Bryan. It'll take him a few minutes to get on the road."

"I've got something to do. I'll meet him back here in an hour."

I'm pleased that Schoppe will be with me. He doesn't say much, but he struck me as having some sense and as being alert. And, besides, I like him. He didn't try to pretend that he wasn't shocked that first day I met him, when we viewed the bodies of those poor kids killed in cold blood.

I'm glad when Alvin Penny answers the door to his house. I didn't want to resort to dragging the information I need out of Zerlene.

"I was afraid I'd see you again."

"I need to know where I can find your son Beaumont. The number you gave me isn't working."

He clamps his lips together and nods for me to follow him inside. He closes the door behind me and asks, "You think he killed those people?"

"I don't have any evidence pointing to him, but I think he knows who did."

"If he tells you, it's likely to get him killed."

He's right. "But If he doesn't, an innocent boy is going to sit in jail for a long time."

"Truly is a good boy. Known him my whole life." He looks off into a corner of his tidy front room. "Wonder what causes one man to take the low road and another to turn out all right?"

His question hits close to home, with my brother in the same league with his son. "I wish I knew. But I don't. Now I have to ask you for Beaumont's whereabouts."

"You'd go all the way to Houston to track him down?"

"I'm prepared to do that, yes."

"So you're not afraid to get yourself killed?"

"I'm going to do everything I can to make sure that doesn't happen."

He runs his hand along his jaw. "Young man like you. Willing to do what you can to get that boy out of jail. Different generation."

I hold still, letting him come to his conclusion.

"Truth is, you don't have to go all the way to Houston. Beaumont is around here."

"Where?"

"He's keeping with a lady over in Bobtail."

"You know where? And why he's staying here?"

"No, on both counts. But I can tell you that the lady goes by the name of Betty. And she's a white woman."

I head back to the station to wait for Schoppe. I'm grateful that I don't have to root around in Houston to locate Penny. I have only the name Betty to go on, but Bobtail is a lot smaller than Houston. I should be able to track Penny down.

When Schoppe arrives, I tell him what led me to conclude that Penny is the man with answers—his drug connections in Houston and my suspicion that he brought the Wortham family here. I leave out that I think he's supplying my brother with drugs to sell. "I appreciate that you're willing to throw in with me."

"I can tell my boss likes you, or he wouldn't send me over here. Said he thought I might learn something."

"Uh oh, I was thinking the same thing. Sounds like we're quite a pair."

We grin at each other. Part of me knows we could get ourselves killed, but if I don't take that risk, I won't be able to face myself.

CHAPTER 38

Schoppe and I head for the Bobtail Police Department. If there's a white woman living with a black man, it's likely the police are aware of it. Bobtail is bigger than Jarrett Creek, but it's still small enough for word of a mixed-race situation to get around pretty fast. Not to mention that with Penny being in the drug-peddling business, his girlfriend is probably hooked on something, which the police might know about, too.

"You mean Betty Whitehorse?" The duty cop nods. "Sure I know her. She says she's an Indian, but she's only one by marriage and divorce. She just claims to be an Indian so she can get extra money from the government."

The cop is leaning on his forearms and enjoying this gossip session. In the few months of training I had, one of our instructors told us that police departments have gossip lines that put old ladies to shame.

"Do you know if she has a black boyfriend?"

"Boyfriend? That's a good one." He looks closer at me. "Aren't you the man who brought in that beat-up prostitute the other night?"

"That was me. Why?"

"You better look out. People are going to think you're a regular over in that part of town." He guffaws. Seeing that I don't join in the merriment, he says, "As to your question, I haven't heard anything like that, but anything is possible. If he has money in his pocket, she'll be after it along with his pecker."

He finally gets around to looking up her last known address and gives us directions. As soon as we get close to her house, I recognize the neighborhood for what it is. Bobtail is generally free of slum areas, but this qualifies, with little houses slumped close together like they're trying to hold each other up.

The once-green exterior of Betty Whitehorse's house has peeled off to gray wood. Luckily the front porch and steps are concrete, so they haven't disintegrated like the rest of the house.

It's ten o'clock, and Betty opens the door in a short robe, rubbing sleep from her eyes. She's a big-boned woman with plenty of padding. Her long, black hair is in wild disarray, and her dark eyes are bloodshot. "What do you want? I'm off work." The sweet smell of marijuana wafts out into the open air.

I identify myself and Luke Schoppe. "We're looking for a man by the name of Beaumont Penny. It's a matter of some urgency, and I understand he's staying here with you."

She runs her tongue over her teeth, an unattractive sight. "I don't know who told you that, but I don't know anybody by that name. What kind of a name is Beaumont anyway?" The way she smirks, I'm pretty sure Penny is listening and she's jerking his chain.

"If I asked your neighbors, would they have seen him?"

"If they said they did, you couldn't trust them. Not one of them wouldn't lie for the hell of it. Jealous." She reaches up and blots at perspiration glistening between her big breasts.

"I'm not looking to get Mr. Penny in trouble. I just need some information." Speaking of lying.

"Trouble or not, he still ain't here."

Schoppe says, "Tell you what, Craddock. I'll stay here and watch the place, and you go back to the police station and arrange for a search warrant. And while you're at it, maybe get a warrant to look for drugs, too. I think I smell a little whiff of something on the air."

"Hold on, now," Betty says. "There's no need for all that."

"Betty, let me talk to these men." A man I take to be Penny steps up next to Betty. He's as skinny as she is hefty, with his hair puffed up in an afro that makes his head look like a flower on top of a lean stalk. I have an uncomfortable picture of the two of them nestled up in bed together. Mr. and Mrs. Jack Sprat.

"You Beaumont Penny?" I ask.

"That's me. I guess you're Craddock, the man who has been bothering my daddy."

"Did he say that?"

"He didn't have to. I know what you small-town cops are like. You'll do anything to pin something on a black man."

"I think you'll find I'm trying to do the opposite. Can we come inside?"

"I'd as soon you didn't," Betty says, settling her hands onto her hips.

"It's Betty's abode," Penny says. "If she doesn't want us inside, we'll sit out on the porch."

We sit on three rickety, wooden folding chairs.

"You know Truly Bennett?" I ask. "He's from Jarrett Creek."

He makes a show of looking out at the sky with a puzzled look on his face. "Don't recollect anybody by that name," he says.

"His daddy is Ezekiel Bennett, and his sister is Alva. They live down the street from your daddy in Jarrett Creek." At the mention of Alva's name, his eyes twitch.

"Now I know who you mean. He's a nice young man. I understand he got himself into some trouble, though."

"He didn't get into it by himself. He's been wrongly accused of a crime."

"That's no surprise. Like I said, it's easy for a black man to find trouble."

"Trouble you can get him out of." It's hot on the porch, and I'm sweating. The street is deserted except for a dog sprawled in the middle. I suspect many of the women and men who live here work nights.

"If I'm not mistaken, he's in jail for killing those people in Jarrett Creek. I don't know what you think I can do for him. I was in Houston at the time of the murders."

"You know Horace Craddock?"

He's startled by the quick change of subject. "The name sounds familiar."

"I'll bet it does." I glance at Schoppe and see that he's wondering the same thing Penny is, except that he doesn't know Horace has been running drugs. "Because you've been supplying him with drugs to sell to the high school kids around here."

"Whoa now, that's a mighty high-flyin' accusation. Where do you get an idea like that?" He sits up tall. His jovial manner has turned suddenly menacing. "If he told you that, he's lying."

"I'm not at liberty to tell you where I got the information."

"An accusation of that kind could get a man killed, you know." His smile could freeze blood.

"Is that a threat?" Schoppe asks. His voice has steel in it.

"Statin' a fact, that's all."

"Let me state another fact for you." I move my hand to my gun. Although I've always been a good shot, I don't often carry the Colt, but I figured it might be a good idea until things settle down. "I can always see to it that you spend a little time in jail on suspicion of murder and selling drugs. Even if it doesn't stick, I can make your life difficult."

"You can't do that. You don't have a thing to go on, and I'll make a claim against you for false arrest."

"I'll cross that bridge when we get to it. It ought to be interesting to find out what your Houston drug connection will do when he finds out you're in jail."

"They won't do nothing because there's no such animal." He stands up. "Matter of fact, I need to call my lawyer before I say another word. I was trying to help you out, but this has gone too far."

Schoppe and I stand up, too. Schoppe says, "You can make the call at the station. Right now, you need to come with us." He nods to me. "You want to read him the words?"

"I guess I ought to." I get my card out and read the *Miranda* words to him. He looks bored.

When I'm done, he says, "At least let me tell my lady where I'm going."

"I'll tell her myself when we get you safe inside the squad car," Schoppe says.

We escort Penny down the steps between the two of us and secure him in the backseat of the squad car. Schoppe goes back up to tell Betty Whitehorse what's going on, although I expect she has been listening.

I'm sweating fully now. I'm way out of my depth. I thought maybe the fear of arrest would shake something loose from Beaumont Penny, but he's a lot slicker a character than I am. I know I can't hold him long, but at least I can rattle the cage of his dealer.

Schoppe motions that he wants to speak to me out of range of Penny's hearing. We walk down the street a ways. He grins at me. "I hope you know what you're doing."

"Not a clue."

We laugh.

"What next?" he asks. "He looks like a hard case to me. Not likely to volunteer much."

"I agree. He's a decoy. I said before that all I'm after is getting Bennett released. But that's not completely true. There's more. We've got a drug problem in Jarrett Creek. I believe whoever killed those people are connected to the drug trade as well. I hope that bringing Penny in will put them on notice that I'm not going to tolerate illegal drugs."

"I thought you were steering clear of the Houston drug business. That's a nest of hornets."

"I don't expect a bunch of big-time drug dealers from Houston to descend on Jarrett Creek and shoot up the place, but they've extended their territory this way, recruiting no-account people out to make a buck to sell drugs to school kids. What I hope is that if they think the law in this county gets stirred up enough, they'll back off."

For the first time, Schoppe looks worried. "I hope you're right."

When we get Penny back to the station in Jarrett Creek, he's all bluff and swagger. Tilley stands up when we walk in, and he eyes Penny with alarm. "What's he doing here?"

I explain who he is. Tilley can't keep his eyes off Penny. I guess he's impressed that we have a minor celebrity in custody.

I take Penny to the jail and put him in a cell.

"This place is mighty nasty," he says. His lips curl as he looks at the stained mattress.

He's right. It's an old building that has seen a lot of drunks and minor criminals who had nothing better to do than draw on the walls when they weren't puking or sweating out alcohol. "I know this isn't the first time you've seen the inside of a jail."

"When am I going to get my phone call?"

"Soon. I need to go get some lunch. You want anything? Enchiladas at the café are pretty good."

His mouth falls open. "I don't need any damn lunch. I need to call my lawyer."

"Suit yourself. I'll be back in a little bit."

I close the door behind me. Tilley is sitting up straight at his desk, eyes trained on the door I came out of. "You think he's the one that murdered those people?" His voice is hushed.

"No. I think he knows who did, though."

I ask Tilley if he wants to join Schoppe and me at the café, but he tells me he's going home for lunch. Schoppe and I stroll over to the café and take our time eating and exchanging cop talk. Although we know Penny is a small fry, we're both as keyed up as if we have made a major arrest.

I take a plate of enchiladas wrapped in foil back for Penny. He waves it away. I tell him to take the plate because he may find that he's hungry later.

"There's not going to be any later," he says. "My lawyer will have me out of here this afternoon."

I make another attempt to get him to talk to me, but he's adamant that he won't say another word without a lawyer.

Handcuffing his hands behind him, I bring him into the front room and ask him the lawyer's telephone number.

"If you'll take these cuffs off, I can dial it for myself," he says.

"I'd better do it for you. Wouldn't want you to misdial." It has occurred to me that he might call someone who pretends to be his lawyer.

He gives me a number, and the man who answers doesn't identify himself as a lawyer. "Who am I speaking with?" I ask.

"Who is it you're calling?"

"Hold on." I cover the mouthpiece and say, "I think this is the wrong number. What did you say your lawyer's name is?"

"Milton Consecci."

"I'm looking for an attorney by the name of Consecci," I say.

There's a moment of silence.

"You still there?" I ask.

"I'm here. Who did you say you were?"

"This is Chief Samuel Craddock of the Jarrett Creek Police, and I have a man here in custody who wants to speak with Mr. Consecci."

"Who is it?"

"His name is Beaumont Penny." I raise my eyebrows at Penny, along with a fake smile, and he looks murder at me.

"Why didn't you say so? Hold on. I'll get Consecci."

"He's coming," I say to Penny. If he could shoot nails out of his eyes, I'd be attached to the wall.

A man comes on the line with a deep, authoritative voice. "Let me speak with Penny," he says.

"Are you Mr. Consecci?"

"Yes. Put him on."

I hold the phone to Penny's ear.

Penny's tone is less arrogant with the man who is supposedly his lawyer. He tells Consecci what happened and asks him to come and get him out of "this no-good hick police station."

He listens and his eyes narrow. "What do you mean 'tomorrow'? You're supposed to be available any time." Penny is quiet for a bit, then says, "All right. First thing in the morning."

He leans back, indicating the call is over, and I hang up the phone. "I expect you'll want those enchiladas now," I say.

He doesn't reply, but I didn't think he would.

I call Wills to find out if he's gotten any forensic information on the bullets from Sutherland. He sounds aggravated. "No, but I'm ready to go to his higher-ups and get some satisfaction. I don't know what good it will do, but I'm tired of him dragging his feet."

I tell Schoppe he ought to get back to Bryan, that I don't have big plans for the afternoon except to work on Penny a little more. As soon as he's gone, I go back to the cell. Penny is sitting on the cot, forearms on his knees. When he sees me, he rises. "I don't suppose you'd let me call Betty. She could bring me some cigarettes."

"No, but I'll call your daddy, and he can bring you some."

His expression is pained. "Don't call Daddy. He doesn't need to see me behind bars."

"You should have thought of that a long time ago."

"Listen here, I've got some advice for you. You're getting into something you don't want to mess with."

I open my mouth to reply, but he holds up his hand. "I know who you are, and I know you're trying to help get this kid out of jail. It's not every lawman who's willing to step up. If I could help you, I would, but I'm not in a position to do that."

"It's not just about Truly," I say. "It's about drugs being sold to the high school kids. I want it stopped."

"You're trying to push the wind," he says.

"A girl overdosed this week. If I turn a blind eye, before I know it, somebody will die, and then it will be my fault for being a coward. You can tell that to your drug connection. I want this town left alone."

"Big talk." He sits back down on the cot.

It's the first time he's been straight with me, and the first time I've had a chance to let people outside of Jarrett Creek know my mission. I go over to the gas station and buy him a pack of cigarettes. I spend what's left of the afternoon at my desk, waiting for a sign of trouble, but it's quiet. Even the petty criminals seem to have taken the day off.

CHAPTER 39

I don't know how long I've been asleep when the sound of my front door squeaking and the door closing wakes me. For a second, I think I'm dreaming, and then I wonder if Jeanne has decided to come home. Quiet footsteps approach my bedroom, and I reach under my pillow and grab the Colt. "Hold it right there," I say, as I swing my legs off the side of the bed and grope for my pants. My hands are sweating. Have I been a fool to lie down and sleep as if everything is normal?

"Samuel, it's me."

"Horace, why can't you knock the way most people do?"

"I didn't want to wake Jeanne."

"She isn't here." I reach over and turn on the bedside lamp.

My older brother is my height, but a lot leaner, almost emaciated. In the shadows, his face looks like a skull, and I wonder why I haven't noticed that he looks like a drug addict. His clothes, a black T-shirt and khaki pants, look like they haven't been changed in a good while.

I put on my pants and get a T-shirt out of the chest of drawers and pull it on. "Let's go in the kitchen." I don't want my brother in my bedroom.

When we get to the kitchen I square off with him. "Now what do you want?"

"You have a beer?"

"What time is it?"

"Midnight."

I grab a couple of beers, and we go sit on the front porch.

"Samuel, you've pissed off some people, and I'm scared you're going to get yourself killed."

"What people?"

"People that have an interest in Beaumont Penny."

"I'm touched at your concern, but you should have thought of that before you started dealing drugs with him."

"You've got it all wrong."

"Oh, come on, Horace, who do you think you're talking to? Everybody in town knows you're selling drugs to high school kids. That's why they hired me to be police chief. They thought I could corral you."

"Where did you hear that?"

"Never mind. Did you know that a young girl overdosed a couple of days ago? And I caught the kid who supplied her with her pills smoking dope out at the lake last weekend. This has got to stop."

"It's got nothing to do with me. The kid out at the lake you're talking about was Charlie Ostrand, is that right?"

"Yes, you know him?"

"Sort of."

I can't sit anymore, and I'm so mad I could haul off and punch Horace. I walk over to the porch rail and lean against the post. "I told you that the other night I went to the drug drop-off point and got knocked out for my trouble, but not before I heard your voice."

He stays still as a stone.

"You can't deny that."

"All right, but it has nothing to do with Beaumont Penny."

"He's not supplying you with drugs?"

He leans over with his elbows on his knees. His voice is desolate. "No, he's way over my head."

"What does that mean?"

"It means he's one of the big guns from Houston." He gets up and walks over close to me, keeping his voice low. "The only reason I'm here is that I'm trying to keep you from getting yourself killed. Hell, I may get myself killed by interfering."

"You'll forgive me if I find it hard to be too concerned. You brought this on both of us. You're lazy and looking for easy money."

He groans. "You don't need to be so all-fired holier-than-thou, Samuel. I was looking for a way to keep a roof over my family's head."

"There are other ways, Horace, but they involve work." All of a sudden I realize that I sound like our mamma. Maybe she was always disgusted at our daddy after he started drinking. Maybe I inherited some lucky genes that bypassed Horace. "Look, you've put me in a spot. I ought to arrest you. How do you think I'd feel handcuffing you and marching you down to the jailhouse?"

"It would be a damn sight better than you poking your nose in where it doesn't belong. You have to let Penny go."

"Horace, there are two issues here. One, I want the drug dealing to stop here in Jarrett Creek. Bobtail can do what they want with it, but I want it out of my town. And two, I want Truly Bennett out of jail. That's why I've got Beaumont Penny in custody. And I told him the same thing this afternoon."

"Are you kidding me? You really do have a death wish."

"I don't give a damn what Penny does in Houston. I just don't want it here. I figured if he was supplying drugs, I could stop it. Now you tell me Penny isn't supplying you with drugs? Who is?"

"You sure you want to know?"

"Of course I do."

His voice goes hard. "Sometimes you're not as smart as you think you are. Why don't you think on it a minute? Who has a finger in every single thing that happens in this town and can move around as he pleases, no questions asked?"

It sounds like he could be describing me, but I know I'm not the culprit. My head starts to pound as the implication hits me. "A cop."

I already know before he says, "Tilley. You said everybody knows I was dealing drugs, but did you ever wonder why Tilley didn't take the job as chief?"

"They told me he was moving to Waco."

"That was his excuse, but you'll notice he didn't go nowhere."

"Seems like it would have been more convenient for him to be supplying drugs if he was chief."

"Not at all. He has to move around a good bit, all over the county, and as a deputy nobody pays a bit of attention to what he does or where he goes. Not to mention he's all up in the volunteer fire department. Makes hisself look good."

"Where does he get the drugs?"

"That's where Penny comes in. I'm not up on the details. I'm not that high in the food chain."

I remember Tilley's face when he saw Penny this afternoon, and his warnings. "That son of a bitch."

"What are you going to do?"

"That's not your concern. Where is Donna?"

"She's back at our place. For tonight."

"Why are you two planning to move to Houston?"

"What do you care? We'll be out of your way."

"I care because if you're getting deeper into peddling drugs, you can't take Tom with you. Look what they did to that poor family that moved here. They won't think twice about killing him if you cross them."

"I don't plan to get crossways with any of those people."

"I'm going to make you an offer, and I want you to take me up on it."

He's quiet, and seconds roll past, giving me the chance to consider what I will do if he refuses, which he may well do.

"I'm listening."

"I want to give you the money to get out of here. Leave the state, or at least the area, and get started somewhere else. I'll give you enough to live on while you figure out what you want to do."

He snickers. "You're mighty handy at spending your wife's money."

"I know Jeanne wants a good life for Tom, and she'll be glad to make that happen."

"If I say no?"

"Give yourself tonight to think about it. Talk it over with Donna."

He stomps down the front steps and is gone. The air has cooled off some. I go inside and pour myself two fingers of bourbon and go back out on the porch to sip it. I have plenty to think about, but one thought tops all the others. Not once did he ask where Tom was.

CHAPTER 40

I wake up exhausted, although I slept straight through once I fell asleep. The air last night was cool, but this morning it's heavy. When I go down to tend to the cows, they seem as listless as I feel. The sun is out, but there's a haze in the air, and I expect it will be clouding up soon.

I'm not looking forward to the day. The only bright spot is thinking that Jeanne and Tom are having a blast in California.

Usually I eat a good breakfast, but this morning I make do with two cups of strong coffee and a couple pieces of toast. I want to be sure I get to the station before anyone else. I'm there by seven thirty, which makes me laugh at myself. Eldridge is on duty today, and he won't be in until nine at the earliest.

I poke my head into the jail and find Penny snoring, so I close the door quietly. Who says the guilty don't get a good night's sleep?

I make a pot of coffee and put my feet up on the desk and think. Tilley. Cato. Beaumont Penny. My brother, Horace. And of course there's John Sutherland. What to do with them? I've done what I can to invite the drug dealers to leave town, but how do I get Truly Bennett freed? I wish there was some way to broadcast to the cutthroats in Houston that I don't want too much. Just that. The rest of it—figuring out who killed that family—that's somebody else's job. I wish there was somebody to tell me what to do. I could talk it over with Wills, or maybe Bonnie Bedichek, or even Sheriff Newberry. But each of them has their own agenda. This is what being a lawman is all about. Taking the responsibility on my shoulders. If I hadn't planned to do that, I shouldn't have taken the job.

If I were smart, I'd let Beaumont Penny go, arrest my brother, and pretend he never told me about Tilley. I'd call John Sutherland and politely ask if he'd change his mind about dropping charges against Truly Bennett, and act regretful when he declined. I'd call Ezekiel Bennett and tell him I'm sorry that I couldn't help Truly, but that I know eventually he'll be cleared. I'd let the police corruption investigation take its course. I might even call Jeanne and tell her I'm taking the first plane to join her in Disneyland. I imagine her face lighting up when I say the words.

Of course, if I did all that, I would have to lay my badge on the desk as I walked out. I wouldn't feel like much of a man.

I take out Sutherland's business card and pull the phone toward me. He answers after a few rings. "I'd like to come by your office."

"What for? I'm busy." He's surly, but so am I.

"I have some information that might be important to you."

He pauses a couple of beats. I imagine him puzzling over what I could possibly know that would be of interest to him.

"Tell me on the phone."

"No." I would normally say something like, I'd rather tell him in person—something friendly. A friendly puppy talking to a big dog. But I don't feel friendly, and I don't feel like a puppy.

I expect him to snarl back at me, but he says, "All right, if you're so all-fired determined to take a drive, come on."

Thirty minutes later, I'm in his office. I've thought out carefully the way I'm going to handle this, and when he asks me what I've got for him, I say, "First of all, when I'm done with what I've got to tell you, I want you to release Truly Bennett."

He guffaws. "You've really got a hard-on for this Bennett boy, don't you?"

"He didn't kill those people, and you know it."

"What makes you think I know that?"

"You would have turned over the forensics on the bullets."

"How do you figure that?"

"I expect the bullets recovered in those murders were from the same gun that killed a drug dealer in Houston after Bennett was in jail."

"You really are wet behind the ears. Anybody with the slightest experience would know that whoever murdered the people in your town would get rid of the weapon as soon as they could."

"They would if they thought there was a chance of somebody making the connection. But my guess is they thought a hick cop and a disinterested member of the highway patrol wouldn't make the connection. Why get rid of a perfectly good weapon if you don't have to?" I call him "disinterested" rather than crooked because I don't want him to get the slightest hint that anyone suspects he is corrupt. He might not be. He might just be lazy and looking for an easy way to seem like he's solved the murder case.

"So you want me to say the word to get Bennett out of jail."

"That's not the only thing I want. I want the drug business out of Jarrett Creek."

"That doesn't have anything to do with me."

"I'm telling you what I'm after. I've already put them on notice."

He blinks. "What do you mean?"

"Just what I said." I'm not ready to drop Penny's name yet.

"You don't care who killed those people on your turf?" he asks.

"Of course I care, but everything I've uncovered tells me it was done by people involved in a drug dispute in Houston. I can't pursue that. It's out of my jurisdiction. That's up to Houston law enforcement."

"Fair enough. Now, what information do you have that's important enough to sell me on the idea of letting Bennett go?"

"Information that could make your career. I've got the name of the person in this county who is the dealer for the illicit drugs being sold around here, and his Houston connection."

"How do I know the information is real?"

"I'll give it to you, and you can check it out."

"You better believe I will."

So I tell him what I know about Beaumont Penny and my own deputy, Doug Tilley. If Sutherland is crooked, he already knows about Penny, and he won't want the information to go any farther than his office. If he doesn't know, it gives him a chance to make a name for himself. And either way, it gives him a good excuse for letting Truly Bennett go.

Leaving his office, I'm sweating and my hands are shaking. I don't know whether I've killed myself or not with what I've set in motion.

When I get back to the station, I'm not happy to find Tilley there. I had planned to call Wills right away and describe my meeting with Sutherland. I'm not ready to confront Tilley yet.

"What are you doing here?" I ask. "Eldridge is on today."

"He wasn't feeling too good, and I said I'd come by in his place."

"Nice of you."

He gestures toward the back. "Why is Beaumont Penny still back there? I thought you were going to call his lawyer."

"Lawyer said he was going to be here first thing this morning. I guess first thing means different things to different people. Anyway, I'm going to let him go."

"He shouldn't have been here to begin with." There's an edge to his voice. Have I heard it before and ignored it, or is it a new development?

"I'm sure he'd agree." I look at my watch. "Matter of fact, would you be good enough to do the honors? I'm supposed to be somewhere."

His relief shows on his face, and now he's all innocence. "What should I tell him?"

"Give him my sincere apologies, and tell him I'm young and don't know what the hell I'm doing."

His laugh grates on me. "Don't be too hard on yourself."

I'd like to hit him, but now is not the time to play my hand.

I drive home and call Wills from there. When I tell him the information my brother divulged about Tilley and Penny, and about my visit to Sutherland this morning, he whistles. "I like it when I don't overestimate people, but you're exceeding expectations. The Feds will be interested to know what Sutherland does with the information you gave him."

"That's what I was hoping you'd say."

When I hang up, I feel at loose ends. It's a waiting game to see if Sutherland or my brother rises to the bait I've handed them. I dread my brother's answer. I don't relish the idea of handcuffing him and hauling him off to jail, but he may leave me no choice. I consider whether I ought to drive over to his apartment and nudge him, but instead I walk down to spend a few minutes with my cows. It's peaceful in the pasture, and I am pleased to see that they seem to have settled in. The full-grown ones pay no attention to me, but the yearlings come to the fence to take a look at me. I rub a couple of noses.

My plan was to go back to headquarters, but when I get back to the house, Horace's car is sitting out front. I round the corner to the front of the house and find Horace and Donna sitting on the porch steps.

"You could have gone on in," I say. "It's hot out here."

Donna's eyes and the tip of her nose are red. Her bruises have faded to a dull yellow and lavender. "Where's Tom?"

"He's not here right now."

"They told us at school that he won't be in this week. What have you done with him?" Her voice is full of tears and aggravation.

"I've had a few problems here in town, and I was concerned about danger, so I sent him and Jeanne off for a few days. They're in California."

"You had no right to send him off without telling us. That's kidnapping."

"Not exactly, since you brought him to my house to stay with me. I didn't know how to get in touch with you, and I thought it was a matter of some urgency to get him and Jeanne out of here." I glance over at Horace, and he's staring at the floor near his feet.

"Horace, did you and Donna talk about my offer?"

He shoves his hands in his pockets and meets my eyes, glaring.

"What offer?" Donna asks.

"Doesn't matter, we're not going to do it," Horace says. "I came by to tell you we're headed for Houston. We want to ask you and Jeanne if you'd mind taking care of Tom until we get settled."

Donna's eyes are wild. "I thought I'd get to say good-bye, though. And what kind of offer are you talking about?"

"It was nothing." Horace's tone is sharp. "I'll bring you back to see Tom when he gets back here."

"Donna, Jeanne or I will bring Tom to see you. He'll want to see you, I know."

She stands up, lips clamped together, her eyes welling with tears. "I guess we'd better get on." She walks off the porch, headed toward the car. I notice now that the backseat is filled with household goods.

"Horace, I . . ." I was going to say I want him to reconsider, but he puts his hand up to stop me.

"I'll call you when we get settled," he says.

I stick my hand out to shake his, and he reluctantly takes it. "Have you told Mamma?" I ask.

He looks toward the car and brings his hand up to brush the top of his head. "I didn't want to upset her."

Fury wells up in me. He's a coward. How did I never see that? How did that happen? How did he become someone who sneaks out on his son and his mamma and decides to make a living on the wrong side of the law? But it won't do me any good to let loose on him. He's had plenty of that in his life from our mamma. Maybe there's an answer in there somewhere.

As they drive away, I get a lump in my throat, not for myself, but for the sake of their boy. How would he feel, knowing they've just taken off without him?

CHAPTER 41

I'm not in a good mood to go back to headquarters, but I can't think what else to do. I need to wait to hear from Sutherland, and he's not likely to call me at home. I've struck out with one deal. My brother has opted for the dark side. It would be easy enough for Sutherland to ignore me, and then I'd be faced with failure all around. I don't think I'm asking so much. It's not like I'll ever solve the question of who murdered that family. All I'm asking is that the wrong man not be convicted and that drug dealers leave this place alone.

On the way to the station, I stop by the café and pick up some enchiladas to go. I'm at my desk with a mouthful when the phone rings. It's the school principal.

"Haven't heard from you since that incident with the girl," Gilpin says. "I wondered what the status is."

"She got out of the hospital. Is she back in school?"

"Not yet. But I'm getting some pressure from Ostrand. I'd like to tell him if his son is off the hook."

"Can I get back to you tomorrow?"

"Can't you tell me how things are going now?"

"Tomorrow," I say.

"If you say so." He sounds startled at my sharp tone. He no longer intimidates me. Nothing like feeling like you may be killed by drug dealers to put everyday life in perspective.

I've mopped up the last of the enchiladas, and I am staring at the phone, waiting for it to ring, when I hear a car outside. I hope it's not Tilley.

I hear two sets of footsteps crunching on the gravel outside, and then the door opens. Ezekiel Bennett looms in the doorway, with someone behind him. "Look who's here," he says. He steps aside, and Truly Bennett steps into the room.

I jump up and walk over to shake his hand. "What in the world happened? How did you get out?"

"That's what I'd like to know," he says. "They came in two hours ago and told me the highway patrol had directed them to let me go. They didn't need to tell me twice. Didn't take ten minutes for them to push me out the front door."

I look at Ezekiel and grin. It's the first time I've felt like smiling in a while. It's taking a minute to sink in that my talk with Sutherland succeeded. "You must have been surprised."

"I was and I wasn't. You know I've been keeping myself outside the jailhouse every day, waiting for him to walk out of there, so in a way I knew it would happen. I knew because I believed you were serious about getting him out. But I didn't think it would be quite this fast." His expression is somber. It would be the right time for a smile, but I don't think he's allowed himself to really believe Truly is out yet.

I turn to Truly. "Does your sister know?"

"We stopped by the motel where she works so Daddy could tell her. She said we're going to have a celebration tonight. She wanted me to invite you."

"I appreciate that. I may stop by, but this is your celebration. I won't interrupt."

"No, sir, you won't get off that easy," Ezekiel says.

Finally he smiles. It seems like there ought to be some kind of fanfare. I've noticed that when big things happen in life, often it seems commonplace after a nervous wait. "Truly, you look like you could use some rest. You better be prepared. I expect reporters are going to descend on you the minute they find out you've been released." I'm thinking particularly of Bonnie Bedichek, whom I'm going to call the minute they're gone.

"I am tired and I'm going home, but first I want to know what you did to get me out."

I don't know what to tell him. That I made a deal with the devil? That I stood up to a man who may or not be corrupt? Or that maybe Sutherland was just a racist and pigheaded? I finally tell him the only thing that makes sense, "Persevered."

"How can I ever pay you?"

"Truly, it's my job. But there is one thing. As soon as you've had time to celebrate, come on over to the pasture and take a look at my cows. I think they look pretty good, but I need an expert eye."

"Tomorrow morning, first thing."

Ezekiel leads his son out the door as if he's afraid to let go of him for fear he'll be snatched back.

I want to bask in the pleasure of one success, but there is something I have to do. I put in a call to Tilley's house, and his wife says he isn't home.

"You know where he is?"

"He said he had a couple of errands to run, and then he'd swing back by work."

I wish I had been here when he let Beaumont Penny go. I wonder if I ought to go to Alvin Penny's house and find out if Beaumont is holed up there, or if he's gone back to his girlfriend's place. I'm going to have to have a talk with Alvin Penny and tell him I don't want his son back here in town. I'm losing a brother, and he'll lose a son. It's an even deal.

It occurs to me that if I do my job right, I need to write up a report on all that has happened. There needs to be a record of things. I should file it with Newberry. I don't know if Eldridge ever did anything like that. It strikes me how little I know about the administrative end of being a police chief.

There's another car pulling into the parking lot. I steel myself for Tilley, and sure enough it's him. His face is red, and his shirt is rumpled, with sweat stains under the arms. The fact that I turned Tilley's name over to Sutherland, and that Tilley is still walking around, tells me all I need to know with regard to Sutherland. I'll tell Wills, and he can add the information to the corruption investigation.

I don't say a word, just watch him stride across the floor and plop down in his chair. He pulls the chair up to the front of my desk and says, "What the hell do you think you're doing?"

"With regard to what?"

"You think you're pretty clever, don't you? Ratting me out to John Sutherland."

I lean forward across the desk. This man has at least ten years on me, but he's a fool and I'm not. "Here's what I think. At one time you planned to move to Waco. Apparently you changed your mind. Now it's time to change it back. Wherever you go, I want to see the last of you."

"How am I supposed to do that?"

"That's not my concern. You have until tomorrow morning. If you're gone by then, you leave with your raggedy-ass reputation. If you don't, I'll see to it that this town knows what you were up to. Now get out of my police station."

He snickers. "That's pretty big talk."

I turn away from him and start writing my report. After a minute, he gets up, but remains standing in front of me, and waits. I don't look up, and in a minute, he stalks out. I let out a breath I've been holding. I know he won't defy me and stick around.

CHAPTER 42

After I settle down, I call the school principal. "Gilpin, this is Samuel Craddock. As it happens, I don't have to wait until tomorrow to tell you that you shouldn't have any more problems with outside drug dealers. I can't stop kids from stealing drugs out of their folks' medicine cabinets, but that no-good kid Charlie Ostrand is out of business."

"How did that happen?"

"I Iad a meeting of the minds with a few people. You can let Charlie back on the football team. That is, if the coach wants him back."

"What should I tell his daddy?"

"Leave him to me."

"Craddock, I'd appreciate it if you'd be diplomatic."

"I'll do my best, but I wouldn't count on it. If you have any more problems, be sure and let me know."

I dial Raymond Ostrand's telephone number. His secretary says he isn't available, but I tell her I'll bet he'll want to know I called. While I wait for him to call back, I stare at Tilley's desk and think of the two deputies I'm left with. I wonder if Eldridge had the slightest idea that Tilley was using his position on the police force to cover up his drug dealing. I'm sure poor Johnny Pat had no idea. Who am I going to get to replace Tilley?

Ostrand's call comes within a few minutes. "This better be a conversation with you telling me you're done picking on my son."

"You're probably going to want to increase his allowance."

"Why is that?"

"He won't be making spending money selling drugs anymore."

"Now you listen here . . ."

"No, you listen. I have a message for you to give him. Tell him the drug supply line is no longer operational. I've plugged it up."

"He won't have any idea what you're talking about."

"Oh, really? He's the one who told me how he got the drugs to begin with, so he'll want to know that it's closed down. And there's one more thing. If I hear that he's mixed up with any more drug dealing, I'll haul him in."

"Craddock, I'll pass that off as hotheaded words from a man too young to be in your position. I believe a suggestion from me to Sheriff Newberry will knock you back a peg. You'll be answering to another chief of police before you know it."

"We'll see." I have no idea if he'll try to make good on his threat or if Newberry would comply, but if either of them does, I'll fight it.

I have to wait until tonight to call Jeanne and tell her she and Tom can come home whenever she's ready. But right now I have another task that gives me pleasure.

Bonnie Bedichek's car is in her driveway, and before I get to the door, she comes charging out with a board in one hand and a hammer in the other.

"Whoa! Where are you going? You almost knocked me down," I say, jumping back.

She has a funny look on her face, like I've caught her at something she wants to keep hidden. "What are you doing here?" she asks.

"I promised you a scoop, and I'm here to deliver."

Her mouth falls open. "Okay." She lays the board and hammer down on the steps. "Come on inside."

If anything, her place is more chaotic than it was, but it looks like she's doing some heavy cleaning. There are boxes open on the floor, some of them half filled.

She gets iced tea for both of us, and we sit down in the clutter. "What kind of scoop?"

I can't help but grin. "First off, Truly Bennett has been released."

Bonnie laughs. "That's a relief. How did you manage that?"

On the way over, I thought about how much to tell her. I can't tell her the whole story, but I can give her some good copy. "I can't tell you the details, but I found evidence that meant Truly couldn't have killed them. I took the evidence to John Sutherland, and he agreed to free Truly." I'm stretching the truth, but it's the only way to tell the story without revealing the ongoing corruption investigation. It will give her enough to write about anyway.

She smiles at me in the way I think a proud big sister would smile. "I'm really pleased for you. You stepped up."

"I'll be honest with you, Bonnie. I doubt I would have stuck my neck out if you hadn't poked me."

"No, you get the credit. Now what's happening with the drug situation? Have you gotten anywhere with figuring out who has been selling to the kids?"

I've thought this over, too, and I'm pretty sure I'm right. "You already knew my brother was mixed up in that, didn't you?"

She nods.

"Why didn't you tell me?"

"I didn't know how much you knew. I figured you'd get the picture sooner or later. Have you arrested him?"

I tell her that Horace and Donna have taken off. "I wish I could say I think they're going to get themselves on a better track, but I doubt it."

"I heard a rumor that you had Beaumont Penny in jail overnight."

I run my hand along my jaw. I'd love to be able to brag on that part of it, but I can't. "It was a misunderstanding." I can't resist adding, "But I doubt he'll be around much anymore."

"Ah. I see."

"And you might also want to know that I'll be looking for a new deputy. Doug Tilley has decided to get on up to Waco after all."

I see by her expression that she understands what I mean, that

Tilley was involved. She reaches over and grabs my hand. "You've cleaned house! Good for you." She stands up. "That's a good scoop." Her lips are trembling. "It will make a good final edition." Her voice wobbles and her eyes tear up.

I get to my feet. "What do you mean?"

"Samuel, I'm done. I'm tired of holding a small-town newspaper together on my own. I'm out of money and out of enthusiasm. I applied to work at the city newspaper in Corpus Christi, and they hired me. I've had the offer for a couple of weeks, but I finally made up my mind." She laughs and dabs at her eyes. "They hired me for the women's section. Can you imagine that?"

So that's what the half full boxes mean. She's packing. I shove one with my foot. "You're going to hate working for an editor after being your own boss."

"Ha! You'd be surprised. I've struggled with this damned rag of a newspaper for ten years, and I don't want to do it anymore."

"Who's going to take over?"

She shakes her head. "I doubt if anybody will be as stubborn as I am, and there sure isn't any money in it. But maybe somebody will go for it."

"I don't even know how it gets printed," I say.

"Most people think it's magic. I contract with a printing operation in Bryan–College Station. But I do all the work myself. I won't say it wasn't satisfying on some level, but I'm worn out."

I'm genuinely sorry to see her go. "I'm going to miss you. I barely got acquainted with you."

"We made a good team." Her smile is sad. "It's sort of your fault I decided to go."

"What did I have to do with it?"

"You made me see how I'd been spinning my wheels with George Cato all these years. I knew if I stayed here, I'd get old waiting for him to come around. I need something new in my life." She gestures toward the front door. "Come on outside. I was just about to put up the 'For Sale' sign."

We go out, and I get her to let me pound the sign into the ground in front of her house. For a wild minute I envy her going off for a new adventure, but the feeling subsides by the time I get back to headquarters.

There's a message from Letitia Sandler that this time goats have gotten in her garden. Who needs more excitement than that?

ACKNOWLEDGMENTS

This book is loosely based on a real-life crime that had been in my mind for a long time as the basis for a story. When I started to write the book, I looked up the details and found out that the man who was originally convicted of the crime had recently been freed through the hard work of the Innocence Project. My deepest admiration for this amazing group, which in 1992 was founded by Peter Neufeld and Barry Scheck at Cardozo School of Law, and which, according to its mission statement, "exonerates the wrongly convicted through DNA testing and reforms the criminal justice system to prevent future injustice."

I have a wonderful writers group, and once again would like to thank them for keeping me on track. Staci, Robert, and Laird, you are the best.

Thank you always to my agent, Janet Reid, whose use of the carrot and the stick is masterful.

ABOUT THE AUTHOR

Terry Shames grew up in Texas, a vast and varied landscape that still drives her imagination. She is the author of the bestselling Samuel Craddock series. *A Killing at Cotton Hill* was awarded the Macavity Award for Best First Novel of 2013, and *The Last Death of Jack Harbin* was nominated for the Macavity Award for Best Mystery Novel of 2014. She is a member of Sisters in Crime and Mystery Writers of America. Follow her at www.TerryShames.com.

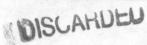

DATE DUE

This item is Due on
or before Date shown.

FEB - - 2017